As effervescent as the signature cocktail in the American Bar of its posh hotel setting, Prudence Emery and Ron Base's highly entertaining *Death at the Savoy* is a swiftly paced whodunit set in mid-'60s London—the perfect backdrop for a pedigreed supporting cast that includes the Battling Burtons, the ever-sage Noël Coward, a wisecracking Bob Hope, and a certain high-living Royal, not to mention an ex-cop gangster's widow from New York. What begins as an innocent caviar tasting soon escalates into a...well, to spoil the fun would be a crime.
  — Stephen M. Silverman, author of *David Lean* and *The Amusement Park*

A totally page-turning, entertaining romp through 1960s London. I loved it, read it in one sitting, and look forward to reading more of Priscilla Tempest's adventures at the Savoy.
  —Alma Lee, founder and first Artistic Director of Vancouver Writers Festival

With a supporting cast of characters including Noël Coward, Elizabeth Taylor, Richard Burton, Princess Margaret, and Mountbatten, how could the unlikely protagonist Pricilla Tempest do anything but sparkle and shine? Set at the Savoy Hotel in the 1960s, this novel transports you to another time and place, all the while making murder great fun! If you are like me, someone who adored the character Phryne Fisher, then this book is for you. There is wit, style, and humour buoying up the mystery page after page in this joyful madcap murder mystery!
  —Heidi von Palleske, author of *Two White Queens and the One-Eyed Jack*

This is a terrific read, with its delicious, backstairs view of one of the great hotels of the world. The plot has more twists and turns than the River Thames. Its cast of characters includes Noël Coward, Bob Hope, and Princess Margaret, apart from the long-limbed Canadian heroine, aptly named Miss Tempest. A younger, sexier version of Miss Marple herself. I know which one I prefer.
  —Hilary Brown, former foreign correspondent for ABC News,
    former anchor for CBC Toronto, author of *War Tourist*

Death at the Savoy is funny, sexy, a little camp, and you want to know more. With a nod to Agatha Christie and rooted in Prudence Emery's real-life experiences at the Savoy, the intrigue keeps coming. As a young actor in London, I paid my way through drama school by working as head receptionist at the Park Lane Hotel, so I recognize the canvas and characters. If you're looking for a fun read and a sprinkling of gossip, look no further. *Death At the Savoy* is a must!

—Matt Frewer, star of *Max Headroom*

The glitzy '60s come alive in this riveting, star-studded whodunit. Base and Emery dazzle with their evocative portrayal of the Savoy Hotel and a dynamic plot that'll leave you wanting more. Can't wait for my next adventure with the irresistible Priscilla Tempest!

—Erin Ruddy, bestselling author of *Tell Me My Name*

Death at the Savoy starts with a bang—lots of characters, entertaining scenes, posh setting...and hints of more to come. It all moves swiftly and promises to be fun as you canter along with the characters.

—Anna Porter, co-founder of Key Porter Books, author of *Deceptions*

This book is a flashy, exhilarating ride—fizzy as a flute of champagne, brimming with intriguing twists and turns that are at once hilarious and dark. With her background at the Savoy in the Swinging Sixties, Prudence Emery is admirably equipped to dish delicious dirt!

—David Young, award-winning playwright, screenwriter, and novelist

A wonderfully sophisticated romp through the hallways of London's most famous hotel in 1968, where Priscilla Tempest takes on murder in a miniskirt. Told with an artful wit and precision that blends just the right amount of cheek with chic, *Death at the Savoy* is as deliciously decadent as 2,000-thread count Egyptian cotton sheets.

—C.S. O'Cinneide, bestselling author of The Candace Starr mysteries

SE &
PRUDENCE EMERY

DEATH
AT THE
SAVOY

A Priscilla Tempest Mystery, Book 1

Douglas & McIntyre

1   2   3   4   5   —   26   25   24   23   22

Douglas & McIntyre (2013) Ltd.
4437 Rondeview Road, P.O. Box 219, Madeira Park, BC, V0N 2H0
www.douglas-mcintyre.com

Edited by Pam Robertson
Cover illustration by Glenn Brucker
Text design by Carleton Wilson
Printed and bound in Canada
Printed on 100% recycled paper

Supported by the Province of British Columbia

Douglas & McIntyre acknowledges the support of the Canada Council for the Arts,
the Government of Canada, and the Province of British Columbia through the
BC Arts Council.

Library and Archives Canada Cataloguing in Publication
Title: Death at the Savoy / Prudence Emery and Ron Base.
Names: Emery, Prudence, 1936- author. | Base, Ron, 1948- author.
Description: Series statement: A Priscilla Tempest mystery ; book 1
Identifiers: Canadiana (print) 20220150842 | Canadiana (ebook) 20220150893 |
        ISBN 9781771623216 (softcover) | ISBN 9781771623223 (EPUB)
Classification: LCC PS8609.M495 D43 2022 | DDC C813/.6—dc23

For Mollie Patterson and Elisa McLaren who have been stalwart friends over the years of dramatic ups and downs, including adventures at the Savoy. And to Carl Jongbloed who joined me in other adventures.
    —P.E.

For Kathy who makes it all worthwhile.
    —R.B.

*All good hotels tend to lead people to do things
they wouldn't necessarily do at home.*

André Balazs

*If you drink much from a bottle marked 'poison' it is certain
to disagree with you sooner or later.*

Lewis Carroll, *Alice's Adventures in Wonderland*

Contents

Authors' Note

There is the twenty-first century Savoy Hotel that continues its splendid traditions of fine service in a modern era that does not always value such things. There is the Savoy Hotel that existed in the late sixties, a much different hotel back then, but certainly no less dedicated to the high standards first set out by Richard D'Oyly Carte, the Savoy's founder.

And then there is the authors' Savoy, the fictional hotel that we have created within the pages of this novel. Our Savoy is fashioned with great fondness and endless admiration, but at the same time it is not real. It is populated by made-up characters who exist only in the world that we shaped for them. The royal, rich, and famous who inhabit this imagined world live no further than the edges of our imaginations.

We had a wonderful time living in our version of the Savoy, creating portrayals of iconic personalities as they and the hotel existed more than half a century ago. Our hope is that we can be forgiven for the occasional misbehaving princess and the odd dead body that somehow got on the premises while our backs were turned.

CHAPTER ONE

The Body in Suite 705

The Savoy Hotel's head housekeeper discovered the body lying on the carpet in River Suite 705 at 9:30 a.m.

Millicent Holmes first called the Savoy's security office and when no one picked up, she called reception.

"There is a dead body here in 705."

"I'm sorry, what did you just say, Mrs. Holmes?" asked Vincent Tomberry, the assistant reception manager on duty that morning. The Savoy's strict etiquette forbade calling staff members by their first names.

"I said a body, a dead body," repeated Mrs. Holmes.

"Did you not call Major O'Hara?" Tomberry asked calmly. Given the age of much of its clientele, a dead body in one of the suites was not unheard of.

"I did, but no one answered so I called you."

"What were you doing in the suite this early?"

That was the part that, if Millicent wasn't careful, could get her into trouble. "I was checking that he had everything he needed. They were supposed to send up extra pillows. I wanted to make sure he received them."

There, Millicent thought, that was explained well. After all, such a request was hardly unusual in a luxury hotel that prided itself on serving its guests' needs at all hours of the night and day. The story had recently made the rounds among staff about the duchess who had ordered dinner in her room at three a.m. One of the two kitchens in continuous operation was more than happy to oblige. Such requests from Savoy clients were stored in a card index system for future reference.

Major Jack O'Hara, Retired, the head of the Savoy's security staff, had just come in to work and was carefully trimming his moustache using the hand mirror he kept in his desk when Mr. Tomberry interrupted him.

"I've had a call from housekeeping," Mr. Tomberry said. "Apparently there is a dead body in Suite 705."

Major O'Hara wasn't certain he had heard correctly. "What did you just say?"

"A body," Mr. Tomberry repeated.

"Dead?"

"I cannot imagine there is any other kind," replied Mr. Tomberry archly.

"You're sure there's not some mistake," the major stated.

"The point is, I need you to get up to 705 and have a look."

"Very well," Major O'Hara said with a resigned sigh. Honestly, the staff was impossible at times. "Who is registered in the room?"

"That's the thing," Tomberry said impatiently. "It's Mr. Amir Abrahim."

"The foreign arms dealer," Major O'Hara pronounced.

"In fact, Mr. Abrahim is a *regular* guest."

"I'll be along shortly," the major said.

Major O'Hara finished with his moustache, tucked the mirror away in his desk, straightened his bespoke suit jacket, adjusted his tie, and then left his office and marched down the hall to the lift up to the seventh floor.

Mrs. Holmes waited outside the suite. Major O'Hara noticed she was shaking. "In there," she said, pointing to the river suite door. He rapped his knuckles against the door's surface and when there was no answer, opened it and stepped in.

The body lay face up in a shaft of morning sunlight. Major O'Hara bent down on one knee to make sure Mr. Amir Abrahim, a regular guest apparently, was indeed dead. As far as Major O'Hara was concerned, he was. Full rigor mortis had set in.

The major exhaled as he lifted himself up and said out loud, "Jesus Christ!"

He looked around, seeing the bottle of Moët & Chandon champagne in its watery ice bucket, the two champagne glasses on the coffee table, one of them tipped on its side, spilling liquid across the surface.

He went to the house phone, picked up the receiver, and dialed the general manager's extension. When Clive Banville came on the line, Major O'Hara said, "Sir, I'm afraid we have a problem."

CHAPTER TWO

Welcome to the Savoy

The...*Savoy*! The very name could leave one breathless with antici-pation. After all, that name had come to denote the luxury and fine service available only to a certain kind of very special guest, a guest who understood the best and therefore demanded it. A guest, in short, who had lots and lots of money. The Savoy prided itself on delivering that very best to those very rich and very well connected, twenty-four hours a day.

Knowing of the Savoy's impeccable reputation, even the most jaded of guests could not arrive in its rarefied world without a cer-tain amount of awe. After all, here was...the *Savoy*. And here you were, a part of it, if only for a brief period of time. The Savoy said you were not like everyone else—and thus, you *were not*!

Once entered via the Strand courtyard, haughtily inspected by the statue of Count Peter of Savoy atop the stainless-steel art-deco canopy. The count was given the land the hotel stood on by King Henry III in the mid-thirteenth century. Having received Count Peter's blessing, there would be a friendly nod from the head doorman who recognized immediately the kind of guest you were—deserving the best, remember. The doorman ushered you through the revolving doors of the front entrance, passing the porters in dove-grey suits poised to help with your voluminous Louis Vuitton luggage.

Once through the doors, one arrived in the lobby, known as the Front Hall, admiring the mixture of Edwardian and art-deco stylings, mahogany woodwork reflecting from polished black-and-white checkerboard marble floor tiles. Opposite the main entrance, the wide staircase led to the restaurant overlooking the Embankment.

Over by reception, page boys were stationed should errands of any kind be required. To the left of the entrance, the concierge was ready to help with reservations at London's finest restaurants or theatre tickets to the biggest West End hits—you know, the ones where tickets were impossible to get *unless* one was a guest of the Savoy. Should one wish flowers sent—to a mistress, for example—the Savoy employed a staff of twenty in the florist shop.

To the right, the Enquiry Desk was only too happy to keep track of one's mail and messages or arrange to send a telegram.

It would be pointed out as one checked in that the nearby Resident's Lounge remained open at all times of the day or night to serve one's needs. Here, it should be warned, the American singer and actress Elaine Stritch might show up unexpectedly and rather famously—or infamously, depending on your point of view—hold court, as well as a drink, into the wee hours.

Next to the Resident's Lounge, a set of stairs rose to the American Bar, one of London's great watering holes and the first, legend has it, to add ice to its drinks, hence its name. En route to the bar, one could keep in mind the nearby Grill for one's dining pleasure, with its own kitchen, naturally.

And once one decided to retire, the lift, off the Front Hall and lacquered a dazzling Chinese red, was at one's disposal.

Now if one was more than simply a special guest of the Savoy, if one had been anointed a god or goddess of popular culture—a celebrity, as those gods and goddesses were known—then one would wish to be introduced to the Savoy Press Office. To access the press office, a climb of three steps was necessary and then a brief walk along the corridor, past the theatre ticket desk to the left and the hair salon to the right, to Room 205, known simply as 205. A second lift was opposite the door.

Once inside 205, a visiting celebrity or—heaven forbid!—a member of the press in search of a free drink—would be confronted by two offices of blond wood panelling, with a wall devoted to autographed photographs of other gods and goddesses who over the years had blessed the Savoy with their presence.

In one of those offices, you would find the hotel's young—some would say *too* young—press officer, Miss Priscilla Tempest. Ah, yes, Miss Tempest. Well, she doesn't quite fit in, does she? But then it was the press office, so not a great deal was expected.

Whatever Miss Tempest's shortcomings, she was certainly easy on the eye, as most male members of the Savoy's staff were quick to acknowledge, most members of the staff being male. That was part of the problem for Miss Tempest, you see. When all was said and done, despite what one heard about the free and easy Swinging London of 1968, the Savoy remained a luxurious bastion overseen by men.

You had only to catch a glimpse of her as she hurried through the Front Hall to see that she was, well, *different*. She had fashionably short reddish-blond hair, a fashionably pixie-like face that most men found irresistible, and fashionably long legs she liked to display in a series of fashionable miniskirts. It should be said that men usually found her legs even more irresistible—fashionably speaking.

There was nothing much Miss Tempest could do about this even if she had wanted to. It was, you understand, the strict policy of the Savoy not to allow women in any of its restaurants if they wore trousers. Famously, Katharine Hepburn had been turned away for lunch at Claridge's, one of the Savoy Group's restaurants, because—*horrors!*—she was wearing her trademark trousers.

Ironically then, even within the stuffy, tradition-bound culture of the Savoy, the shortest skirt imaginable was permissible and unremarked upon. Thus Priscilla. Thus her skirts. Thus the admiring men.

It should be pointed out, however, that in addition to her long legs and that delightfully pixieish face that had allowed her to get away with so much more than she otherwise might have, Priscilla was Canadian and consequently even more suspect. A foreigner in the press office, of all things, albeit a charming and attractive foreigner. But still. Eyebrows were raised as questions were whispered, speculating on how a twenty-something young woman who previously only briefly worked at a small public relations firm had landed such a prestigious job at the world's finest hotel.

That morning Priscilla was preoccupied with the impending visit of Bob Hope, who was doing a series of shows at the London Palladium. He would be checking in the next day, and had agreed to a press conference to promote the performances. Members of the press had to be phoned to confirm their attendance.

The Australian prime minister and his entourage were arriving at the end of the week. Louis Armstrong would soon be back, requiring his usual soundproof suite, as would Tony Bennett. The Queen Mother was due for a luncheon. The Marchioness of Lothian had telephoned seeking publicity for her upcoming charity event to be held in the Gondoliers Room.

On it went, the famous and rich, royalty and aristocracy, arriving as they had ever since the theatrical impresario Richard D'Oyly Carte, who had made a fortune presenting Gilbert and Sullivan operettas, first built the Savoy Theatre off the Strand in 1881 and then opened the hotel next door in 1889.

Even though D'Oyly Carte had been inspired by the luxury hotels and restaurants he had visited on the Continent and in America, where regular dining out had become popular, no one thought the concept would ever work in London. After all, the rich and aristocratic entertained in their lavish homes. Why would they ever travel to a hotel in order to do it? And besides, only— dare one say?—foreigners stayed in hotels. Such visitors were fine for local commerce but certainly high society would not care to mingle with them. Undaunted by his critics, D'Oyly Carte bull-dozed ahead, creating a hotel with a view of the Embankment and the Houses of Parliament so impressive Manet painted it from an upstairs window.

All London was soon atwitter about the Savoy's lifts, called ascending rooms, its bathrooms (every suite with its own, previously unheard of), and—heavens, was it safe?—*electricity*! Twenty-four hours a day! And imagine, a telephone in every room, including the bathroom.

And please, let us not forget the gastronomic invention, the culinary delights that drew high society from their lavish homes. These were overseen by the Swiss general manager, César Ritz, with recipes devised by the legendary Georges Auguste Escoffier and a small army of imported French cooks—men only, *s'il vous plaît*. Women would only distract the men, and besides, they could not lift the stockpots. Truffles! Foie gras! Caviar! Six hundred egg dishes! And, of course, Escoffier's signature dessert, Pêche Melba (after the Australian singer, Dame Nellie Melba) spun from gold leaf and served on a swan made of ice!

Given the Savoy's rich history, its lofty tradition, its frosty, austere male overseers with their permanent frowns where women were concerned, Priscilla, a nervous year after starting, could only marvel that, somehow, she still had a job. She was a fraud, she told herself during moments of self-doubt, a fraud who would soon be found out and summarily dismissed. No wonder she had a headache this morning, she thought.

Headaches at the press office were not unusual, occasioned not so much by the workload as by the ongoing demand to entertain the press and celebrities who constantly dropped by expecting refreshment.

When Priscilla required that refreshment, she had only to press the "waiter" button on an oval silver plaque. It was also known as the booze button. Two other buttons were designated for maid and valet service. In the press office, those buttons were never required.

The waiter button summoned Karl Steiner, an elegant, silver-haired Austrian with piercing blue eyes, dressed in a cutaway jacket and black trousers. If he recognized the guest, and he usually did, Karl would simply say, "the usual sir?" or "the usual madam?" And without further question, the usual, borne on a silver tray, would shortly appear.

Priscilla's headache this morning, she had to admit, had a great deal to do with the champagne she had drunk the night before at the Covent Garden opening of Luciano Pavarotti's starring turn in Verdi's *Rigoletto*. It was delightful to see the great Pavarotti on stage and she liked him personally, but sitting through the opera was an endurance. The experience was somewhat mitigated by the champagne at the afterparty. Too much champagne, actually.

The telephone rang, making Priscilla jump. Her nerves this morning were shot. She picked up the receiver. "Savoy Press Office, Priscilla Tempest here. How may I help you?"

"Get up to 705 now!" The cultivated but highly agitated voice of hotel manager Clive Banville. Before Priscilla could ask him why, he hung up.

Gawd, she thought, what's all that about? Her nervousness about job security notwithstanding, Priscilla had a penchant for getting herself into Banville's bad books, particularly since he had played no role in her hiring.

Her assistant, Susie Gore-Langton, shoulder-length hair the colour of honey, a figure to die for, and a habit of turning up late, burst into view. Susie came from an aristocratic family whose luck had more or less run out in the last few years. Given her background, Susie could not imagine working anywhere but at the Savoy. More than anything, she feared losing her job, thus shaming her parents and, even worse, forcing her to look for something below her perceived status in life. Even so, arriving for work at a designated hour was a concept she had yet to fully embrace. Out of breath, she asked brightly, "Where are you off to?"

"The GM wants to see me."

"Trouble?"

"Naturally," Priscilla answered. "Man the phones while I'm gone, will you? I need you to call around and remind the papers about the Bob Hope press conference tomorrow."

"Jolly good," Susie said. "You're looking the worse for wear if you don't mind my saying."

"I do mind your saying," Priscilla replied, slightly irritated, thinking she had successfully masked any excesses from the night before.

"A bad night at the opera?" Susie, as usual, was undaunted by Priscilla's tone.

"Don't ask," Priscilla said with a groan.

She took the lift up to the river suite, hurrying along the corridor as Major O'Hara came into view. He looked unusually grim, even for him, Priscilla thought.

"Prepare yourself," the major announced as she approached.

"Prepare for what?"

Instead of answering, he opened the door to the suite and motioned for her to enter. The first thing she saw was tall, whipthin Clive Banville, pale, looking even more perplexed than usual. The second thing was tiny, delicately featured Millicent Holmes, pressed against the wall, her dark eyes darting nervously between her boss and the body twisted on the floor.

"My God," Priscilla gasped.

"Unfortunately, God is not going to be much help," Banville said dolefully. He gave her a look. "Are you going to be all right?"

How could she possibly be all right? Priscilla thought. After all, she was staring at the dead man, who had been her date the night before.

CHAPTER THREE

Mystery Woman

"What happened?" Priscilla asked, once she had recovered. Major O'Hara, ramrod straight, his face gravely set, had stepped back into the room and closed the door.

"We don't know," Banville said. "There's no sign of foul play, right Major?"

"Nothing evident at the moment," Major O'Hara replied. "But one never knows, of course, and Mr. Amir is a rather notorious personage."

Banville looked unhappy with that answer. "I'd prefer to hear there was no foul play."

"We shouldn't jump to conclusions just yet," Major O'Hara said.

"What do you suggest we do about this?" It took Priscilla a moment to realize Banville was talking to her.

"Do?" She was desperately trying to refocus, suppressing any notion that she had absolutely no experience dealing with dead people in hotel rooms.

Finally, she pulled her thoughts together. "Unless this situation is handled correctly, it could reflect very badly on the Savoy and we certainly don't want that," Priscilla ventured.

The two men appeared to take her statement with grave seriousness. Major O'Hara nodded and then said, "The question is, how do we avoid the bad publicity?"

"That's why I've called Miss Tempest here," Banville said. "To help us navigate through with the least damage to the reputation of the hotel."

"Naturally," said Major O'Hara.

Priscilla cleared her throat and said the only thing she could think of to say, "Well, the first thing is to call the police."

Banville looked at her in surprise. "The police?"

Major O'Hara stepped forward, speaking with authority. "After all, this is Amir Abrahim."

"You keep saying that." Banville sounded angry, as though Amir's name should not be spoken.

"Yes, it's worth remembering that this chap is rather notorious in the international business world." It struck Priscilla, taken aback to learn that the man lying on the floor might be described as "notorious," that Major O'Hara was enjoying his quickly adopted role of knowledgeable lecturer on a guest's dubious background.

"Among his associates," the major continued, "Mr. Abrahim is—or was—known as Mister Three Per Cent. That's due to the fact that he and members of his family act as middlemen bringing together Western arms merchants and their Arab clients in exchange for a three per cent commission."

Banville eyed Priscilla. "Don't just stand there, Miss Tempest. A valued guest has died in our hotel. We take special care of our guests, dead or alive. Thus, no matter what, we must exercise the utmost discretion in handling our Mr. Abrahim. What do you suggest?"

Priscilla, once again momentarily at a loss for words, nonplussed at being called out by the general manager, inhaled deeply and got herself together enough to say, "It is only a matter of time before the press gets wind of what's happened. There is no way, in my estimation, around that reality, particularly after the police are called in. The best we can hope for is that Mr. Abrahim died of natural causes. In the meantime, we let it be known that the hotel's staff did all it could, faced with a tragic situation such as this, and that we are here to co-operate in any way we can because the peace and security of our guests will always come first."

"I think Miss Tempest has it right," chimed in Major O'Hara to Priscilla's immense relief.

"What should properly happen," Banville said, employing the authoritative tone of his office, "is that the chairman is informed along with all heads of department so that we can evolve a strategy to deal with this in the efficient way troublesome events are always dealt with."

"Unfortunately, there is a dead man lying on the floor," noted the major. "I would suggest there is not a lot of time for strategy sessions."

"The police," said Banville, as though still getting his head around the idea of doing something without the approval of the hotel's chairman. "Are we absolutely certain the police are necessary?"

"I have a contact at New Scotland Yard, DCI Robert Lightfoot. Discreet fellow, Bobby," Major O'Hara said. "He knows how to handle these kinds of delicate situations. I'll get on to him."

Priscilla turned to Millicent Holmes, all but forgotten until now, but still poised against the wall. "What about you, Mrs. Holmes? Can I ask you if you saw anything suspicious when you came to the suite?"

"Suspicious?" Mrs. Holmes looked rattled.

"Anything out of place. Anything that struck you as unusual?"

"You mean other than the dead man lying on the carpet?" She paused, as though struggling with what to say next.

"Speak up, woman," Banville ordered. "This is no time to obfuscate."

"Well, there was the lady..." Mrs. Holmes sounded more hesitant and frightened than ever.

"Lady? What lady?"

"Just as I got off the lift, she came along the corridor, running along, actually. It crossed my mind at the time that she had come from Mr. Abrahim's suite. I mean, it's not the first time, you know, that the ladies have been...with him."

"And what time was this?" Major O'Hara asked.

"Around 9:30 a.m., a couple of minutes before I entered the suite."

"What did this person look like?"

Mrs. Holmes replied, "Young, naturally, but not as young as some I've seen with him."

"Anything else, Mrs. Holmes?" Banville asked with surprising gentleness. "Anything that might help?"

"It couldn't have been, of course." Mrs. Holmes was starting to sound panicky.

"Who?" Banville's voice was not so gentle. Now it was like a whip cracking in the room.

Mrs. Holmes gulped and in a rush of words stated: "The lady in question looked quite a bit like HRH the Princess Margaret."

Spanish Caviar

When Priscilla returned to 205, Susie was occupied on the phone reminding the world—or the world contained on Fleet Street—about the Bob Hope press conference.

Still in a state of shock, Priscilla seated herself at her desk, coming to terms with what she had just seen and heard in Suite 705. Amir, dead? Princess Margaret fleeing his suite? How was that possible? Given what Priscilla knew, how could Princess Margaret possibly have been with him? Yet the head housekeeper had seen something and there was no reason to believe she was lying.

Susie finally got off the phone. She came and peeked into Priscilla's office. "Is anything wrong?"

"Nothing except for the body upstairs in 705."

"A body?" Susie looked stunned. "You mean, *dead*?"

Priscilla nodded.

"Suite 705 is occupied by Mr. Abrahim, isn't it?"

"It's him on the floor," Priscilla acknowledged.

"Oh, my God," Susie cried. "He was here yesterday afternoon when Pavarotti came by. He wanted you to go to the opera with him."

"I *went* to the opera with him," Priscilla said.

Susie's eyes widened more. "Was he all right?"

Fine, Priscilla thought. Better than fine. Far too frisky. What was it about her that made the men in her life act...friskily?

That display of friskiness had actually originated in the afternoon at the hotel's historic Abraham Lincoln Room, where

Winston Churchill had once pleaded the case for American entry into the First World War.

"The statistics are actually quite amazing," Priscilla had been explaining at the time to a small group of guests. "We imported thirty-nine tons of butter from Norway last year along with two tons of foie gras, a half million oysters, and three thousand five hundred quarts of champagne. Much of it consumed, I fear, by our press office—"

Priscilla had paused for laughter, but had gotten disappointing titters instead.

"But most importantly, and why we are gathered here today," she had continued, "the Savoy proudly serves *half a ton* of fresh beluga caviar annually. The caviar is an example of what sets us apart from other establishments. A taste of caviar is a taste of what makes us the world's premier luxury hotel."

"Beluga caviar comes from the roe or eggs of the beluga sturgeon. The beluga sturgeon is a species found mainly in the Caspian Sea, the area of Russia from which we get most of our supply, thanks to people like Mr. Grégoire Balandin who is with us this afternoon to answer any questions you might have—and that I, with my very limited knowledge, can't."

Grégoire Balandin stood at the back of the room, a bearded fellow with jet-black hair and the hard body of a wrestler barely contained in his sombre blue suit. He nodded imperiously at Priscilla's mention of his name, not bothering with any kind of smile. Very Russian, Priscilla thought. Not exactly exuding charm or giving off any suggestion that he welcomed questions.

Priscilla went on: "It takes twenty years for the beluga sturgeon to mature, and in fact it's the lighter-coloured eggs from older fish that are most valuable. The rarest caviar of all, and one of the samples that will be available this afternoon, is beluga-Albino caviar, a golden caviar that comes from the eggs of a female albino.

These fish are as much as one hundred years old." Priscilla turned to Balandin. "Have I got that right, Mr. Balandin?"

As Balandin had stepped forward, Priscilla couldn't help notice the blackness of his eyes, perhaps, she reflected, embodying the enduring mystery of the Soviet Union. And perhaps, too, the sense of danger. Ridiculous, she quickly thought. The man supplied caviar, for heaven's sake. She really had to do something about that wandering mind of hers.

"We call it black gold," Balandin announced in a heavily accented voice. "The most expensive, the most delicious."

Balandin fell silent, presumably feeling he had said enough. Priscilla resumed: "We will be tasting several varieties today. Note, please, that you will be tasting the products with mother-of-pearl spoons. We never use metal spoons because the metal interferes with the caviar's delicate taste."

Guests moved along the tables where servers had laid out varieties of caviar. Shortly, Priscilla was approached by the sort of blue-eyed, darkly good-looking young man she had been known to find far too desirable. So even before he opened his mouth, she had decided this was someone definitely worth resisting. Or trying to resist.

"Spanish caviar," were the first words out of what Priscilla had decided was a damnably attractive mouth.

"I beg your pardon?"

"Spanish caviar," he repeated. "Just as good as the beluga but much less expensive."

"And are you in charge of the world's Spanish caviar production?" Priscilla asked.

"I am Amir Abrahim," he said.

"That doesn't sound very Spanish."

"It isn't. I am Egyptian by birth. But I am very interested in the caviar of Spain. The beluga sturgeons you have here are soon to become endangered. The Russians are crazy bastards. They are overfishing the Caspian. The future is Spanish caviar."

"I will keep that in mind," Priscilla had said. "Are you a guest in the hotel?"

"How could I stay anywhere else?"

"Then I'm surprised we haven't met before," Priscilla said.

"I am not surprised so much as shocked," Amir said. "But thankfully we now have met, and that changes everything."

"Does it?" Priscilla wasn't so sure. She reminded herself that she was a hotel employee and he was a hotel guest. She should not be flirting with hotel guests, no matter how blue the eyes or how firm and smooth the jawline.

Except that she was not thinking about any of that later in the evening when he whispered in her ear to confirm, "I am most attracted to you, Priscilla."

At that point they were sipping champagne together amid the crush of opera goers in the Royal Opera House's Champagne Bar during the *Rigoletto* interval. By now she had ascertained that her blue-eyed companion was the sort of wealthy London playboy a single young woman like herself should stay far away from. But then, that was her problem, wasn't it? *not* staying away from the kind of men a single young woman like herself should stay away from.

"You have that gamine quality I find irresistible," he told her. "A slender English rose."

"I'm actually a Canadian rose," Priscilla countered.

"Canada? I know nothing of Canada."

"It's that large mass of land directly above the United States."

"You can teach me all about your Canada, as long as we do not have to sit through the rest of this opera. It's boring."

"It's *Rigoletto*," Priscilla had replied. "And it's Pavarotti and he's always marvellous."

"Let's forget Pavarotti and leave."

"I certainly can't do that," Priscilla said. "Luciano would never forgive me. Besides, he's invited me to the opening night party."

"What will you say to him?"

She grinned and said, "I will not lie. I will say the Great Pavarotti was wonderful as the Duke of Mantua—which is true. And I will say nothing about the opera."

"I believe he wants to sleep with you," Amir said.

"He's a regular guest at the hotel, that's all."

"I am a regular guest at the hotel, and I want to sleep with you," Amir said.

"And?" Susie asked, bringing Priscilla abruptly out of her reverie and back to the present. She had plunked herself down on the sofa adjacent to Priscilla's desk.

"And what?" Priscilla was reluctant, but saw that Susie would settle for nothing less than the full story.

"Did you sleep with him?"

"He did get me back to his suite," Priscilla conceded.

Susie's eyes were now so wide they were practically popping out of her head. "Then what?" she demanded, leaning forward intently.

"Then there was champagne," Priscilla went on. "In these situations, there is always champagne. More's the pity, seeing as how I have a weakness for champagne—and occasionally for the men pouring it."

"*And?*" prodded Susie.

"And I know what you're thinking, but no, I didn't sleep with him. I was tempted, I suppose. But he was drunk and I wasn't and therefore didn't."

Susie's eyes had settled a bit. She was not leaning forward quite so intently. "Still, you may have been the last person to see him alive."

"Unless he was murdered."

"*Murdered?*" Susie's eyes were bulging again. "You're not serious."

"Amir was fine when I left him. This morning he's dead. No one's saying anything, but I can't imagine a healthy man suddenly expiring even if he's had too much to drink. Something must have happened."

"*Murder?* At the Savoy?" Susie's voice had dropped to a murmur. "Who could ever imagine such a thing?"

"Major O'Hara is calling Scotland Yard, so we'll see."

"The *police*," Susie breathed.

"Listen, for the moment we keep this very quiet, all right?"

"Including where you were last night?" Susie asked.

"Definitely, including where I was. Mr. Banville is already concerned about the hotel's reputation and he's expecting us to keep a lid on any bad publicity."

"How do we do that?"

"We do it by keeping our mouths shut," Priscilla said as her telephone rang. She picked up the receiver. "Savoy Hotel Press Office. How may I help you?"

"Priscilla!"

Priscilla froze. It was the familiar voice of Percy Hoskins, who, if you didn't already think he was the *Evening Standard's* best reporter, was more than willing to confirm it for you.

"Percy, what can I do for you?"

"Why don't you tell me, Priscilla."

"Tell you what?"

"Tell me about the murder at the Savoy," Percy said.

An Inspector Calls

Priscilla allowed herself a moment to sharply draw in her breath before she said, "I have no idea what you're talking about."

"Yes you do, luv," Percy replied in that growl of a voice that, depending on her mood, could either seduce or irritate her. Today, it scared her.

"Percy, you're delusional," Priscilla said, finding her firm speaking-to-the-press voice. "This is the Savoy Hotel. There is no murder at the Savoy."

"A body was found this morning in one of the suites," Percy continued in the tired I-know-it-all voice he used when talking to people like Priscilla whose job it was to keep information from him. "Maybe it isn't murder. But there is a body and the police are on the way."

Across the room, Susie got off the phone. Her eyes were once again large as she mouthed to Priscilla: "The police are here!"

"There are no police at the Savoy," Priscilla intoned. "Really, Percy, it's a busy time. I thought you were calling about the Bob Hope press conference."

"Is Bob dead at the Savoy?"

"No, of course not."

"Then I'm not interested," Percy said.

"I don't have time for this," Priscilla snapped.

"I'm on my way over," Percy said.

"Goodbye, Percy," Priscilla said, hanging up.

She looked over at Susie, still goggle-eyed at the news of the arrival of the police. "Percy Hoskins at the *Evening Standard*. He knows something is up."

"Oh, dear," Susie said.

Priscilla's telephone rang again. She closed her eyes briefly before answering it. "Would you be so kind as to meet us in 705?" Clive Banville, demanding.

"I have to go back upstairs," Priscilla said to Susie. "Man the fort. If reporters call, tell them you don't know anything, particularly when it comes to dead bodies."

Susie nodded.

In the Front Hall, Priscilla could see uniformed bobbies moving about. If Percy Hoskins was nosing around, it would not be long before a mob of Fleet Street's finest descended. She steeled herself as she got into the lift and once again rode to the seventh floor.

A uniformed police officer stood guard in the corridor as Priscilla emerged from the lift. She was attempting to explain to the officer who she was and what she was doing there when Clive Banville appeared, said it was all right, and motioned for her to come to him.

"This way, please, Miss Tempest," he said formally.

She was ushered into the suite, now filled with grim-looking men in dark suits. One of those dark suits separated himself from the others and came over to Clive Banville and Priscilla. Banville said, "Miss Tempest, this is Scotland Yard Detective Chief Inspector Robert Lightfoot."

A heavyset man with the firm jaw and iron-grey hair that lend themselves to the image of a Scotland Yard inspector, Robert Lightfoot even possessed steely eyes, which now focused on Priscilla. Not in a very friendly manner, Priscilla thought.

"Miss Tempest," he said in a gravelly voice that, again considering his employment, perfectly suited him, and which she found oddly attractive. The quiet rumble of that voice could calm you in the night, she thought. She quickly dismissed that thought. The owner of that voice was much more likely to get her into trouble than calm her in the night.

"Detective Inspector," Priscilla said, trying not to sound as nervous as she was feeling. After all, she told herself, she had nothing to hide. Well, not *too* much to hide.

Behind the inspector, Priscilla caught a glimpse of Amir Abrahim's body now covered by a sheet and then quickly averted her eyes. Come to think of it, she had plenty to hide.

"I have a few questions for you if you don't mind," Inspector Lightfoot was saying.

"Not at all," Priscilla replied, thinking that there was no way she could lie her way through a police interrogation.

"Where were you last night?"

There, Priscilla thought, what was she supposed to say to that? The truth? Unavoidable, considering where she and Amir were and the number of people who would have seen them. "I was at the opera."

"So we understand," Inspector Lightfoot said, and Priscilla was silently thankful that at least she hadn't tried to lie about that. "And who did you attend the opera with?"

"Mister Luciano Pavarotti." That came out a lot more easily. "Mr. Pavarotti is performing in *Rigoletto* at the Royal Opera House in Covent Garden. He invited me to attend."

"Yes?"

"Mister Amir Abrahim happened to be in the press office at the same time as Mr. Pavarotti."

"Go on."

"Although I had no wish to take Mr. Abrahim with me, Mr. Pavarotti responded to Mr. Abrahim's desire to see the production and suggested that I accompany Mr. Abrahim."

Her breathing was better. The answers to the inspector's questions were coming much more naturally. Truth, she decided, was so much easier than a lie.

"In other words, you attended the opera with Amir Abrahim. Is that correct?"

"It is," Priscilla agreed.

"And what happened after that?"

"There was an opening night party at the opera house and again at the invitation of Mr. Pavarotti, I attended."

"And was Mr. Abrahim with you?"

"He was at the party, yes."

"And following the party?"

"I returned to the Savoy," Priscilla answered. Now they were entering darker territory, the edge of the rabbit hole that could soon descend into a web of lies.

"With Mr. Abrahim?"

There was no way around it, was there? She nodded and softly said, "Yes."

"You came here to his suite?"

Priscilla caught a glimpse of Clive Banville's unhappy face, that you-are-out-of-a-job look she was certain she saw. She gulped and said, "Briefly, yes."

"Briefly. How long would you say you were in the suite?"

"Perhaps twenty minutes."

"And what happened during that time?"

"Not much," Priscilla said. "Mr. Abrahim had a bottle of champagne he said someone had delivered to his suite."

"Did he say who had delivered this bottle?"

"No, he didn't," Priscilla answered.

At the time, she hadn't believed him. She suspected he had the champagne ready in the event he could lure her back to his suite.

"Although," she added, "I recall that he did seem somewhat intrigued as to the identity of the person who sent the champagne."

"All right. Then what happened?"

"He proceeded to open the bottle."

"Did you consume any of the champagne?"

"No, I felt I'd had enough to drink and I wanted to get out of there."

"But he drank the champagne."

"Yes, quite a bit, actually. Why?"

"We will not know for certain until tests come back from our lab, but right now it appears as though Mr. Abrahim succumbed after ingesting some sort of poison, likely in the champagne he drank."

"But he was all right when I left," Priscilla said, once again doing her best to stifle the growing sense of apprehension she was feeling, and not doing much of a job.

"You're sure of that?" Inspector Lightfoot asked in what sounded to Priscilla like a skeptical tone.

"He'd had too much to drink and he was not happy that I was leaving. But otherwise..." Otherwise, what? she thought. Amir was a drunken man anxious to get a young woman into bed and that young woman was just as anxious not to get into bed. A similar scenario that same night undoubtedly had played out all over London. Nothing about it had seemed particularly unusual—until now.

"And what time was it when you left?" asked the inspector.

"I didn't look at my watch, but it must have been a little past midnight."

"And where did you go after you left Mr. Abrahim?"

"The doorman hailed a cab for me and I went home to my flat in Knightsbridge."

"And you saw no one else?"

"No one," Priscilla affirmed.

"No other women?"

Who looked like Princess Margaret? Priscilla thought. "No," she said aloud.

For a time, there was silence, enabling Priscilla to notice two things: the deepening frown on Clive Banville's face, and the young detective close by scribbling away into a notebook.

Inspector Lightfoot drew in his breath and said, "Very well, Miss Tempest. That will be all for now. If you could keep yourself available, we may have more questions for you later. Further, at some point, we will ask you to make a formal statement at Scotland Yard."

"And I will want to speak to you in my office," Banville added sternly.

"Yes, of course," Priscilla said.

Feeling numb and slightly nauseous, Priscilla went out into the corridor. There were more police, all eyes on her—accusatory? Wondering if they were observing the progress of a murderess?

If not a murderess, a young fool certainly, easily swayed into doing the sort of things she shouldn't do. She tormented herself with feelings of guilt for being so weak as to even consider going back to Amir's suite, let alone allowing herself to actually do so. Every time she swore that she would be more careful, do nothing that would jeopardize her job, she ended up doing exactly the opposite. There was no hope for her she decided as she entered the Front Hall.

Major O'Hara was there, stroking his moustache and giving her a neutral, but to Priscilla's eye, somewhat suspicious look. He stopped his moustache-stroking and self-consciously straightened his suit jacket as though preparing himself for something particularly nasty and wanting to ensure he was properly dressed for it.

"The police are keeping the press outside," he announced gruffly. "How the devil these bastards get wind of things, I'll never know."

"Someone tips them off," Priscilla said and immediately regretted the words, since they caused Major O'Hara to cast an even more suspicious glance in her direction. This time he seemed concerned with straightening his tie.

"How are things upstairs?" the major inquired once the Windsor knot had been checked satisfactorily.

"Unfolding," Priscilla said.

"My understanding is that Scotland Yard believes he was poisoned."

"Sorry, Major," Priscilla said, cutting him off. "I really must get to the office."

She pushed past him, noting the tension in his body language as though ready, if necessary, to spring into action in order to bring her to a stop. Thankfully, he remained rigidly in place, his previously suspicious expression having deteriorated into outright accusation.

She opened the door to 205, a refuge from demanding, suspicious eyes.

Except, it wasn't.

"Priscilla, my luv!" With his shock of unkempt hair, his loosened tie at his frayed collar, the chin that only intermittently felt a razor, Percy Hoskins failed to hide his rumpled attractiveness while at the same time providing irrefutable evidence that he was that unique creation of God and Fleet Street—a reporter.

CHAPTER SIX

Ink-Stained Wretch

"What are you doing here?" Priscilla demanded. She shot Susie an accusatory look—silently cursing her for allowing Percy into the office to make himself far too comfortable on her sofa.

"I just stepped out for a moment," Susie protested, lingering sheepishly in the doorway. "He was already here when I got back."

"Don't blame Susie," Percy said. "The office was unguarded. I slipped through enemy lines."

"I want you out of here," Priscilla said venturing further into her office, employing the most demanding voice she could muster at short notice.

"That's no way to treat a much-admired member of the Fourth Estate," said Percy with a grin, in no hurry to leave.

"If a much-admired member of the Fourth Estate were present, it might be different. But since it's you, Percy, get out."

"And here I thought you held me in higher esteem."

"Percy, I'm not kidding. I want you out of this office."

"As soon as you tell me who is dead in one of the river suites."

"No comment," Priscilla said.

"Someone is dead then."

"I didn't say that," Priscilla protested.

"Tell me who it is, off the record, and I'm out of here in a flash," said Percy.

"I'm not telling you anything—now, out or I call security."

"Not the maintainer of proper decorum, that enemy of a free press, Major Jack O'Hara? Why, shiver me timbers."

But at least Percy was on his feet, in all his six-foot-two, shaggy, unkempt splendour, Priscilla reflected. One could be attracted, she supposed. Perhaps if he were the last heterosexual male on earth.

Or maybe the second-last.

The jangle of the phone on her desk ended any further debate concerning Percy's possible attractiveness. She snapped up the receiver. "Mr. Banville will see you at your earliest convenience." The snotty, arrogant voice of Sidney Stopford, the general manager's assistant, dubbed El Sid by the staff.

"I'll be right along," Priscilla said.

"I will inform Mr. Banville."

The line went dead. Priscilla hung up. Percy was looking at her expectantly. "That sounds like the boss wants to see you," he stated. "I wonder what it's about."

"Percy, get out of here. Now. No more arguments. You can leave by the Savoy Hill entrance so no one will see you and I won't lose my job."

"Are you in trouble, Priscilla?"

"Percy—"

"Because of the dead body?"

"One minute more and I really am calling Major O'Hara."

"Okay, okay, I'm going, luv, not to worry," Percy said. He took her elbow and darting a glance in Susie's direction said to Priscilla, "Step outside with me for a minute, will you?"

Priscilla gave him an exasperated look but then allowed Percy to lead her into the hall.

"What's this about?" she demanded.

"Who is on the case? Is it Charger Lightfoot?"

"Who?"

"Inspector Robert Lightfoot. They call him Charger—Charger Lightfoot. He thinks he's Jack Hawkins in *Gideon of Scotland Yard* but he's a bit of a dolt as far as I'm concerned, possibly deep in the pockets of the establishment to boot. Is that who has caught this case?"

"I can't say."

"If it is, sure as hell whatever happened upstairs will be swept under the carpet." Percy leaned into her, dropping his voice to a conspiratorial whisper. "I know you can't say anything, but I'm pretty certain that the dead man is a bloke named Amir Abrahim. I've been trying to get in touch with Amir for days, chasing a story on him. Amir, his older brother, and his father—these guys are big-time bad."

"He told me he was involved with caviar."

"Caviar?"

"That's what he said. Spanish caviar."

"Are you kidding? Amir is part of the Abrahim family. They are Egyptian, notorious international arms dealers. They have nothing to do with caviar, that's for sure."

"If he's so bad, why wasn't he in jail?"

Percy leaned in even closer when he said, "Because there is a belief that he is having an affair with Princess Margaret. They've got Charger Lightfoot on a tight leash. They're afraid if they arrest Amir, it will create a huge scandal involving the princess. Buckingham Palace has been applying pressure to keep a lid on things, and Charger is only too happy to oblige them."

Priscilla thought of Millicent Holmes's suspicion that the woman she saw outside Amir's suite was Princess Margaret.

Percy caught the look on her face. "That means something to you, doesn't it? It is Amir who's dead, right?"

"I'm not saying anything."

"But if I use his name in my story, I won't be wrong?"

Priscilla didn't respond—didn't dare respond.

"Okay," Percy said. "If I'm right, don't say anything. If I'm wrong just say 'no comment,' and I'm out of your hair—your gorgeous hair, incidentally."

"I have a meeting I must get to," she snapped.

As she brushed past him, she noted the satisfied smirk on Percy's somewhat—she simply must stop thinking like this—appealing face. Damn her attraction to this guy. What was wrong with her, anyway?

"I wasn't kidding about the hair," he called to her.

"Go to hell," she called back. She felt better after she said it.

CHAPTER SEVEN

The Place of Execution

Heart thumping, Priscilla steeled herself for entry into the Place of Execution, otherwise known as the office of the general manager. A summons to his office was never a good thing, and particularly bad since one of his employees—namely Priscilla—was not exactly a favourite and, further, had been out with a guest found dead in one of the river suites.

Not good at all. She was having trouble breathing as she entered the outer office. The Keeper of the Gate, Sidney Stopford, El Sid, adjusted his round, gold-rimmed spectacles so that he could properly give her the same dead-eye look she got from the cod at the Billingsgate Fish Market.

"What took you so long?" Sidney's short red hair complemented the moustache that seemed out of place perched above a small, moist mouth perpetually twisted into a sneer of disdain, particularly when Priscilla was around.

"Would you please tell him I'm here?"

He shook his head in apparent despair at the likes of women such as Priscilla before he spoke into an intercom. "Miss Tempest is *finally* here."

"Send her in," Banville's amplified voice came back.

Sidney nodded at her. "You may enter."

She opened one of the oak-panelled doors and stepped into the inner office where Clive Banville stood, an imposing, elegant statue, immaculate in his morning suit with striped trousers and tails, the de rigueur costume for those fortunate enough to toil at the Savoy in managerial positions. Priscilla did not wear a morning suit, so in the estimation of people like Banville, she worked for the Savoy but she was not *of* the Savoy—would never be *of* the Savoy.

It occurred to Priscilla that she might do better if she simply ordered a morning suit and wore it to work. But then she could not enter any of the Savoy's restaurants because, after all, women in trousers were not permitted. Damned if she did, Priscilla thought, and even more damned if she didn't.

"You may remain standing, Miss Tempest," Banville announced, taking his seat behind the vast desk that kept him safely separated from his underlings.

"Yes, sir," Priscilla replied.

"Miss Tempest, I believe you are aware that I was not in favour of your being hired at the Savoy."

"You have informed me of your feelings in the past," Priscilla acknowledged.

"By great good fortune, you happen to know people who know people who know the people who persuaded me not to stand in the way of your being taken on in your present position. I heard the rumours, of course…"

"What rumours were those, sir?" Priscilla blurted out the question before she could stop herself.

"I never listen to rumours and gossip," Banville snapped. "Never!"

"Of course not." Priscilla seethed but fought to maintain a neutral expression.

"Against my better judgment, I went along with your engagement. Perhaps that was my mistake."

"I'm sorry you feel that way, sir," Priscilla said.

"In the months since you joined us, I have seen nothing to alter my view that a mistake has been made." The statement was accompanied by a dismissive swish of a bony hand. "One must quickly learn to fit in at the Savoy," Banville continued solemnly. "It is my belief that is the lesson you have failed to learn."

Banville paused to take a breath before continuing. "This belief has been further confirmed by your behaviour last night. Not only did you attend the opera with a hotel guest, but by your own admission you returned to this hotel and spent time in his suite. Now that guest is lying dead upstairs and this hotel, the premier luxury hotel in the world, I might add, is full of police, trailed by the usual snarling pack of press dogs. And at the centre of it all, potentially about to plunge us into a world of scandal, is our own Miss Tempest!"

Banville remained still, but his voice had risen to an angry crescendo. If he had chosen that moment to toss her bodily out of his office, it would not have surprised Priscilla.

"If I might, sir," she ventured in a voice that to her sounded squeaky and ineffective, more suited to an animated cartoon than to a general manager's office. "I had little choice but to attend the opera. It is as I told the Scotland Yard inspector upstairs, I attended the opera at the insistence of Mr. Pavarotti. I had met Mr. Abrahim earlier in the afternoon at a caviar tasting in the Abraham Lincoln Room—it was very successful, I should add. Later, Mr. Abrahim happened to be in the press office and was invited to the opera by Mr. Pavarotti."

Banville seemed unimpressed by her explanation. "That still doesn't explain what the devil were you doing in that man's suite at all hours of the morning."

"It wasn't all hours," Priscilla protested. "Mr. Abrahim became quite intoxicated at the party after the performance. I thought I was doing both this gentleman and the hotel a favour by helping him back to his room. He opened a bottle of champagne and wanted me to drink with him, but I refused."

"And that is all that happened?"

Was that all that happened? Priscilla asked herself. Oh, God, she thought. It wasn't quite *all* that happened. Why wasn't it ever simple? Why wasn't all that happened, *all* that happened. Why was it always...more?

"Come, my sweet Priscilla, you must have champagne with me."

Priscilla wasn't sure she liked being described as sweet. But at this time of night, she concluded, given Amir's condition, she had to take the compliments where she could get them.

"This is Moët, the finest of champagnes," Amir continued. "Sent to me by a lovely friend, I suspect. A pleasant late-night surprise."

"Women sending you champagne, Amir, remarkable," Priscilla said.

"Does it not make you jealous, Priscilla?"

Hardly, Priscilla thought. More like relieved. Out loud she stated diplomatically, "It fills me with delight to know the hotel's wonderful room service is being utilized by one of our guests."

"But I cannot drink the bottle by myself. Well, I can, but better to share it with you, my sweet beauty."

"Your sweet beauty has to leave," Priscilla countered. She made a mental note to herself to stay away in the future from mysterious men prone to drinking too much champagne, although it occurred to her that she had made such notes before and then ignored them.

"Please," Amir said in a pleading voice. "This could be my last night on earth. The least you could do is drink with me."

"How could it possibly be your last night?"

"Unfortunately, Amir has many enemies."

"Does Amir really?" Priscilla said, not certain how seriously to take him in his current inebriated state.

"I'm very serious. So very serious..." He had begun to slur his words, showing the effects after a long evening of over-indulgence. "The business I am in, you see, for every friend you make, there is an enemy. And the trouble with making enemies in my world, the enemies have guns."

"How dangerous is Spanish caviar?"

"It is my experience that it is the people with guns who are most willing to use them in order to kill you."

"But surely no one would kill you for caviar."

"Ah, but you don't know the Russians," he said. "Where caviar and Russians are concerned, there is no end to the peril. They are bastards who don't like competition."

"If I take you at your word, which I probably shouldn't do," Priscilla said, playing along with him, "tell me who wants to kill you. Russians?"

In response, Amir had flopped onto a nearby sofa, spilling the champagne in his glass.

"Please be careful," Priscilla scolded. "You're going to ruin a very expensive carpet."

"For what I am paying these buggers, I can ruin the damn carpet," Amir said sleepily. "My beautiful Priscilla, protector of the Savoy's reputation—and its carpets."

"Definitely the carpets."

"If only you knew the crooks and scoundrels from all over the world London welcomes," Amir mumbled.

"I'm sure that's not true," Priscilla said, feeling that even at this late hour it was her duty to defend the city's reputation.

Amir waved his hand contemptuously. "Crooks and scoundrels—and killers, too. The killers coming for me."

"Tell me, who is threatening you?"

"Like I said, bastards. My own fault, I suppose, allowing myself to be too easily seduced."

"Who has seduced you, Amir? The person who sent you the champagne?"

"You seduce me, and you don't need to send champagne." Amir lifted his head up and motioned to her. "Come over here."

"Amir, I'm not coming near you. I have to leave." This is where trouble starts, Priscilla told herself.

"My willowy, seductive beauty...Come, please." His words had become even more garbled.

Willowy? She wasn't sure about willowy either. What did that mean? Was she too thin? Reluctantly, against what passed for her better judgment, she advanced. When she was close, he suddenly reached up and pulled her down on top of him. Before she had a chance to struggle away, his mouth was on hers. She told herself that she would break the kiss. She would not allow him to kiss her.

She kept telling herself that as she kissed him.

Finally, she pushed away, out of breath. "Stop," she declared. "We can't do this."

"We can't, but we are," Amir mumbled. He had reached for her again, but this time, she pulled together the intestinal fortitude to draw away and stumble to her feet, yanking down the hem of an already far-too-revealing skirt.

"My killer," Amir said, lying back and closing his eyes.

"There is no killer," she said.

"There is," he murmured. "My last night. My killer comes..."

"No," she said.

"I must tell you..." he had mumbled.

"Who?"

"It's—"

CHAPTER EIGHT

The Killer Inside

"Miss Tempest, are you listening?" Banville's impatience was all too evident.

Priscilla forced herself to refocus. "Yes, I am, sir."

Banville lowered his head, pinching at the bridge of his nose with his thumb and forefinger. Then he started up again: "You said that you left Mr. Abrahim's suite shortly after you arrived and that nothing untoward happened. Is that correct?"

Priscilla nodded. "Mr. Abrahim was falling asleep on the sofa when I left twenty minutes or so after I got him to the suite."

"Nonetheless, your motives aside, you exercised poor judgment. No matter what the excuse, you are a young lady, an employee of this hotel, who ended up in a room with a man who, shall we say, was known for his questionable behaviour, particularly where women are concerned. In so doing, you put your own reputation, and, more grievously, the reputation of this hotel in jeopardy. Do you understand that?"

"Yes, sir, I do."

"If this were any other circumstance, you would be immediately discharged. However, for the moment, I will allow you to continue with your duties. We are getting more than enough attention as it is."

Priscilla heaved a silent sigh of relief. "Thank you, sir," she said aloud.

"When the dust settles, I will be reviewing your employment with the chairman. At that time, I must warn you, all options are open as to your future here at the Savoy."

"I understand, sir. Will that be all?"

"For now, yes. Get back to work. Do your job. Don't let us down."

"I won't, sir."

Priscilla turned to leave. Banville called after her. "Miss Tempest. One more thing..."

She turned to face him, marvelling at his stillness, watching that thin mouth opening just enough to issue a final warning. "It is important that I see nothing of your involvement with Mr. Abrahim in the papers. Is that clear?"

"Yes, sir."

"Finally, I do want to make sure you have told the police and myself all that you know about this situation, that you are not holding anything back."

"I'm not, sir," she said.

"Are you certain about that?"

"I am, sir." Working hard not to sound as though she was lying. Knowing full well she was.

Before Amir had been able to finish his sentence, Priscilla had interrupted him. "Stop it, Amir. This is a joke. I'm not going to kiss you anymore, no matter how many killers you tell me about."

He had struggled to sit up and that's when she saw something in his eyes that disconcerted her. "I am finished," he had said. "It's over..."

"Amir, you're scaring me. Tell me what you are talking about."

His lips had moved, fighting to get words out as he sank back on the sofa.

"What?" she asked.

"My killer..."

"Yes, yes," she said impatiently. "Tell me. Who is your killer?"

"You," he had breathed. "You've killed me..."

CHAPTER NINE

A Case of Mistaken Identity

By four o'clock, the body of Amir Abrahim had been removed from the hotel and most of the police had left the premises, although an officer had been assigned to guard Suite 705, still designated a crime scene.

To keep the press out of the corridors and maintain discretion, Priscilla hastily booked the Pinafore Room, named, in the D'Oyly Carte tradition, after a Gilbert and Sullivan operetta.

Inspector Robert Lightfoot addressed the impatient press. Priscilla could see no sign of Percy Hoskins as she squeezed in behind the inspector in order to hear what he had to say.

"At approximately 9:30 a.m. today, a member of the Savoy's housekeeping staff discovered the body of a male individual in one of the river suites. We will not be identifying this person until next of kin has been notified. At the moment, we are treating this as a suspicious death, pending the outcome of a postmortem investigation."

Flashbulbs popped as reporters erupted into a cacophony of noisy questions, demanding answers Inspector Lightfoot was not prepared to provide. He excused himself and quickly disappeared, leaving Priscilla momentarily the focus of attention. "I can't add anything to what the police have already told you," she announced. "I would say only that the health and safety of our guests remains of utmost importance to the staff here at the Savoy."

"But are you prepared to deny the rumours we are hearing that there has been a murder at the Savoy?" called out one of the reporters, his voice rising about the cacophony of shouted questions.

"The police have said no such thing," Priscilla pointed out tersely. "It is, as Inspector Lightfoot told you, an ongoing investigation."

The statement failed to quell the flood of questions that followed. "That's all for now," Priscilla managed to declare before following the inspector and making a hasty retreat.

She was crossing the Front Hall when Major O'Hara, looking even grimmer than usual, intercepted her.

"Miss Tempest. A word?"

Now what? Priscilla groaned inwardly. "Of course," she said, allowing herself to be drawn into the Resident's Lounge, an area strictly reserved for the Savoy's clients but deserted at that time of day.

"You've had a conversation with Mr. Banville, I take it," Major O'Hara stated brusquely.

She saw no reason to say anything but "Yes."

"Very good. There is one more issue that should be discussed, that I assume did not come up during your time with Mr. Banville."

"I don't know, Major," Priscilla said, not at all certain what he was getting at. "What is the issue you're talking about?"

"I'm talking about this nonsense about HRH the Princess Margaret." O'Hara said this in a manner that suggested Priscilla should already have known about the nonsense.

"Nonsense?" Priscilla's mind was drawing a blank. What nonsense?

"A case of mistaken identity, it seems."

"Oh? Is that what it is?" It had become clearer what the major was getting at. "Do you mean the nonsense about the princess being spotted outside Mr. Abrahim's suite?"

That made O'Hara look unhappier than ever. "I've had a word with Mrs. Holmes. She has had time to reconsider her story."

"Has she? Why did she do that, do you suppose?"

"It appears that in the rush of the moment, she believed she saw someone who in fact she didn't see at all." O'Hara spoke as though this was the most rational explanation imaginable.

"You mean she didn't see Princess Margaret outside Amir Abrahim's suite?"

"That is correct. Thus, I think you'll agree it isn't necessary to talk about this any further." O'Hara spoke in a manner that did not brook disagreement, so Priscilla decided it best not to provide any.

"After all," he continued, "given the truth of the situation, the last thing we want to do is embarrass the royal family in any way. Right?"

"Definitely not," Priscilla said.

"You should know, Miss Tempest..."

"Yes?"

"In view of the events this morning and the part you seem to have played in those events, I must tell you that as head of security at the Savoy, I have my eye on you."

"I see, Major." Keeping her tone level and reasonable. Trying hard to do it. "Now is that good or bad?"

"There is a sense here that you are not fitting in the way we had hoped."

Despite her best effort, Priscilla could not stop her stomach from falling. "I'm sorry to hear that."

"Not spreading rumours about HRH the Princess Margaret would go a long way in the direction of improving your standing at this hotel—fitting in, as it were."

"And would the same apply to Mrs. Holmes?"

"Yes, I think that's fair to say," Major O'Hara agreed.

"I'm sure Mrs. Holmes and myself want nothing more than to improve our standing here at the Savoy," Priscilla said, thinking, You bastard...

"Well, that's all I wanted to say. Have a good evening."

And off marched Major O'Hara, leaving Priscilla at once seething with anger and despairing of ever being able to hold onto her job in the face of men such as Major O'Hara, who obviously wanted her gone.

She straightened her shoulders, taking a deep breath. She would not let them get to her. She would persevere. Priscilla was tough, taking on all comers.

Yeah, right, she thought. Good luck with that.

CHAPTER TEN

A Buck's Fizz Solves the Problem

By the time Priscilla got back to the press office, the afternoon edition of the *Evening Standard* had been delivered. It lay on her desk, its big black headline leaping off the front page:

NOTORIOUS ARMS DEALER
FOUND DEAD AT THE SAVOY

Percy Hoskins's story identified Amir Abrahim as the dead man. "Sources close to the scene" had revealed his identity according to Percy's story. Priscilla briefly closed her eyes. That revelation would almost certainly raise suspicions from the likes of Clive Banville and Major O'Hara as to who that source "close to the scene" might be.

She was on thin enough ice as it was; she certainly didn't need this. She tossed the paper aside and sat at her desk, her mind whirling, inhaling deeply, thankful for the first quiet moments of the day. Susie had escaped to the ladies' room, and that might well take forever. Priscilla was finally alone with her thoughts, rifling through a dozen apocalyptic scenarios, furious all over again with herself for revealing too much to Percy Hoskins, and conflicted as to whether she should have told the police that Amir had drunkenly predicted his own death.

Someone was going to kill him, he had said. It was the nature of the business he was in. The people who didn't like you tended to kill you. But then when she had pressed him as to who exactly might commit such an act, he had said *she* would do it. That, Priscilla surmised, would not sit well with the police, even though when she left him saying she had had enough, thanks, he was fine. Groggy but awake, and certainly not close to the death he was predicting for himself. She had arrived back at her flat, thankful that for once she had behaved herself. A small but notable victory.

Still, there was the business of the woman who had sent Amir the champagne, the woman who might or might not be Princess Margaret—no matter how much Major O'Hara insisted it wasn't.

God knows what would happen if she told all this to the police. That would be the end of her at the Savoy.

No, for the moment, best to keep quiet. About everything.

"Miss Tempest," a voice announced as the office door opened and a balding head like an egg-shaped chocolate poked into view.

"Mr. Coward," Priscilla said delightedly.

"Is it safe to come in?" Noël Coward asked in that nasal drawl that Priscilla—not to mention the rest of the English-speaking world—would instantly recognize anywhere.

"Perhaps the safest place in the hotel," Priscilla said. "Come in, Noël, by all means."

Tall and tanned, dapper in a perfectly tailored dark blue suit fitted at his tailor, Ede & Ravenscroft of Savile Row, Noël raised insouciant eyebrows as he crossed to Priscilla's desk. He had become an unexpected friend soon after Priscilla arrived at the Savoy, wandering into the press office one afternoon in search of a pen with which to autograph for a waiting fan the print edition of *Blithe Spirit*. Nonplussed by the appearance of such a famous personage at a time when she hadn't met many famous personages, Priscilla had handed him her fountain pen.

Noël had gripped it in his hand, surprised eyebrows raised. "A lovely young woman who uses a fountain pen," he had said admiringly. "Most unusual."

"Please, don't ruin the nib, it's a new pen." The words were out of her mouth before she could think to stop them.

Noël had given her a sharp, reproving look. Then, eyebrows leaping high on his endless forehead, he broke into laughter. Vastly relieved that he found her impertinence amusing, she had offered a glass of champagne. That did it. Fast friends over a fountain pen and champagne. Noël had been wandering into the press office ever since.

"Just back from Jamaica," Noël was saying, "in search of a likely suspect with whom I could share a Buck's Fizz, I immediately thought of you, Priscilla. But then the police were keeping me out of the hotel, and in my paranoia I thought perhaps you'd decided never again to have anything to do with me."

"Not a chance," Priscilla said brightly. "I am so glad to see you. I'm in desperate need of a Buck's Fizz—or three, after what I've been through today. I suppose you've heard what happened."

"A dead Egyptian, I understand. Dead at the Savoy, my goodness. Murder most foul, do you suppose?"

"The police don't know yet," Priscilla said. "For now, it's being treated as a suspicious death."

"Not the first time an Egyptian has been found dead in the hotel, incidentally," Noël replied. "Prince and Princess Fahmy, although whether Fahmy was an actual prince is open to question. The couple arrived at the Savoy in 1923 when the hotel was at the height of its luxuriousness and yours truly had become a regular guest while playing the juvenile lead in *London Calling!* and putting the finishing touches to *The Vortex*. The prince and princess no sooner checked in than the princess took it upon herself to shoot the prince. Three times, in fact."

"I hadn't heard that," Priscilla said.

"Hardly surprising. Certainly the hotel management doesn't like to memorialize such things, and you can hardly blame them. I've been loitering at the Savoy since 1922, so it is left to old goats like myself to remember."

"What happened to the princess?"

"During her trial she let it be known that the prince enjoyed buggering her. She didn't like that so she shot him. Naturally the English jury, firmly opposed to such behaviour—particularly when foreigners are involved—let her off."

"Nothing like that is involved this time," Priscilla ventured.

"As far as you know." Noël punctuated the statement with dramatically raised eyebrows.

Yes, except as far as she knew, Priscilla thought, was much further than she chose to let on.

Aloud, she said, "Come along. Let's get out of here."

Gathering her shoulder bag, Priscilla led the way across the Front Hall and up the stairs to the Savoy's American Bar. Art-deco inspired, done in shades of cream and burgundy, the oldest surviving cocktail bar in Britain—it had opened in 1893—was presided over by barman extraordinaire Joe Gilmore. Resplendent in his trademark white waist jacket, Joe offered a welcoming smile as Priscilla entered. "Buck's Fizz coming up," he announced. "And I've saved the corner table for Mr. Coward."

"Many thanks, Joe," Noël called. Joe knew his clientele all too well.

They moved through tables filled with the well-dressed early evening crowd, the low buzz of conversation wrapping comfortably around Priscilla as she and Noël occupied their regular table near the window. Outside, the Thames was a bluish grey at this time of day. For the first time since she arrived at work that morning, Priscilla began to feel somewhat relaxed. Thank goodness for Noël and a Buck's Fizz, she thought.

Noël was lighting a cigarette as the black-suited waiter arrived with their drinks. "Champagne and orange juice, the perfect late afternoon pick-me-up," Noël remarked.

He blew out a cloud of smoke before extending a comforting hand to Priscilla's arm. "You look stressed, my dear."

"A dead body at the Savoy puts everyone on edge, me included."

"Most impertinent," Noël said. "Didn't this gentleman understand? It's the Savoy. Dying at the Savoy is simply not allowed."

He allowed himself another drag on his cigarette, then coughed a bit, before laying it carefully on an ashtray. "Smoking too damn much lately."

"There's something else," Priscilla said.

"Yes, my dear?" Noël leaned in expectantly.

"You mustn't say a word."

"Your secrets are safe with me."

Priscilla took a quick look around, dropping her voice. "I was with him last night."

"With who?"

"Between the two of us?"

"My lips are sealed—at least where our little secrets are concerned."

"Amir Abrahim. He's the dead man in question."

"The rumoured Egyptian. Why does that name sound familiar?"

"He sells guns to people who probably shouldn't have them— he *did* sell guns."

"I see."

"We were at the Royal Opera House together."

Noël made a face. "You poor thing. People are wrong when they say the opera isn't what it used to be. It *is* what it used to be— that's what's wrong with it. This fellow Amir probably returned to his room and in despair over what he had just seen, he killed himself."

Priscilla leaned further into him, dropping her voice even more. "Scotland Yard believes he was poisoned."

Noël raised his eyebrows in surprise. "Then it truly may have been murder most foul."

"That's strictly between us, Noël."

"It goes without saying, dear girl. And you were with this chap?"

"I'm afraid so. As a result, I might be a bit of a suspect."

"Oh, dear. What does it mean to be a 'bit' of a suspect?"

"It doesn't mean anything good."

Noël raised his glass. "Chin, chin. A Buck's Fizz doesn't solve all the world's problems, but it does wrap them in a lovely glow."

Priscilla lifted her glass and took a long sip from it. "That's better," she announced.

"There you go, didn't I tell you?"

"Let me ask you something, Noël," Priscilla said.

"Ask me anything, dear girl. Except perhaps what has happened to my latest play."

"*Suite in Three Keys* has done well, has it not?"

"It ain't *Private Lives*, put it that way," he said, finishing his drink and summoning the waiter for another. "Now, what did you want to ask me?"

"About Princess Margaret."

That renewed the up-and-down movement of Noël's eyebrows. "What about her?"

"You know her?"

"My dear girl, I know *everyone*."

"Tell me what you know about her."

"I know Margaret is impossible, erratic, not to mention spoiled. Worst of all, she's unhappy. Can't say as I blame her. Trapped in a musty old castle with a cold-fish sister and a complete ass for a husband. Little wonder she has affairs."

"Does she?"

Noël's eyebrows did another dance. "Doesn't everyone? It's London, it's 1968, everyone is sleeping with everyone else. Why should she be any different?"

"Supposing she was having an affair that threatened to become public, what do you think would happen?"

"With this Amir?"

"It's possible."

"The princess with a notorious arms dealer who has turned up dead. Not good at all. If that were the case, Buckingham Palace would do what it usually does in these sorts of shoddy situations."

"What's that?"

"The Grey Men who run things over there would proceed to move heaven and earth to ensure her affair doesn't become public."

"How far would they go, do you think?"

"To keep Margaret's...shall we say...*transgressions* out of the press and the public view? I would suggest they would stop at nothing."

"Even murder?"

Noël didn't answer immediately. The waiter arrived with two more Buck's Fizzes. Noël contemplated the flute in his hand.

"You must understand, dear girl, much has changed in Jolly Old England, the Beatles and swinging London and all that, but the establishment in this country still runs things, and they are all interconnected in one way or another. From Buck House to Downing Street to the doors of the Savoy, they all move in the same rarefied circles. They stick together, even when they don't particularly want to."

Noël put his glass aside and returned that comforting hand to Priscilla's arm. "Whatever you're thinking, I would stop thinking it. I'm a bit of a gadfly around these parts and getting old, so I can get away with tweaking that establishment from time to time. They find me amusing in their way and so keep me in the fold. But you, dear girl, you are different. Where the Grey Men of Buck House are concerned, I would be very, very careful if I were you."

"I believe," Priscilla said, swallowing hard, "I'm in need of another Buck's Fizz."

CHAPTER ELEVEN

Overheated

Feeling somewhat woozy from the day and the two Buck's Fizzes Noël Coward had poured into her, Priscilla decided a walk home might be just the thing to clear her head.

She made her way across the Savoy forecourt, along the Strand and then through Admiralty Arch down the Mall along St. James's Park. The sun was setting over her tiny slice of the British Empire, an untypically cloudless evening to warm the troubled soul of a young Canadian in London who was feeling somewhat lost, having to confront, in no particular order, dead bodies, famous people, general managers threatening to fire her, and suspicious police.

Ah, well, she thought, another day in the life of the unsinkable Priscilla Tempest. Except as she cut obliquely across Green Park aiming for Hyde Park Corner, she was feeling absolutely sinkable.

Ordering herself not to be pessimistic, reminding herself that she must always remain positive, she walked along Knightsbridge, approaching No. 37–39, the eight-storey building owned by the Savoy where she lived. The manager of Simpson's-in-the Strand lived above her fifth-floor flat. A sitting room gave Priscilla a grand view of Hyde Park, which she particularly liked in the spring when daffodils were in bloom. There was a small kitchen and bathroom, and in back a single bedroom with a double bed. The guests who didn't end up in bed with her slept on a sofa bed in the sitting room. In all, Priscilla thought, it was like a three-star hotel suite. She loved living there and groaned at the prospect of not only losing her job but at the same time, her lovely flat.

Ahead, not far from the entrance to 37–39, a forest-green MGB two-seater roadster was at the curb with its hood up and a driver radiating the frustrated look of all MG owners. "It's overheated," the driver declared as Priscilla approached.

The driver was slim and tall with dark brown hair, a particularly square jaw, and, Priscilla noted, blazing green eyes that somewhat matched the car's exterior.

"I'm sorry?" Priscilla said.

"The car overheated." The declaration was followed by what Priscilla had to concede was a rather dazzling smile. "It's always overheating."

"Men who buy MGs," Priscilla said with a shake of her head.

"We are a sorry breed," the driver agreed sadly.

"A foolish breed."

"Do you by any chance live around here?"

"Just along the street," Priscilla said, wondering if she was giving too much away—if she wasn't prone to giving too much away to attractive men generally.

"I don't suppose I could trouble you for some water—for the car. It's—"

"Yes, overheated," Priscilla said, smiling.

"I hate to impose."

"No imposition," Priscilla said. "I'll bring it out to you."

"If you have a pail..."

Priscilla frowned. *Pail?* What would she be doing with a pail? "I don't have a pail—I don't *think* I have pail."

"Actually, I probably shouldn't have said that."

"No?"

"You don't strike me as a pail-type girl."

"As a matter of fact, I'm not."

"I knew it." Accompanied by another smile designed to dazzle.

"Let me see what I can do."

"My name's Mark Ryde, incidentally."

She thought to provide her name and then decided it was best not to hurry things. Aloud, she said, "I'll be right back, Mark Ryde."

The tiny lift with its folding metal door rattled and shook as it slowly rose to the fifth floor. Priscilla stepped out and crossed the hall to her flat. She unlocked the door and entered, lamenting the scattered clothes, the dirty dishes on the kitchen counter that militated against inviting strangers with MGBs inside, even if their names were Mark Ryde and they were slim with square jaws and eyes that matched the colour of their car.

She found a big pot in the cupboard beneath the counter, filled it full of water, and then lugged it back down to the street where Mark waited.

"Thanks," he said, taking the pot from her. She followed him to the car and watched over his shoulder as he balanced the pot on the edge of the engine block, twisted the cap off the radiator, and carefully poured in the water.

"Is that enough?" Priscilla asked. "I can get more."

"No, that should do the trick," he said, replacing the radiator cap and then handing back the empty pot. "You're a lifesaver."

"All part of my good-neighbour policy," Priscilla said.

"Makes me wish I was a neighbour," Mark flashed another of those highly attractive smiles. Having him as a neighbour might not be such a bad thing.

"You haven't told me your name," Mark added.

That's right, she thought. She hadn't. Should she? "Priscilla," she said.

"Ah, Priscilla." She enjoyed the way Mark's eyes seemed to light up as he said her name. "Do they call you Prissy?"

Priscilla frowned. "No one calls me Prissy."

"Right. Priscilla it is," Mark acknowledged with a nod. "Do you work around here?"

How to answer that question, she thought. "At the Savoy. Not too far away."

"The Savoy?" Mark looked impressed. "What do you do there? Change the sheets?"

"Only a couple of days a week. Otherwise, I'm in the press office."

"Pressing?"

"Something like that," Priscilla said.

"Tell me, do you have a lot of influence at the Savoy?"

An honest answer was in order, she decided. "Not a whole lot, I'm afraid."

"Damn," Mark said, feigning a disappointed look. "I was hoping I might get a reduction on the room rate."

"Why? Do you need a room?" Were they flirting? Definitely, she concluded.

"In case a girlfriend throws me out," Mark said.

"Do you have a girlfriend?" Kidding around, of course. Or was she?

He grinned and shook his head. "She threw me out."

"I'm afraid there are no reductions at the Savoy."

"What about you, Priscilla?"

Yes, what about her? What was she supposed to say to that? "I don't have a girlfriend so she can't throw me out."

"What about boys? I don't see a lineup down the street or anything."

"They're all waiting at the pub."

"That's too bad. I never stand in line."

"There's no lineup," Priscilla assured him. "They're all gathered at the bar."

"I don't like crowds either."

"More's the pity," Priscilla said, adopting a regretful expression.

"Perhaps I'll see you around. I'm at the Savoy from time to time."

"Then by all means, drop into the press office and say hello."

Mark got into the car. She debated whether to say something else. But what? The car's engine growled to life.

"That does it," he called. "Good as new. Thank you again."

And with a wave, he was off down Knightsbridge, leaving Priscilla feeling slightly...well, kind of disappointed, if she was being honest. Mark Ryde might have offered to buy her a drink as a reward for her public service. What's more, he never did say whether he would actually drop into the press office. Maybe her invitation was too blatant. Or not blatant enough.

Or perhaps it was just as well he didn't drop in. Or buy her a drink. Or pursue her in any way. He was far too handsome, and handsome young men who might well get her into something— no, thank you. She had been involved lately in far too many some-things. That was London for you.

Too many somethings that amounted to nothing.

CHAPTER TWELVE

Mr. Hope's Request

Bob Hope, accompanied by a small entourage, arrived in the Savoy forecourt and swung through the revolving doors into the Front Hall where he was met by Clive Banville and Priscilla. Hope, wearing a dark blue suit, radiated the certain energy of a man accustomed to his fame and entirely satisfied with it. Banville greeted him warmly and then introduced Priscilla.

"We just got out of Nam," Hope said. "We were entertaining the troops over there."

"Nam," Priscilla said. "Oh, dear. That must have been very dangerous."

"Not at all," Hope replied. "In fact, when we flew in, they gave us a twenty-one-gun salute. Three of them were ours."

Priscilla laughed and said, "That's very funny." Even Banville managed a smile before taking his leave.

Hope addressed Priscilla. "Tell me, sweetheart, what's the plan for this morning?"

"Well, we have members of the press waiting for you in the River Room in advance of your appearance at the Palladium. You'll speak to them, answer a few questions, and then I'll escort you up to your suite. You're staying with us for a few days, I understand."

"Okay, and yeah, that all sounds good," Hope said. Passersby stared in amazement as the comedian stopped and turned to Priscilla. "I don't mind talking to these press fellas. But do me a favour will you, sweetheart? As soon as we get started, go up and check my suite, make sure everything's in order. I'm dead tired, and I probably look it."

"You look fantastic, Mr. Hope," Priscilla enthused.

"Yes, I have a wonderful makeup crew. They're the same people who restored the Statue of Liberty."

"This is the Savoy. We pride ourselves on ensuring everything is perfect, but I'll be very happy to make certain that perfection has been maintained in your suite. Is there anything specific you require?"

"Only a good bed so I can get some sleep as soon as this is over," Hope said.

"Consider it done."

"You're a doll," he said, delivering one of his knifelike smiles.

Priscilla led the way into the River Room, aptly named since it overlooked the Thames. Members of the London press were crowded onto chairs lined in rows before a podium. There was applause and the pop of flashbulbs as Hope entered. He smiled genially and waved as Priscilla stepped to the microphone mounted on the podium.

"Good morning, ladies and gentlemen. Usually, at one of these affairs, I have to spend time introducing our guest. But this morning, our guest needs no introduction, certainly not from me, other than to say the Savoy Hotel is so proud and delighted to once again be hosting Mr. Bob Hope."

There was more applause as Hope, that trademark cocky grin in place, stepped to the podium. "Thank you for that introduction, Priscilla," Hope said. "It was short and sweet—just like you."

"She's pretty tall, Bob," someone called out.

"My mistake. When you get to be my age, you make plenty of mistakes. You start to realize on your birthday that the candles cost more than the cake."

Amid laughter, he went on: "Listen, it's great to be back here in the home country. As some of you know, I was born in Eltham in the southeast part of London. The doctor took one look at me, turned to my mother, and said, 'Congratulations, you have an eight-pound ham.'"

A chorus of laughter followed. One of the reporters shouted, "What made you leave England, Bob?"

"I found out I could never be King."

More laughter and Priscilla realized that Hope might be dead tired, but he was in his element, on stage in a room full of people laughing at his jokes. Someone asked him about hosting the recent Academy Awards ceremony in Los Angeles.

"I've never seen six hours whiz by so fast," Hope said.

Priscilla slipped out of the room and hurried to the reception desk, where Vincent Tomberry was presiding. "Mr. Hope wants me to make sure everything is in order in his suite," Priscilla explained in the face of Tomberry's questioning look.

"This is the Savoy, Miss Tempest," he pronounced. "Everything is always in order."

"Do you know if Mr. Hope's luggage has arrived?"

"It has arrived and has been taken up to his suite," Tomberry stated.

"The key, please." Priscilla held out her hand.

"This is unnecessary."

"Nonetheless, Mr. Hope has made a request and it is up to us to honour that request."

With a final frown of disapproval, the assistant reception manager dropped the key into the palm of Priscilla's hand.

She went to the lift and stood waiting for its arrival, relieved that Hope had been so co-operative, the press so charmed and responsive. Surely someone in management would notice that she was doing a good job and not want to fire her.

I will be in the Grill wearing trousers before that happens, she thought as the lift doors opened.

Arriving on the sixth floor, Priscilla hurried to Suite 611 and used the key to unlock the door. She stepped inside and closed the door, then heard a sound that seemed to be coming from the bathroom. Was someone already in here? "Hullo?" she called out.

More sounds came from the bathroom. "Is someone there?"

Suddenly, the door opened and a naked man burst out in a blur of movement, lurching toward her. Priscilla screamed as the man, wild-eyed, his greying hair dishevelled, attacked, grabbing at her throat, his mouth open and foaming, pushing her backward. She screamed a second time as she clawed at the man's face.

He fell away, his wild eyes filled with uncomprehending confusion. He let out a loud gasp before collapsing to his knees and then falling forward on his face.

Priscilla watched in horror as the man writhed on the carpet and then lay still—in much the same position, she thought fleetingly, as Amir Abrahim.

No sooner had she knelt to the man to try to help him than a door leading to the suite's bedroom opened and a woman whisked out. She wore a short black cocktail dress and carried a hand purse. She sped past Priscilla without a downward glance.

Priscilla caught a glimpse of dark hair piled on her head and high cheekbones before she disappeared out the door, slamming it behind her.

On the floor, the man stirred, and Priscilla focused her attention on him as his lips, caked with some sort of white substance, began to move. He mumbled something unintelligible. Priscilla leaned down. His breath escaping from his partially open mouth smelled rank. "What is it?" she urged. "What are you saying?"

But there was nothing. The man grew still. "No," Priscilla cried, "don't you die...don't you dare ..."

The man wasn't listening. His eyes glazed over and his lips stopped moving. Priscilla was in shock, coming to the realization that she was in Bob Hope's suite holding an unconscious man, tumbling into a world of trouble.

The Suspect Is Questioned

This time there were none of the niceties present during Priscilla's previous encounter with Detective Inspector Robert Lightfoot. This time it was a hustle out of the hotel and down to the turreted Victorian pile overlooking the Thames that was the headquarters of New Scotland Yard.

This time it was sweating it out in an anonymous office filled with the smell of stale tobacco, Priscilla still shaken, mind a blur, trembling on the edge of an uncomfortable straight-backed chair. Inspector Lightfoot glowered from behind a gunmetal-grey desk, the looming forms of other members of his squad somewhere in the background. A skeleton-thin stenographer was taking down her every word.

"The wrong key?" Inspector Lightfoot glared at her as he asked the question.

"That's right," Priscilla said. "It was supposed to be the key to the suite occupied by Mr. Bob Hope. Only it wasn't. It was for the suite next to his."

"And tell us again what you were doing up there in the first place."

Was she incriminating herself by talking to these police officers? Surely not. Or would they take down what she said and use it in court, like they always did in those black-and-white British crime movies? But she hadn't done anything. She was innocent!

Except, as Priscilla sat there, the black looks of her inquisitors suggested they did not for a moment believe that.

"As I explained to the other officers, Mr. Hope is in town for a performance at the London Palladium. He said he was tired after a long flight from Vietnam where he had been entertaining American troops. He wanted me to check his suite to ensure that everything was in order so he could get some sleep immediately after the press conference."

"And so...?"

"I went to the desk, asked the assistant reception manager for the key to Mr. Hope's suite. I assumed I had the correct key. It turned out, I didn't..."

"When you opened the door, is that when you realized you were in the wrong suite?"

Priscilla shook her head. "I believed I was in the right suite. When I heard noises coming from the bathroom, I immediately thought a guest somehow was in the wrong suite."

Was she making any sense at all? Every word out of her mouth sounded like gibberish.

"And when this man appeared?"

"I was shocked, of course—still am."

"You had no idea who this person was?"

"A naked man screaming and lurching toward me, then grabbing my throat—I thought he was about to kill me. I didn't have a lot of time to attempt to identify him."

"Mr. Bernard Bannister is the victim's name," Inspector Lightfoot said.

"How is he doing?"

"Mr. Bannister is in a coma at the Charing Cross Hospital. Tell me, does that name ring a bell? The Honourable Bernard Bannister?"

"No. Should it?"

"You've never heard that name before? Is that what you're saying?"

"Yes, it is," Priscilla said indignantly, angry despite the fear gnawing at her, that she should be expected to know the name of someone when she had no idea who he was—and made to feel guilty about it.

Inspector Lightfoot sat back in his chair, fishing a package of cigarettes out of his inside jacket pocket. He extracted a wooden match from a box, using his thumbnail to produce a burst of flame before directing that flame to the end of his cigarette. Once he had blown a stream of blue-grey smoke into the already choked air, he seemed to remember that Priscilla was still perched tensely before him.

"Miss Tempest," he pronounced, dropping the spent match into the ashtray at his elbow, "in the past week, two men have been found in distress at the Savoy—a place, I'd wager, that in its long history has not had to suffer many similar incidents, let alone two in such a short span of time."

Inspector Lightfoot paused to take a drag on his cigarette. "Now in both these unfortunate occurrences, Miss Tempest, you figure prominently—far too prominently."

"What do you mean by that?" Priscilla demanded.

"I mean simply that you may know more than you are letting on, and if that is the case, I would strongly urge you to stop playing games and tell us what you know about these incidents."

"Inspector, I have told you all I know," Priscilla said in a tired voice. It was one thing to repeatedly question her. It was another thing entirely to suggest she played any part in what had happened to these men. But then she'd been in their suites at the wrong time, hadn't she? Suspicious. Damnably suspicious. Guilty as charged then! *Throw away the key!*

But wait a minute, she thought, there was that woman, wasn't there? The woman with the high cheekbones that Priscilla would kill for, bolting from the room.

"You're forgetting the woman I told you about earlier," Priscilla said out loud.

"The woman." Lightfoot managed to sound as though he was hearing this for the first time.

"As I have now told you a number of times, when I went to the aid of this gentleman, a woman burst out of the bedroom. Before I could stop her—even think to stop her—she dashed from the room."

"And you did not follow her?"

"No," Priscilla said in an irritated voice. "I thought it much more important to get help for a guest I feared was dying right there before my eyes."

Inspector Lightfoot calmly blew out more cigarette smoke. "I'm afraid the prognosis is not good for our Mr. Bannister. We may yet have a second suspicious death on our hands."

Inspector Lightfoot looked pained at the prospect.

"What about Mr. Abrahim? Has it been ascertained what happened to him?"

"I think we're about done here," Inspector Lightfoot said, punctuating the statement by jabbing his half-smoked cigarette decisively into an ashtray, sending butts scattering. He followed up with a hard look. "But make no mistake, Miss Tempest, we are not done with you. As our investigation progresses there will be more questions. And be aware, we have our eyes on you."

Priscilla felt numb. She was having trouble swallowing. "Does that mean," she managed to say, "that you don't want to tell me what happened to Mr. Abrahim, or you don't yet know?"

"It means I ask the questions, Miss Tempest, not you." He nodded to one of the detectives poised behind Priscilla. "Escort Miss Tempest out, please."

CHAPTER FOURTEEN

The Price of Beer

According to the Big Ben clocktower looming against the grey sky further along the street, it was nearing four o'clock as Priscilla exited New Scotland Yard. She came out the iron entrance gates and stood on the street, attempting as best she could to calm rattled nerves that, given what she'd just been through, resisted being calmed.

Those rattled nerves only worsened at the sight of Percy Hoskins slumped on a park bench across the street. As soon as he spotted Priscilla, he tossed away the cigarette he was smoking and sauntered across to where she stood.

"What on earth are you doing here?" she demanded.

Percy looked affronted. "I was worried about you, Priscilla. Came to make sure you're all right. Those Scotland Yard lads can be real bastards."

"How did you know I was here?"

"Friends in high places," Percy said with a crooked grin.

"Yes, well, I'm not speaking to the press."

Priscilla started along Whitehall. Percy caught up to her declaring, "I'm not asking you to say anything."

"Ha," she said.

"Come on, luv, don't be like that. There's a pub nearby. Let's go for a drink. Off the record. You look as though you could use one."

Priscilla could certainly use a drink. She came to a stop and turned to face him. "Just a drink," she said. "No questions. Nasty people have been asking me questions all day. I'm sick of them."

"In fact, I can let you in on a thing or two—and what's more, I'll pay."

"The thought of being present when a reporter actually opens his wallet is irresistible," Priscilla said. "Lead on."

They found a pub just off the Victoria Embankment that had a minimal number of patrons at this time of the day, mostly civil service types.

Percy got a couple of pints from the bar while Priscilla seated herself in a corner. He joined her, heaving a pleased sigh. "End of day, luv. Cheers." He clicked her glass and then took a deep swallow. "That's better," he pronounced.

"Late night last night?" Priscilla asked.

"Always a late night, luv, chasing the stories that keep the British public informed."

"Right," said Priscilla doubtfully, taking a sip from her own beer.

"How are you doing?" Percy asked. "Charger didn't bring out his rubber hose or anything like that, did he?"

"Not yet," Priscilla said. "But they seem to think I'm somehow involved in what's happened."

"Well, it is Bernard Bannister, isn't it?"

Priscilla gave him a quizzical look. "Inspector Lightfoot thought I should know who he is, and I have absolutely no idea—and how do you know?"

"Like I said, late nights chasing the stories that keep the British public informed," Percy said with a knowing smile. "You really don't know who he is?"

"Should I?"

"Member of parliament. Top Tory. Rumoured to be in the running for the party leadership what with the Wilson government sinking in the polls and certain Conservatives wondering if Ted Heath is the man for the job."

"I don't follow politics," Priscilla said. "What's the thinking, then, that Bernard Bannister is the man for the job?"

"Until he ended up in a coma in Charing Cross Hospital, having been discovered near death by our own Priscilla Tempest."

Priscilla made a face and drank more beer. Her head was beginning to ache. This was all too much. A twenty-something with great legs whose ambitions ran no further than ensuring everyone's glass was filled and that the likes of Bob Hope got to the press conference on time, and here she was finding bodies everywhere, suddenly a person of interest at Scotland Yard.

How did all this happen?

Percy was saying, "In a matter of days, you have a notorious arms dealer dead at the Savoy and now a prominent Tory fighting for his life."

"Inspector Lightfoot wouldn't say anything about what had happened to Amir or to this Mr. Bannister."

"That's because Charger doesn't know. I don't think they know what to make of the Bannister situation, but they're very concerned about it."

"If you ask me, considering what happened to Amir Abrahim, I would say that someone did something to Mr. Bannister as well," Priscilla offered.

"Maybe it's you, Priscilla, going about poisoning guests at the Savoy."

She was relieved to see that Percy was smiling when he said this. At least, he seemed to be smiling.

Priscilla made another face. "I'm afraid that may be what the police are thinking."

"Maybe it's up to you and me to get to the bottom of this," Percy said.

Priscilla eyed him suspiciously. "I'm not sure what you mean by 'you and me.'"

"Look, I have certain information and I believe you know things you're not telling me," Percy said, pushing his beer to one side so he could lean closer. "Let's pool our information and resources. That way we can figure out what's happening at the Savoy."

"Why would I want to do that?"

"To clear your name for one thing."

"Do you think my name needs to be cleared?"

"What do you think?"

She hesitated. What did she think? That she was in a lot of trouble, was her first thought. Her second dealt with what she knew—Amir's declaration that his enemies were out to kill him, his assertion that she was the enemy who might do it; the mysterious woman in the black cocktail dress escaping Bernard Bannister's suite.

Things that she hesitated to tell Percy Hoskins, given that his motives were dubious at best.

"Well?" Percy drew her out of her thoughts.

"I'd better think about it," Priscilla declared.

Percy adopted a disappointed expression that Priscilla immediately suspected was counterfeit.

"Why do I suspect this is all about getting me to tell you things I shouldn't tell you?"

"That means you do know things you're not telling me." Percy was far too smooth when it came to countering her allegations.

"I didn't say that."

"In a way you did, luv."

There was no use continuing to waste her time, Priscilla decided. She looked at her watch impatiently. "I have to get back to the office."

Percy finished what was left of his beer and then plunked it down decisively on the table. "Here's what I'm about to do," he announced. "There's a phone on the bar. I'm going to use it to call the paper and break the story about the Honourable Bernard Bannister, the Tory MP found unconscious at the Savoy Hotel under mysterious circumstances. Now I can either use the name of the hotel employee who found him and the fact that she has been questioned by police. Or, I can leave it out."

Priscilla looked at him in astonishment. "Percy, you're not blackmailing me, are you?"

"Heavens no," Percy said in mock horror. "Put it this way: I am merely trying to make you understand that with the two of us working together, co-operating together, we can solve the mystery of the suspicious events at the Savoy."

"Bastard," she said.

"A newspaperman," Percy replied.

"It's the same thing," Priscilla said.

"Have we got a deal or not?"

Priscilla thought of the ramifications of her name appearing in the *Evening Standard* for the second time in a week. The glowering countenance of General Manager Clive Banville floated in front of her eyes.

Priscilla swallowed hard and nodded.

CHAPTER FIFTEEN

Meet the Burtons

Still furious with Percy Hoskins for forcing her to co-operate with him in what was certain to be a disastrous collaboration, she braced herself as she entered the Savoy, expecting to find the Front Hall full of suspicious police and ravenous press anxious to blame her for the latest scandal at the hotel.

But instead, the Front Hall was oddly quiet and nearly deserted—except for Assistant Reception Manager Vincent Tomberry, the frown on his face seemingly set in stone. He stiffened behind the reception desk as she approached. "I gave you the right key," he hissed out of the corner of his mouth.

"No, you did not," she hissed right back.

If looks could kill, Priscilla thought, then Vincent's glare would certainly do the trick. She moved away and that's when she saw a familiar figure rise from one of the upholstered armchairs, smiling broadly as he came over. Was that the sound of her heart picking up speed? No, it couldn't be.

Mark Ryde said, "I wondered if I might run into you."

"Did you?" Priscilla thought of how awful she must look after an afternoon of being interrogated at Scotland Yard.

"You do remember me." Mark spoke with the authority of a man who had fully expected to be remembered.

"Mark—the gentleman with the thirsty MGB." Priscilla's tone suggested she remembered—but only vaguely. She added, "How is it doing?"

"The car is fine, thanks for asking."

"What brings you to the Savoy?"

"Well, you did invite me to drop by."

"Did I?" she replied with a nonchalance that belied the pleasure she was feeling now that he had actually showed up.

"Also, as it happens, I'm here to meet a friend," he went on. Not to see her, she noted, but to meet someone else. Who? she wondered as she focused on Mark saying, "I understand there was some trouble here earlier. Have you heard anything?"

"Trouble at the Savoy?" Priscilla arranged to look astonished. "Impossible. There is no such thing as trouble at the Savoy."

"An oasis of tranquility, is it?"

"Always. Absolutely."

"Well, then," Mark said, "I guess I've come to the right place. I'm constantly on the lookout for oases of tranquility."

"Look no further."

"Perfect." Mark peered at his watch. "Now if only my friend shows up."

"I'd better get to the office," Priscilla said. "Enjoy your visit."

"It's great to see you," Mark said.

"Good to see you," Priscilla said in the artificially sincere voice she employed suggesting lunch with someone she never intended to have lunch with in a million years.

Except, as she left him, she wasn't sure that was how she felt about Mark Ryde. Be still my beating-too-fast heart, Priscilla thought.

Except it wouldn't be still—until she entered 205 and was confronted by Susie in full panic mode. "Bob Hope has *left* the Savoy," she exclaimed.

"What?"

"Apparently, he's moved over to the Dorchester Hotel—can you believe it? He says there are fewer bodies lying around the Dorchester. Everyone is up in arms. I mean Bob Hope—at the *Dorchester*! It's a nightmare! Can you imagine?"

Unfortunately, Priscilla could.

"Also, the Burtons have arrived."

"The Burtons?"

"Elizabeth and Richard," Susie said as though everyone in the world should know who they are—and as it happened, everyone did.

"They're here? Now?"

"They checked in a couple of hours ago, huge entourage. A great deal of fuss and bother."

"No one told us," Priscilla said.

"Apparently it was all very hush-hush. No one knew they were coming. They arrived on their yacht. It's parked on the Thames. They suddenly appeared and then all hell broke loose."

The phone on Priscilla's desk began to ring. She stared at it. What fresh hell could this be? she thought, paraphrasing Dorothy Parker, another put-upon woman who drank too much. She picked up the receiver.

"Buck's Fizz time!" the voice of Noël Coward announced.

"Where are you, Noël?"

"The American Bar. Where else would I be at this time of day? Come, join me. I won't take Noël for an answer. Why, I won't even take no."

Before Priscilla could offer any objections, Noël hung up.

Priscilla thought that if she had any brains, she would steer clear of Noël Coward and the American Bar. But she didn't have any brains, and besides, the police suspected she was a murderer. Damned good excuse for a Buck's Fizz. Maybe more than one.

"Hold the fort," Priscilla said to Susie. "I'm being summoned to the American Bar."

"A summons hard to resist," said Susie.

"Given what's happened today, impossible," agreed Priscilla.

There was an excited buzz in the air as Priscilla entered the bar, patrons straining to look blasé over their drinks, but unable to restrain themselves from continually glancing at the far corner where Noël Coward sat with a couple she instantly recognized—the Burtons, Liz and Dick, as tabloids the world over had nicknamed them.

It was startling to see the reality of the couple turning to Priscilla as she approached. Elizabeth Taylor's two most distinctive assets, those violet eyes and that impressive bosom, were on full display. Richard Burton, his pockmarked face deeply tanned, inspected Priscilla with sad, watchful eyes. Everyone, naturally, was drinking Buck's Fizzes. From the look of things, several had already been consumed.

Noël was on his feet kissing Priscilla's cheeks, making introductions, indicating that she should take the chair next to him, summoning the waiter to bring more drinks. Elizabeth unfurled a dazzling smile in Priscilla's direction.

"Noël tells me you're in charge of the press here at the hotel."

"That's right."

"Do you know how to keep them away?" Richard asked with an ironic smile.

"I'm afraid not, at least where the two of you are concerned."

"Bloody nuisance," Richard said.

"He loves it." Elizabeth said to Priscilla. "He won't admit it, of course." She glanced at Richard. "Otherwise, darling, you're just another Shakespearean actor wishing he were Olivier and worried about the rent."

"I never worry about the rent." Richard shot her an icy smile.

"Not anymore you don't—as long as you stick with me."

"No worries there, pet." Another icy smile. Richard finished the last of his Buck's Fizz.

Noël stepped in to fill the uneasy silence. "Elizabeth and Richard are in town to shoot a movie in which they co-star with yours truly."

"Noël is the real star of *Boom!*," Elizabeth said brightly. "We're just here to support him as best we can."

"*Boom*?" said Priscilla to Noël. "Did you write it?"

"Ghastly thing. Noël couldn't possibly have touched it," Richard said.

"It was originally a play by Tennessee Williams," Noël added. "Joe Losey's directing. We're all off to the island of Sardinia in a few days. Should be fun."

"Ghastly," Richard repeated. The waiter set another Buck's Fizz in front of him.

"Don't drink too many of those," Elizabeth warned.

"Just trying to keep up with you, pet."

"You can't keep up with me," Elizabeth snapped.

Richard regarded Priscilla with glassy eyes and a crooked grin. "You wouldn't know it, but we really do love each other."

"Indubitably. Forever," Elizabeth said.

"Now pet, I've warned you about using big words. There you go, showing off your MGM education again."

"Piss off," Elizabeth said. She finished her Buck's Fizz.

"What did I tell you?" Richard announced to the table with a wry grin. "An MGM education."

Priscilla's attention was diverted by movement at the entrance to the bar. It was Mark Ryde trailing a tall young woman in a short black dress with black hair and high cheekbones. Priscilla immediately recognized her.

She had seen the woman that morning hurrying out of Bernard Bannister's suite as he writhed on the floor.

CHAPTER SIXTEEN

With Richard Burton in a Rolls-Royce

"I did not shag Warren Beatty." Elizabeth Taylor's proclamation made Priscilla refocus on the world's most famous couple.

"Luv, you married Eddie Fisher. After that, anything's possible," Richard retorted in a somewhat slurred voice.

"You really are a bastard, you know that?"

"Indubitably."

Elizabeth glared.

From her vantage point, peering through the tables filled with patrons, Priscilla could just make out the woman in the black dress. She was seated on the far side of the bar, leaning forward, so that Priscilla had only a partial view of her face. She couldn't quite see Mark Ryde.

"I hear there has been more trouble at the Savoy." Noël Coward's voice caused Priscilla to once again refocus.

"I heard something about that, too," Richard said. "A dead body in one of the rooms."

"This morning, I believe. A member of parliament who became deathly ill and was rushed to hospital," Noël said. "Is that true, Priscilla?"

"Yes, I believe so," Priscilla said non-committally.

"Becoming downright dangerous to stay at the Savoy," Richard said.

"Not at all," Priscilla said, feeling she must say something in defence of the hotel. "Everyone is safe at the Savoy, Mr. Burton."

"Please, call me Richard." He gave her one of his sad smiles, the one, Priscilla had concluded in the short time since she had met him, designed to signal that although it looked as though he was having a good time, he wasn't.

On the other side of the bar, the woman in the black dress rose to her feet. Mark Ryde followed. The woman kissed him on the cheek and then grabbed her purse and made her way out of the bar. There was no sign of Mark leaving with her.

"I must go," Priscilla announced suddenly. The others at the table looked surprised. They were all famous. How could anyone possibly decide to leave their company?

"So sorry," Priscilla said, standing. "There's something I have to take care of back at the office."

The Burtons gave her slack-jawed, bleary looks. Noël was on his feet, kissing the air in the vicinity of her cheeks. "We must do it again soon," he said. "Buck's Fizz, forever!"

"Forever and ever," Priscilla said. With a wave in the direction of the Burtons, she headed out of the bar, noticing that Mark Ryde remained in place. He didn't see her.

Priscilla went down the steps and crossed the Front Hall to the entrance. She was about to go through the revolving doors when she spotted the woman in the black dress waiting outside. She stepped back, keeping her eyes on the woman. A black cab pulled up and the woman started for it as Priscilla pushed through the doors. She came out under the hotel's portico in time to see the woman in the black dress entering the cab, the rear door held by the doorman. The cab had pulled up behind a Rolls-Royce Silver Shadow saloon car. A uniformed chauffeur leaned against its hood.

"Do you need a ride?" Priscilla turned to see Richard Burton stagger out of the hotel.

"Where's your wife?"

One of Richard's small hands made circles in the air. "Off with Noël. He adores her. She adores him. A match made in heaven. They'll be very happy together, I'm sure. I'm out of it, left to my own devices, alas. My car is just over there. I'll drive you to the moon and back or anywhere else you'd like to go."

"I want to follow the black cab that just left," Priscilla blurted.

Richard gave her a glassy, unfocused look before producing a crooked, Buck's Fizz–induced grin and turning to his waiting driver. "Bob, you heard the lady, follow that cab."

"Yessir," Bob replied as though Richard Burton ordered him to follow London cabs all the time. He held the rear door open and Burton ushered Priscilla into the beige leather interior. A couple of moments later they were turning onto the Strand, Priscilla peering across the seats through the windscreen at the cab's taillights. "Do you see it?" Priscilla asked.

Bob's head bobbed up and down. "I see him, ma'am."

Richard's hand moved onto Priscilla's bare leg, "You smell lovely, like spring in the hills of Pontrhydyfen."

"Do you really think so?"

"Indubitably."

Priscilla gently removed his hand. "It looks like the cab is turning onto Trafalgar Square."

Richard leaned over to press his lips against her neck. She pulled away. "We're following that cab," she said, as if that was a reasonable explanation for not allowing a famous actor to kiss her neck.

"Of course we are, pet," Richard replied. He collapsed against her, mumbling, "Following that cab…"

They were on Pall Mall now, Bob having no trouble keeping the cab in sight. "Any idea where he's headed?" he called back to Priscilla.

"I'm afraid not," she answered.

Richard was half asleep, but his hand wasn't. Again, she removed it from her leg. He groaned.

The cab turned onto St. James's Street, Bob following. Priscilla wondered how many young women in London got to follow a cab in a Rolls-Royce with Richard Burton and his groping hand in the back seat. Not many, she surmised.

"I am falling madly in love with you," Richard murmured against her shoulder.

They were on Piccadilly, the traffic heavier. Priscilla had lost sight of the cab's taillights. "Do you see him?" she called to Bob.

"All fine, ma'am," Bob assured. "I've got him in my sights."

"We must run off together," Richard mumbled. "I'll tell Elizabeth. She'll understand."

"I doubt she will," Priscilla said, pushing him away to give herself more breathing space.

"Maybe you're right," he said. His head fell back against the seat. "Ah, sweet anguish."

Bob the driver was keeping up to the cab as it moved along Piccadilly, dipping down into the underpass and exiting onto Knightsbridge. Richard leaned against Priscilla. His hand resumed its probing, this time aiming for her breast. She eased it away. "You must behave," Priscilla said to him.

"I'm a movie star," he mumbled. "At all costs movie stars must not behave. It's in the rule book."

Priscilla caught sight of Bob's look in the rearview mirror. He shook his head slightly.

Knightsbridge became Kensington Road, Bob drawing closer to the cab as it turned onto Palace Avenue. Ahead, Priscilla could make out the back of the elegant redbrick structure that was Kensington Palace.

"He's turning in," Bob announced.

And sure enough, the cab went through gates at the rear of the palace. As it did, Bob slowed the Rolls. "As far as I can go."

Richard jerked awake and peered out the window. "Margaret," he announced. "Is that Margaret's place? A drab hellhole. Worse than Buckingham Palace."

Then he slumped heavily against Priscilla and began to snore loudly.

CHAPTER SEVENTEEN

The Love of His Life

Bob helped Priscilla get Richard Burton back into the hotel through the Savoy Hill entrance and up to the fifth floor.

"Where are we?" Richard demanded as he was helped along the hallway.

"We're back at the Savoy," Priscilla said.

"The Savoy?" Richard appeared dumbfounded. "What the hell are we doing here? We should be at the Dorchester. There's been some terrible mistake."

"The Dorchester was all booked," Bob explained.

"This is unacceptable," Richard muttered. "I'm a Dorchester man. Through and through."

When they reached Suite 511, Bob said to Priscilla, "Here is where I will leave you."

"Are you sure you don't want to stay until he's inside?"

Bob shook his head. "I don't want to be present when that door opens."

"Well," Priscilla said, "thank you for your help tonight."

"My pleasure," Bob said, starting away. Then he stopped and turned back to Priscilla. "None of my business, of course."

Priscilla looked at him questioningly.

"That woman we were following. While I was waiting for Mr. and Mrs. Burton, I saw her come out of the hotel—her name is Alana Wynter."

"How do you know that?"

"I've driven her before."

"Do you know anything about her?"

"I know her name, that's all." He gave her a smile. "In case it helps."

The door to the suite opened. A glowering Elizabeth Taylor said, "There you are, you prick. Get in here."

Priscilla helped Richard into the suite where Noël Coward stood with a cigarette holder in one hand and a drink in the other. "Ah, Priscilla," he said. "I thought we had lost you."

"I have an announcement to make," Richard commanded in a thunderous voice designed to reach the balcony in even the largest theatre.

"You've made enough announcements for one night," snarled Elizabeth.

"I am leaving you," Richard said.

"The best news I've heard today," Elizabeth said.

"I am leaving you because I have fallen in love with—" he turned his hazy gaze to Priscilla. "I'm sorry, my pet. What *is* your name?"

"I think," said Noël, setting aside his drink and taking Priscilla by the arm, "it is time to, as they say, call it a night."

"She is the love of my life!" Richard cried.

"Glad to hear it." Elizabeth's violet eyes sparkled maliciously. Priscilla was thankful that Elizabeth kept her scowl focused on Richard, ignoring the object of his undying desire.

Protestations of love appeared to exhaust Richard. He slumped onto a sofa. "I need a cigarette," he said.

"It's been a delightful evening," Noël said. "Marvellous to see the two of you again, and I am so looking forward to shooting *Boom!* together—a surefire hit, of that I am certain."

Elizabeth was yelling at Richard as they departed. The sound of her harangue followed them to the lift. Noël issued a deep sigh. "What a horror," he pronounced. "I love the two of them dearly, but when they've been drinking..." He allowed the sentence to trail off in a flurry of melodramatically raised and lowered eyebrows. "You know what they say about Elizabeth and Richard? The first hour is enchanting. After that, everyone starts looking for a place to hide."

"He certainly has trouble keeping his hands to himself."

"Can't say as I blame him—*if* you're inclined that way."

The lift arrived and they stepped in.

"I haven't had a chance to tell you," Priscilla said.

"Tell me what?"

"The man who was found unconscious in his room this morning."

"Yes," Noël said.

"His name is Bernard Bannister," Priscilla said.

"My goodness. Bernie Bannister. Possibly the next Tory leader."

"And I'm the one who found him."

Noël's eyebrows were working up and down again. "How the devil did you do that?"

"I was supposed to inspect Bob Hope's suite, but reception gave me the wrong key and I walked into Mr. Bannister's suite."

The lift came to a stop. The Front Hall was mostly deserted at that time of night.

"Bannister *lives* in London," Noël said, coming to a stop. "Whatever was he doing at the Savoy?"

"I don't know—except I sort of do."

"Yes?"

"While I was seeing to Mr. Bannister, a woman appeared from the other room and ran out."

"I see." Noël moved his bald head up and down in acknowledgement.

"The same woman came into the American Bar tonight. That's why I left so quickly. I wanted to see where she went."

"Which, I suppose, explains how you ended up with Richard in his Rolls."

"It turns out this woman's name is Alana Wynter. Does that name mean anything to you?"

Noël paused a bit longer than Priscilla might have expected before he asked, "Should it?"

"I thought you might know her, considering where the cab took her."

"Where did it go?"

"To Kensington Palace."

"And that is important because...?" Noel's eyebrows were drawn up his forehead. His expression was a curious combination of surprise and concern.

"It's where Princess Margaret lives. The same Princess Margaret who was seen leaving Amir Abrahim's suite the morning he was found dead."

Noël became contemplative as he lifted the ivory cigarette holder to his lips and took a long draw. "Tell me something," he said slowly, seeming to strain a bit to make his words come across as delivered nonchalantly. "Have you told anyone else about this?"

"I told the police about the woman, but at that point I didn't know she was Alana Wynter."

"Can I offer a word of advice?" Noël, settling, taking on the role of fatherly mentor.

"Yes, by all means. That's why I'm telling you all this. I'm not sure what to do."

"For now, I would do nothing," he said. "Hopefully, Mr. Bannister recovers and the person who was or was not in his suite won't matter."

"How do you suppose Princess Margaret is involved?"

Again, the pause was unexpectedly long. "I have no idea," he finally answered. "But I do believe talking about it will only needlessly complicate matters, and perhaps cause a scandal which would involve you. I would guess that's the last thing you want."

"It certainly is," Priscilla agreed, not sure what he was getting at.

"Then let it go for the time being." Noël spoke decisively, through a pall of cigarette smoke.

"Yes, you may be right." Priscilla sounded much more certain than she was feeling.

"Come, let's get out of here." The familiar merriment was back in his voice. "I'm tired and have drunk far too many Buck's Fizzes. I'm not Richard Burton in a Rolls-Royce, but we can share a cab if you like."

"You're much better than Richard Burton," Priscilla said. "At least I won't be attacked in the back seat."

"Be careful," Noel grinned, "in the dark, I am capable of anything."

"I'll take my chances," Priscilla said.

They laughed together as they exited the hotel.

Mrs. Banville Is Indisposed

The next morning, Priscilla decided to walk to work, at pains to ignore newsstands displaying tabloids screaming the news of Bernard Bannister in a coma. To her surprise, when she dared glance at the *Evening Standard*, there was nothing about him being discovered in a suite at the Savoy Hotel. To her relief, Percy Hoskins had been true to his word and had not used her name in his story.

Strange, not mentioning the hotel. That was not like Percy at all.

The sun was out, the air cool as she passed the institutions and monuments that reminded her of where she stood in the scheme of things—the Wellington Arch, the Victoria Memorial, and, of course, austere, imposing Buckingham Palace. Their very presence reduced her and shouted a warning: Do not upset those in power or their institutions; if you do, they will simply crush tiny birds named Priscilla, tiny *foreign* birds at that.

Or if not crush, then certainly bring about the loss of a very good job at yet another rock-solid institution in the British hierarchy, the Savoy Hotel. The thought made her shudder as she crossed the Mall, passing the hastening, pin-striped, bowler-hatted guardians of those very institutions that she could jeopardize given what she knew.

Or didn't know, but suspected.

She knew that the Egyptian arms dealer in whose suite she had been in was dead; she *suspected* he might have been murdered; *suspected* Princess Margaret might have been involved.

She *knew* that she had found Bernard Bannister nude in a suite at the hotel, and she *knew* he was a prominent member of parliament. She *suspected*, given the manner in which the police were handling things, that there had been some sort of attempted foul play; she *suspected* that the police believed she was somehow involved.

Further, she *knew* a woman with high cheekbones wearing a short black dress had been in the suite with Bannister. Moreover, she *knew* that the same woman had appeared in the American Bar later in the day with a man she *knew* was Mark Ryde—at least that's who he said he was.

The distraction of Richard Burton and his roaming hands and eager lips had not stopped her from following the woman in the black dress to Kensington Palace, the home of, yes, Princess Margaret. Thanks to Bob the chauffeur she had also learned the woman's name, Alana Wynter.

Then there was Noël Coward's reaction when she told him about following Alana. Not at all what she expected. Why did she have a sneaking feeling he knew who Alana was, despite denying that he did? Or was she becoming paranoid and imagining things?

What she *knew*, then, was too much, she concluded; what she *suspected*...that was too much as well. As she proceeded along the Strand, ignoring passersby, adding up what she knew and what she suspected, a cold fear ran down her spine. She didn't want to think about the fact that with all this information at her disposal, she had told the police practically nothing. What would be their reaction if she ever decided to spill the beans, so to speak? Off to Wormwood Scrubs with her! The menace to the British aristocracy removed and silenced, safely behind bars.

Most mornings the simple act of entering the Savoy's Front Hall filled her with pride and excitement. This morning, though, the feeling was one of trepidation, fearing that she was either going to be fired or that Richard Burton was waiting to whisk her off to—where would Richard Burton likely whisk her to? The South of France? Yes, that might be nice, except she would have to put up with the co-star of *Cleopatra's* groping and perhaps Cleopatra herself armed with a dagger.

There was, thankfully, no sign of the Burtons as she crossed the Front Hall but there was, unexpectedly, Millicent Holmes, the head housekeeper, making her way past the ticket desk. Priscilla called to her: "Mrs. Holmes…" Millicent turned and when she saw Priscilla coming toward her, she looked stricken and then nervous.

"I haven't had a chance to talk to you," Priscilla said. "You know, since—"

Millicent looked even more nervous. "They told me not to talk to anyone," she said.

For the first time, Priscilla noted a slight, hard-to-define accent on the edges of her otherwise very English voice. Had she noticed it before? Probably not, but then she had to admit she had not taken much notice at all of Millicent Holmes. Amid the various calamities of Priscilla's daily life at the Savoy, Mrs. Holmes was merely one of the hundreds of hotel employees moving quietly through the background.

"I wanted to talk to you, make sure you're all right."

"I am fine." But Millicent's darting eyes said otherwise.

"Are you certain of that, Mrs. Holmes?"

Millicent closed her eyes and exhaled before she said, "The police, Major O'Hara, everyone is on me, everyone wants me to say things. I don't know what to say. No one seems happy. It's very confusing. My husband is angry with me. I don't know what to do."

"What do they want you to say?" Priscilla asked.

"They want me to say I didn't see who I saw. Threatening me."

"They're threatening you?"

"Not in so many words. But Major O'Hara makes it clear that it would be much wiser for me to change my story. Then I say, yes,

I didn't see her. If that's what makes you happy, I didn't see her. Just, please, leave me alone."

"You mean you didn't see Princess Margaret? Is that what they want you to say?"

"I told them what they wanted to hear," Millicent said. "That is the end of it. But it isn't the end. It's too much." She stopped again and her eyes darkened. "But I mustn't talk to you, Miss Tempest—I shouldn't talk to anyone. I'm only going to get into more trouble."

"But listen to me, Mrs. Holmes—"

"I have to go, I'm sorry. Please. Leave me alone." Millicent started to brush past her but then stopped. "I would be most cautious if I were you, Miss Tempest. If they are threatening me to be quiet, they will threaten you, too."

She hurried off back into the Front Hall.

With Millicent's warning still ringing ominously, Priscilla entered 205 to find Susie, worry lines etched on her clear face as she rose from her desk. She spoke in an bleak tone, saying exactly what Priscilla was afraid she might say: "Mr. Banville is looking for you."

"You didn't tell me that," Priscilla replied immediately.

Susie blinked a couple times, taken aback. "I didn't?"

"You didn't." Priscilla, decisive.

"But Priscilla, I just told you—"

"No, Susie," Priscilla said with even greater firmness. "You didn't."

"Right," Susie said with a nod. "Jolly good. I didn't."

"I need a minute or two. I walked to work."

"You *walked*?" Susie made it sound as though that was the most impossible thing in the world.

"In preparation for climbing Mount Everest," Priscilla said.

"That's a joke, isn't it?"

"I'm beginning to wonder," Priscilla said as she entered her office, Susie following close behind.

"I suppose it has to do with what happened yesterday," Susie ventured. "You know, finding that gentleman."

"Among other events," Priscilla said, seating herself at her desk.

Susie's eyes widened. "What *other* events?"

"Oh, the usual. I drove around London in a Rolls-Royce with Richard Burton declaring his mad love before telling his wife that he is leaving her for me."

Susie's eyes practically bulged out of their sockets. "You mean he's *dumping* Elizabeth Taylor? For *you*?"

"Don't make it sound so impossible," Priscilla said. "Mind you, there is the fact he was drunk and couldn't remember my name. Small detail when you're madly in love."

Susie settled back, reaching for a cigarette, a knowing smile crossing her face. "Come on, now I know you're pulling my leg. You are, aren't you?"

"Yes, I suppose I am," Priscilla said with a sigh.

Her telephone rang. She allowed it to ring a couple times, gritting her teeth, hoping against hope it might be Richard Burton telling her to meet him in the Front Hall, they were off to her dream villa in the South of France.

But it wasn't.

"Did you not get the message that Mr. Banville wants to see you?" The insinuating voice of the Keeper of the Gate, Sidney Stopford, El Sid himself.

"I just got in," said Priscilla.

"Some of us have been at work for over an hour," Sidney sneered.

"When does Mr. Banville want to see me?"

"Immediately."

The line went dead.

Susie looked over sympathetically. "Is anything wrong?"

"The condemned woman was asked."

Susie's eyes once again grew large. "You're not going to get fired, are you?"

"I'm about to find out," Priscilla said, rising from her desk.

"If you get fired then..." Susie made a horrified face. "That means I would probably be fired, too." A tear ran down her cheek. "I can't lose this job, I just *can't*!"

"Don't panic yet," Priscilla said, heading out of the office. "They may simply horsewhip me."

Crossing the Front Hall, she looked for any sign of Millicent but there was only Major O'Hara giving her the sort of sad-but-resigned look prisoners receive from the hangman at the top of the scaffold.

In the general manager's outer office, the evil El Sid looked up at her as if measuring her for the coffin. "Go straight in," he said grimly. "Mr. Banville is waiting."

Priscilla once again was having difficulty breathing as she opened the door and stepped into Clive Banville's office. This morning he wasn't the statue at his desk she had previously encountered. This morning Banville was standing away from his desk, and—she couldn't quite believe it—*smiling*.

"There you are, Miss Tempest," he said in a surprisingly cheery voice. "How are we this morning?"

We are feeling as though it is moments before the blindfold is in place as the firing squad loads up, Priscilla thought. Out loud, she said, "I'm fine, thank you, sir."

"Good to hear, Miss Tempest. Good to hear." Banville had begun pacing.

Then he stopped. "Miss Tempest," he declared, "we have a problem that needs to be addressed."

Bollocks, she thought, here it comes. The time for smiles was over; the time for shit hitting the fan was nigh.

"What kind of problem, sir?" The words choked in her throat.

"My mother-in-law." Accompanied by what sounded to Priscilla like a nervous cough. "I must tell you that the present Mrs. Banville is some years younger than myself. Some years. Her mother, Mrs. Eunice Kerry of New York, is, therefore, well, younger than one might expect. She has decided to visit her daughter in London but has insisted on staying here at the Savoy."

"A good choice, I would say, sir," Priscilla said and immediately regretted the words since they brought a frown to Banville's previously serene face.

"Quite. The problem is, Mrs. Kerry arrives this afternoon and for various reasons I won't go into, I think it's just as well I don't meet her at Heathrow."

"I understand, sir," Priscilla said, when in fact she didn't understand at all.

"Good, I'm glad, because what I would like you to do, Miss Tempest, is fetch my mother-in-law from Heathrow and get her safely back to the hotel."

"Very well, sir," Priscilla said, trying not to show her disbelief.

"Further, for the next few days, I would like you to be available in order to act as her escort around London, ensure she sees the usual tourist sites, Buckingham Palace, the Tower of London, that sort of thing. She may also want to do some shopping and see a show or two, and you can arrange that for her."

He paused to give Priscilla an expectant look. In shock, she had no idea how to respond, so she simply said, "I see, sir."

"Is all this satisfactory?"

"Sir, naturally I would be happy to assist in any way I can. But would it not be more appropriate if Mrs. Banville herself escorted her mother around London? Would they not want to spend time together?"

"Mrs. Banville will assist where possible," Banville said. "But Mrs. Banville, Daisee—is somewhat indisposed at the moment.

"Very good, sir."

"Now, there is one other issue of which you should be made aware." To Priscilla's surprise, Banville actually looked slightly embarrassed.

"Sir?"

"In case it should come up, please note that Mrs. Banville spells her name a little differently than the usual Daisy."

"And how is that, sir?"

"She spells it *D-a-i-s-e-e*."

"Two e's, got it, sir."

"If I am to be honest with you, Mrs. Banville—Daisee—is usually indisposed where her mother is concerned."

"I see," Priscilla said.

"Therefore, Miss Tempest, your assistance in this matter would be most appreciated, both by me and by Mrs. Banville. I realize on the surface this would appear to be outside the scope of your usual duties. But if you regard my mother-in-law as another visiting VIP in need of your attention, well, then it fits right in, doesn't it?"

Priscilla delivered another "I see," unadorned by any show of enthusiasm. Banville didn't seem to notice.

"Mr. Stopford will provide you with the particulars as to Mrs. Kerry's arrival this afternoon. Check in with our office at the airport. They can arrange a limousine that will bring you back to the hotel. Mr. Stopford will also provide you with an appropriate stipend that may be used for any expenses you incur. You will, of course, provide receipts for all expenditures."

"Certainly."

"Mrs. Banville will be in touch at some point, but meanwhile if there are any difficulties feel free to contact myself or Mr. Stopford." He gave her a pointed look. "Any questions, Miss Tempest?"

"One question, if I may, sir. It's about Mrs. Holmes."

"What about her?" Banville was suddenly frowning.

"I haven't seen much of her since the morning she discovered Mr. Abrahim's body," Priscilla lied. "Do you know if she's all right?"

Banville gave every indication he was not pleased with the question. "As far as I know, Mrs. Holmes is fine," he answered cautiously. "We are not happy with her having made certain allegations that simply are not true. However, I understand from Major O'Hara she is reconsidering those statements."

"You mean about seeing Princess Margaret?"

Banville looked pained. "I'd prefer not to discuss that matter further. It's in the hands of the authorities. Let's now get on with our lives, Miss Tempest. I assume there are no further questions?"

Many questions, but Priscilla decided not to ask them. She shook her head. "No, sir."

"Very well, then. I think that's all for now."

Sidney gave Priscilla a smug look as she emerged from Clive Banville's office. He handed her a manila envelope. "Everything you need is in there," he said.

She took the envelope. Sidney grinned. "Oh, are you in for it."

"You really are an ass, do you know that, Sidney?"

"A word of advice from one ass to another: Don't screw up."

As much as she hated to admit it, El Sid was absolutely right, Priscilla thought. She mustn't screw up.

At Henry Fawcett's Memorial

"Do you still have a job?" Susie's eyes were at full bulge as Priscilla settled behind her desk.

"In fact, I have a new job," Priscilla said.

"A new job? What?"

"Babysitter to Mr. Banville's mother-in-law."

Susie looked perplexed. "I don't understand."

"Neither do I, but the fact is I have to be at Heathrow this afternoon to pick up Mrs. Eunice Kerry."

"Well, Mr. Banville didn't fire you," Susie said, resolutely holding onto the bright side.

"Not so far. Get on the phone to Pan Am and make sure their three o'clock flight from New York is on time, will you?"

"Jolly good," said Susie, picking up the receiver to call the airline.

Priscilla stared at her own phone for a couple of minutes, hoping it would ring so she wouldn't have to call him. But it didn't ring and so Priscilla got his card out of her desk and dialed the number on it.

Percy Hoskins answered almost immediately. "I knew you would call," he said with satisfaction.

"Meet me at the Henry Fawcett Memorial," Priscilla said, keeping an eye on Susie, who by now was preoccupied with someone at Pan Am.

"Where the hell is that?"

"A crack investigative reporter like yourself, Percy, I'm sure you can find it."

"What time?"

"In an hour—and don't be late. I don't have much time."

In fact, when Priscilla arrived, Percy was already flopped on a bench in the Victoria Embankment Gardens near the Henry Fawcett Memorial. The monument, flanked on either side by lilies and thick shrubbery, fronted a stone wall dripping with grape vines and shaded by nearby plane trees.

"He was blind," Percy announced, not bothering to get up, waving a hand at the bronze plaque that displayed Henry in three-quarter view, head heroically raised, eyes closed to a world he never could see. "Yet he defended Darwin's theory of evolution, supported women's suffrage, and as Britain's postmaster-general, invented parcel post and enabled the pay telephone. If Henry's any indication, we should blind all politicians. We'd be a better country for it."

"I'm glad I was able to add to your knowledge base," Priscilla said, plunking herself down beside him, wondering about the last time he got that rumpled jacket dry-cleaned, marvelling at how he could fail to run a comb through that tangle of hair. At least, she thought, from the look of his clean jaw, he had shaved recently.

Percy lifted his gaze from her legs to say, "You look spectacular, incidentally."

She pulled at the hem of a skirt but it was not about to cover more of her long legs no matter how hard she tugged at it. "I know what you're after, Percy, so you don't have to flirt."

"Was that flirting? And here I thought it was a compliment."

"I've been thinking about what you said."

"About looking spectacular?"

"About working together."

"You'll notice I didn't use your name in my story."

"That's the thing, you didn't even mention that Bernard Bannister was found at the Savoy," Priscilla said. "No one did. What happened?"

"Let's say it was part of the story when I turned it in."

"You mean it was removed?"

"Edited for space was the way it was explained to me—the way it is always explained," said Percy unhappily.

"But why?"

"Because someone in a high place got in touch with someone else in a high place and when that happens, things happen—like stories that get 'edited' so people like Bernard Bannister are protected from possible scandal."

"Do you think that's what they're doing?"

"It does avoid having to deal with the question of what a noted member of parliament was doing in a suite at the Savoy in the first place."

"How do you feel?"

"How do you think I feel?" Percy gave a shake of his head. "Pissed off. But there's not much I can do about it—other than complain to a lovely young woman by the Henry Fawcett Memorial."

"Look, since we last talked, a couple of things have come up," Priscilla said. "Things that if we're going to work together—*if* we work together—you should know about."

"What kind of things?" Percy had become less interested in her legs and much more interested in what she was saying.

"To your point about what Mr. Bannister was doing at the Savoy."

"You know?" Percy was sitting up straight.

"When I entered the suite and found Mr. Bannister, a woman ran out after he collapsed. Later that evening, I saw her in the American Bar."

A spark of curiosity flickered in Percy's eyes. "That would certainly explain Bannister's presence at the Savoy," he said, "and why they're trying to cover it up. Did you talk to this woman?"

"No, but later I followed her."

Percy couldn't keep the look of surprise off his face. "Followed her. Where?"

"She took a cab to Kensington Palace. That's where Princess Margaret lives."

"Yes, I know that's where Princess Margaret lives." Surprise had been replaced by impatience.

"I also found out the woman's name," Priscilla went on. "It's Alana Wynter. Does that name mean anything to you?"

Percy appeared to think for a moment before moving his shaggy head slowly up and down. "When I was investigating Amir Abrahim's background, her name came up. An international playgirl. They dated briefly, as I recall. But that would have been a couple of years ago."

"An international playgirl?" Priscilla's tone was skeptical. "What is that? Some sort of profession?"

Percy gave a snort of laughter. "It seems to be for Alana, particularly if it turns out she was the woman with that pillar of English family values, Mr. Bernie Bannister."

Priscilla pondered this, debating how far to go when it came to revealing what she knew to Percy.

"What?" he demanded impatiently.

"There's something else I should tell you that I haven't told anyone else." She had gone this far, she thought. No point in keeping anything from him now.

"The night I was with Amir, he said he was afraid that someone would kill him."

"You're kidding."

Priscilla shook her head. "The thing is, when I asked him who—who was threatening to kill him..."

"He gave you a name?"

"He did."

"Who did he say?"

Priscilla paused before she said, "Me. He said it was me."

Rather than amazement, Percy's expression was full of doubt. "You're sure he said it was *you*?"

"What? You think I'm lying?"

"No, but why would you want to murder Amir Abrahim—or, moreover, why would he believe you wanted to murder him?"

"That's the point, I wouldn't."

Percy took his time digesting what she had told him.

"What do you think?" Priscilla asked.

"I'm wondering if you slept with him."

Priscilla reacted angrily. "You bastard. I certainly did not!"

"Okay, okay." Percy raised a defensive hand. "I thought I'd better ask."

"Why does everyone think that?"

"Come on," Percy said, "a pretty young woman alone with a rich guy in his hotel suite..."

"It's so unfair," Priscilla said sullenly.

"Look," Percy said, working to change the subject, "my police sources have informed me that they still don't know what to make of Amir's death. They think some sort of poison chemical is involved but so far their tests don't show anything. Now they've got Bernie Bannister in a coma and they're thinking whatever was used to kill Amir may also have been employed on Bannister."

"The same person or persons poisoned both men?"

"It's certainly a possibility that my sources tell me has not been discounted."

"But why would someone poison two men who don't seem to have anything to do with one another and do it at the Savoy?"

"Good question," Percy said.

"There is one thing that might connect the two victims."

"What's that?"

"The morning she found Amir's body, the head housekeeper spotted someone she thought she recognized hurrying away down the corridor."

"Not Alana Wynter."

"No, the housekeeper, Millicent Holmes, thought the person looked an awful lot like..." And here Priscilla paused, worried about what kind of abyss she could be about to fall into.

"Who?" demanded Percy.

And off the precipice went Priscilla: "Mrs. Holmes believed she saw Princess Margaret."

"Jesus wept," he breathed.

"Princess Margaret is seen outside Amir's room the morning he's found dead," Priscilla continued. "Then I followed Alana Wynter, the playgirl as you call her, who ran out of Bernard Bannister's suite. She takes a cab to Kensington Palace where Princess Margaret lives."

"And *that's* the connection?"

"You don't think it is?"

"A little iffy," Percy said. "Have you told the police any of this?"

Priscilla shook her head. "I'm not so sure about the police."

"Why? What have the police done?"

"I just spoke to Millicent Holmes. She's the head housekeeper who found Abrahim's body."

"What about her?"

"She's in a terrible state. She told me they are pressuring her to change her story—threatening her, she says. Major O'Hara at the hotel, but the police, too."

"Change her story to what?"

"To say that she was mistaken, that she didn't see Princess Margaret in the corridor outside Amir's suite."

Percy made a face. "They're right bastards so I'm not surprised. That's what they do, they apply pressure and even threats. Even so, they must be pretty concerned if they're going after the house-keeper."

"I don't like that look on your face," Priscilla said in a warning voice.

"What look?" Percy, all innocence.

"The look that suggests you might print what I've been telling you."

"How can you even think such a thing?" Percy, maintaining said innocence.

"Because I know you and therefore, I worry you can't be trusted."

"Of course I can."

"Before you do anything," Priscilla went on, "we must find out more."

"Using that word 'we' again, music to my ears," Percy said with delight.

"I don't have a choice," Priscilla replied glumly. "A dead man tells me he thinks I want to murder him. The police suspect I might be responsible for a second man in a coma. I have to admit you've got a point. We must get to the bottom of this if I'm ever going to clear my name—what's left of it."

"No arguments from me," Percy said, looking supremely satisfied with himself.

"The question is, if we do find something, can you get it into print?"

"If it's solid enough, yeah, my editors could be talked into it—shamed into it, if necessary. Let's see what we can come up with."

Priscilla looked at her watch and stood up. "I've got to get out of here."

"Let me see what I can find out about Alana Wynter and how she might be connected to Princess Margaret," Percy said, also standing.

He noticed Priscilla's dour expression. "What's wrong?"

"I was just thinking about what we're getting ourselves into," Priscilla explained. "Noël Coward believes the British establishment will stop at nothing to keep whatever this is quiet. I didn't think much of what he said at the time, but now I wonder if he isn't right."

"Coward is right," Percy confirmed. "It's the establishment's job to keep things quiet and they are very good at it. They threaten helpless people like this Millicent Holmes. Then they get guys like Coward to warn people like you that they'd better not say anything that rocks the ship of state. However, it's up to guys like me to ignore their threats and tell them to go to hell and make the kind of noise that exposes the establishment for what it is."

"But can you do that?"

"Watch me," Percy said. "A bunch of privileged arseholes think they can get away with anything, including murder."

"Do you think they can?" Priscilla asked.

Percy thought about it and then shrugged. "Yeah, probably."

"Percy," Priscilla said in alarm. "That's not what I want to hear."

"How's this then: Priscilla, my love, we are about to shake up the elitist bastards and prove they can't."

"There," Priscilla said, "that's more like it." She glanced over at Henry Fawcett. His eyes remained closed. He didn't seem to be paying the least bit of attention.

CHAPTER TWENTY

A Force of Nature

According to her cranky cab driver, the traffic out to Heathrow was growing more impossible every day. Priscilla, as usual, was running late, so naturally the Pan Am flight from New York had to be early.

As she hurried along the crowded Terminal Three concourse to the arrivals area, Priscilla realized that she had no idea what Mrs. Eunice Kerry looked like. Not that it made any difference. The slim, scowling woman mounted in a wheelchair amid a sea of luggage could only be her.

"Mrs. Kerry?" Priscilla asked breathlessly.

"Who the hell are you?" The words spit from a thinly set mouth creasing a pale face, artfully smoothed by a very good plastic surgeon, that emphasized large, angry eyes. Her stiffly coiffed hair was like a dark brown helmet set atop her head.

"I'm so sorry to be late, Mrs. Kerry," Priscilla said in her best apologetic voice. "The traffic was terrible. I'm Priscilla Tempest. I work for Mr. Banville at the Savoy. He sent me to meet you and ensure that you get safely to the hotel."

"Where's my daughter? Where's Daisee?"

"I don't know, Mrs. Kerry. But I imagine she will be meeting you once we reach the hotel."

"My gawd," Eunice Kerry drawled grimly. "My own daughter can't even come to the airport to meet her mother. Instead, they send an... *employee!*"

"I am sorry, Mrs. Kerry, but our office at the airport has arranged a car for you. Our representative out here will be along shortly and he will take care of your luggage."

"You should already have arranged for him to be here!"

Yes, she should have, Priscilla thought fleetingly. What was wrong with her? Why couldn't she ever get the details right?

The uniformed Savoy rep finally appeared, out of breath and apologetic. He proceeded to pile Mrs. Kerry's luggage onto a cart and wheel it off toward the exit while Priscilla followed, pushing Mrs. Kerry along in her wheelchair, speculating as to whether Mr. Banville's mother-in-law was permanently confined or simply too lazy to walk.

The answer came as soon as they were outside and Priscilla spotted one of the Daimler Sovereigns the Savoy kept on call. She gave a silent prayer of thanks before saying, "We have a car over here."

"Stop the wheelchair," Mrs. Kerry ordered.

As soon as Priscilla brought the wheelchair to a halt, Mrs. Kerry rose up, and Priscilla got her first look at an impressively toned body swathed in something simple, blue, and beautifully tailored by Givenchy. Cruella de Vil, Priscilla decided, had a mean face and a lovely figure.

"What is that?" Mrs. Kerry demanded pointing at the Daimler.

"It's a Daimler Sovereign, ma'am," said Priscilla.

"A Daimler? I thought the hotel had a Rolls. They sent a Daimler instead of a Rolls?"

"I don't believe the hotel has a Rolls-Royce," Priscilla said. "This is the car we use to drive our guests."

"I prefer a Rolls," grumbled Mrs. Kerry.

"My apologies, ma'am. I will make a note of that for your next visit."

Mr. Cecil Bogans, the ancient chauffeur assigned to drive them, was grinning as he held open the rear door for Mrs. Kerry. She gave him a dark scowl. "What the hell are you smiling about?"

The Bogans grin disappeared. "I beg your pardon, madam. We are glad to see you and welcome you to London is all."

"Welcome." She spat out the word, as though it was a bad taste in her mouth. "Some welcome."

Realizing Mrs. Kerry's luggage was not going to fit into the Daimler's boot, Priscilla directed the nervous rep to arrange for a second car to transport the excess. When that was done, she started into the front passenger seat but was interrupted by Mrs. Kerry's demanding voice. "Ride with me!"

Priscilla climbed in beside her while Mr. Bogans got behind the wheel and started out of the airport.

For a time, they rode in silence, Mrs. Kerry staring with no particular interest out the window at the grey London day, Priscilla wondering how she was ever going to be able to deal with this woman over the next few days.

"It always rains here," Mrs. Kerry declared, finally. "At least in New York the sun comes out once in a while." She turned to face Priscilla. "They don't like me."

That caught Priscilla off guard. "I'm sorry. Who doesn't like you?"

"Who the hell do you think? My daughter and her old-goat husband."

"I'm sure that's not true."

"Yes, it is true," Mrs. Kerry retorted. "I wouldn't say it if it wasn't true. I embarrass them. I remind my daughter she married a man older than I am for God's sake—a husband older than the mother. Think about that."

Priscilla tried not to think about it at all. Instead, she tried desperately to summon something appropriate to respond and couldn't think of a thing.

"I haven't had the pleasure of meeting Mrs. Banville," Priscilla said finally.

"*Daisee*. With two e's. I think she changed the spelling to infuriate me." She glanced over at Priscilla. "She will treat you like shit, incidentally, our catty *Daisee*. You're the help, after all. She doesn't talk about the fact that her father was a gangster, her mother an ex-cop. Nope, you won't hear her say a word about that, let me tell you. Another reason she doesn't like me coming to London. I remind Daisee of her past, and she doesn't like to be reminded."

"You're a former police officer?"

"Surprises you, huh? But yeah, I was with the New York State Police for ten years before I met my husband, Daisee's father. Pulled him over on the interstate. Daniel P. Kerry. Turned out he was a New York developer, not anything really big, but big enough so that his business was a front for the Bonannos, one of New York's five Mafia families. A cop marrying a gangster. How do you like that?"

Priscilla didn't know what to say, not sure what was more mind-blowing: Daisee's mother's past or the fact that she was revealing that past to a complete stranger whom she had just met.

"Now, of course," Mrs. Kerry went on, "Danny didn't like to think of himself as a gangster. He was a businessman as far as he was concerned. But no one told the hitmen who shot him to death one night in our driveway. Joe Bonanno, the head of the family at the time, discovered Danny had been taking kickbacks from the development projects he was overseeing."

"Your husband was actually murdered?"

"He *was* taking the kickbacks to support our lifestyle. Danny always was a bit of a conniving asshole, so I didn't have a lot of sympathy for what happened to him. And he certainly left me a very rich widow."

"That's an amazing story."

"The reason I'm telling you this is so that when Daisee starts to put on airs and act like her shit doesn't smell, keep in mind that she's actually a gangster's daughter—and you, thankfully, are not. Or are you?"

"I don't think so. I'm not sure there are many gangsters in Canada."

"You're from Canada? Where?"

"Outside Toronto."

"Take it from me, honey. There are gangsters in Toronto. It is my experience that there are gangsters everywhere."

"I will keep that in mind," Priscilla said.

"And don't let Daisee lay any crap on you about her friend Margaret."

"Margaret?"

"You know, the princess. What other Margaret counts for anything in this town?"

"You're talking about Princess Margaret? The queen's sister?" Priscilla was having trouble believing what she was hearing. Daisee and Princess Margaret—*friends*?

"What are you, thick or something, child? *Yes*, Princess Margaret. Daisee keeps dropping her name like they're best friends or something."

"Maybe they are," Priscilla said.

"As far as I can make out, they're not," declared Mrs. Kerry adamantly. "Margaret uses Daisee, if you want my opinion, which, of course, my daughter never does."

"The princess uses Mrs. Banville?" Priscilla was exceedingly interested in how the princess would do that.

"Put it this way. Margaret has a taste for the wild side, and Daisee facilitates it, I'm afraid. If what my daughter likes to hint in her letters is true, they do get up to some trouble together."

Mrs. Kerry swivelled to Priscilla, as though suddenly realizing she was there. "But I shouldn't be talking like this." She glared at Priscilla. "You didn't hear any of what I've been telling you, do you understand?"

Priscilla nodded. She understood. But she *had* also heard.

The Suite Thing

No sooner had Eunice Kerry breezed into the Savoy's Front Hall than Vincent Tomberry appeared as though in a puff of smoke, his most obsequious smile solidly in place. "Welcome, Mrs. Kerry, welcome back to your home away from home."

"This sure as hell isn't my home," Eunice snarled. "It's a god-damn hotel, no matter what airs you people put on."

Tomberry went pale, rearing back as though Eunice was infected with a deadly virus.

"Where's my daughter?" Eunice demanded.

The question appeared to throw off Tomberry even more. "Mrs. Banville? I don't know. I imagine she should be along."

The words were barely out of his mouth before a lithe, elegant beauty charged—and there was no other word for it—into view. Even more fashion-resplendent than her mother, this time in what Priscilla suspected was Chanel, Daisee Banville, née Kerry, threw herself into her mother's not-exactly-welcoming arms.

"Mother!" Daisee cried, squeezing herself against Eunice, who looked much less delighted and a great deal more agitated.

"Oh, stop it, Daisee," her mother announced, pushing away. "I'm tired. I want to go to my suite. I hope it's not the same one as the last time. I hated that suite."

"I made sure they reserved you a lovely suite, Mother," Daisee said.

"I will decide how lovely it is. Let's take a look at it."

"Of course, madam," Tomberry interjected.

Daisee swung around to Priscilla. "You," she barked. "What's your name?"

"Priscilla Tempest, ma'am."

"Make sure my mother's luggage gets up to her suite. Do you understand?"

"Yes, ma'am."

A big smile spread across Eunice's face. "You see? I told you."

Daisee immediately looked suspicious. "What? What did you tell her, Mother?"

Eunice started walking away. "Come along," she said to Tomberry. "Show me this suite."

"Mother," Daisee said, rushing after the departing Eunice with Tomberry hurrying to follow. "What did you say? What did you tell her?"

Priscilla heard Eunice say, "I told her you are the daughter of a gangster who puts on airs."

"Mother! Are you crazy? You just got here and you're already embarrassing me!"

"How did it go?" Susie asked when Priscilla finally got back to 205.

"Mrs. Kerry changed her suite three times before she was satisfied," Priscilla said, seating herself at her desk.

"She sounds terrible," Susie opined.

"Mrs. Kerry is demanding, no question," Priscilla said. "But curiously enough, I kind of like her. Which is just as well since it looks as though I'm stuck with her for the duration—however long that is."

"Incidentally, before I forget, some chap dropped in looking for you."

"What do you mean, some chap?"

Susie gave one of the non-committal shrugs that Priscilla found irritating. "Dunno. Handsome enough. He didn't give his name. But he left a note for you."

Susie came over and handed Priscilla an envelope. "An admirer?"

"The world is full of them," Priscilla said, taking the envelope.

"Yes, but this one knows how to write."

"Ha ha," Priscilla said, opening the envelope.

The message inside read: *I'm all alone next door at the Coal Hole. Can I buy you a pint?* It was signed, *The fellow with the thirsty MG.*

"Do you know him?" Susie lingered near Priscilla's desk.

"Sort of," Priscilla said.

Mark Ryde, she thought. The gentleman with the MG—and the suspicious fellow she had seen with Alana Wynter in the American Bar.

In the Victorian era, the Coal Hole served as the coal cellar for the Savoy. Now it was a pub that featured a noisy after-work crowd of young professionals and Mark Ryde leaning casually against the end of the bar as though about to be photographed for an *Esquire* magazine feature about how the perfect young English gentleman should look.

Maybe too perfect, Priscilla thought as she slipped through milling patrons and fell into place beside him. She had to concede, as that far-too-handsome face lit in greeting, that as far as perfect men in her life went, lately, no one had made that list.

"I was beginning to wonder if I hadn't been stood up," Mark said.

"After the day I've had, I decided that what I needed was a knight in shining armour, providing he offered a drink," Priscilla said.

Mark looked amused. "Am I your knight in shining armour?"

"Provided you *are* offering a drink," Priscilla replied.

"Aha," said Mark with a grin. "I believe I can arrange that."

"Champagne absolutely would do the trick," she said.

Mark summoned the barman. A moment later a champagne flute was in her hand. Priscilla saluted Mark, and took a deep drink.

"A woman who orders champagne in a pub," Mark said approvingly.

"Your kind of woman?"

"I'm not sure," Mark said. "I haven't dealt with many champagne-drinking women in pubs."

"I'm happy to inform you that your education is now complete."

"I'm not so sure about that, either." He took a sip from the pint of beer he had been nursing. "I'm not sure about much of anything with you, Priscilla."

"Let's decide that we both remain mysteries," Priscilla said.

"I'm not sure that's a good idea," Mark said.

"No? I would say you enjoy mysteries."

"Oh? What makes you think that?"

"For instance, I no sooner run into you in the Front Hall of the Savoy than you show up at the American Bar."

Mark tried to keep the look of surprise off his face but couldn't quite pull it off. "Were you there? I'm afraid I didn't see you."

"You were obviously preoccupied. I was hiding in a corner." Not adding that she was sitting with the Burtons and the whole place had their eyes glued to their table.

"Far too popular for my taste," Mark said. "We didn't stay long."

Before she could think not to, Priscilla heard herself say, "She looked familiar. I wonder if I might know her. Your girlfriend?"

"She's a friend." Rather abruptly, Priscilla thought.

"Not a girlfriend?"

"A *friend*," he emphasized.

"Does she work with you?" It couldn't hurt to prod him, disrupt that casual air of authority he carried around.

"Does it matter?" Had Mark tensed a bit? She was pretty sure he had.

"Curious, that's all."

"No, we don't work together." He seemed to relax, as though finding firmer ground.

"I see. What about you, Mark?"

"What about me?"

"You said you were a civil servant. What sort of civil servant are you?"

"Boring, unfortunately," he replied, adding one of his disarming grins. "Is there any other kind of civil servant?"

"You don't strike me as the boring type."

"Good. I have successfully fooled you—so far."

"Except in my job, it's not a good idea to allow oneself to be fooled."

"No?"

"I find it helps to have a kind of sixth sense about these things, to suspect when someone professes to be the one thing—a boring civil servant, for example—you must be prepared to learn that he or she could turn out to be something else entirely."

"I'm afraid you've lost me." Mark's smile seemed forced.

"Have I?" Priscilla finished her champagne. "I tend to do that."

"Lose people?"

"I leave them strewn about in confusion all over town."

"Can I get you another glass of champagne?"

"No, I have to get going—but thanks."

"So soon?" Was that a somewhat disappointed look? Priscilla decided it was.

"I'm afraid I'm on babysitting duty this week."

"Babysitting? Aha. Maybe *you* aren't what you seem."

"I'm Canadian. Canadians are *exactly* what they seem."

"That's refreshing in a town where, as you say, everyone pretends to be something they're not. You never really know, do you?"

"No, you never do," Priscilla said. "Thank you for the drink." She started away from the bar. Then she stopped and turned around. "Incidentally."

"Yes?"

"I don't believe you."

"You don't believe what?"

"I don't believe for a minute that you're a boring civil servant."

"I may surprise you," he said.

"You already have," she said. True enough, Priscilla thought as she threaded her way through the crush of increasingly noisy Coal Hole regulars grown happier with life after a drink or two.

Surprised her—and made her all that more wary.

Call Commander Blood

Louis Francis Albert Victor Nicholas Mountbatten, Admiral of the Fleet, sat with Noël Coward over brandy amid the hushed, dark-wood serenity of the Reform Club's library.

"Apparently, there are seventy-five thousand books," Mountbatten said, gazing around at the floor-to-ceiling book-filled shelves.

"Interesting," Noël remarked. "Each time I'm invited here, someone invariably tells me there are seventy-five thousand books in this library, and I invariably wonder if any of them are mine."

"There is talk of a knighthood," Lord Mountbatten said.

"Now there's a sentence I don't often hear at the Reform," Noël said, blowing cigarette smoke in the air, a kind of smoke-screen against any idea that he might long for a knighthood to be more than simply talk. "I usually take these rumours with a sip of brandy," he added, taking a sip of brandy.

"This time, it's more than the usual rumours," Mountbatten said.

"Is that so?" Noël studied Mountbatten's ravaged, handsome face through hooded eyes and a cloud of cigarette smoke.

"I have it on excellent authority."

Noël allowed a smile. "Does any rumour ever come without Excellent Authority's name attached to it?"

"You perhaps forget that I have a direct line to HM," Mountbatten gently countered. "Her Majesty likes you a lot—and appreciates your contributions to the theatre, particularly in light of the rubbish that somehow is allowed on London's stages these days."

"Her Majesty is most kind," Noël said.

"Her Majesty desires to recognize a great talent—and, for my small part, I am anxious to ensure that talent is properly recognized."

"Most kind, Dickie." Noël clasped his hands together so that his cigarette holder was like a spear jabbed in Mountbatten's direction. "But if I may ask, from what well deep within you does your sudden desire to celebrate me spring?"

Mountbatten adopted an expression of mock horror. "Surely, Noël, you can't imagine any ulterior motives on my part."

"I can't imagine, but I can suspect," Noël said.

"There is in fact something you might help us with," Mountbatten went on.

Noël gave a knowing smile, giving silent thanks to the other shoe that had finally begun to drop. "Of course, I am at the disposal of HM."

"That's precisely what I told her." Mountbatten paused to drink from his brandy. "As you are undoubtedly aware, the Palace always has its antenna up when it comes to even the whisper of scandal."

The thud Noël heard was the sound of that other shoe hitting the floor. He said nothing. His skeptically raised eyebrows said it all.

"HM is particularly sensitive to any gossip involving her sister, the Princess Margaret."

"Understandable," Noël interjected. "A lovely woman, incidentally, and a good friend."

"You may not be aware of this, few are, but the Palace has lately created a dedicated team of private investigators to handle any, shall we say, matters of delicacy that should arise. These investigators have been dubbed the Walsinghams, after Sir Francis Walsingham, who protected the first Queen Elizabeth."

"I had no idea," Noël said, and he hadn't.

"The Walsinghams have brought it to my attention that a young woman named Priscilla Tempest has been involved in recent events that could have unpleasant repercussions if they are not properly handled."

The mention of Priscilla's name caught Noël off guard. He wasn't certain what he was expecting, but not this. "What kind of events would they be?" he asked.

"The young woman in question is employed at the Savoy where the body of a man named Amir Abrahim was discovered in one of the suites. Apparently, this woman had been with the deceased man the night before. That wouldn't mean much of anything, except for the scurrilous suggestion this fellow Abrahim may have had some sort of association with HRH the Princess Margaret."

"Oh, dear," said Noël.

"I am led to understand that you know this young lady, this Priscilla Tempest."

"Yes, I have gotten to know Priscilla over the past year or so since she has been in charge of the press office at the Savoy."

"And?"

"And the Savoy is, as we both know, a hotel of discretion. Only those individuals of the highest and most reliable calibre are in their employ. Priscilla is an extremely intelligent young woman of utmost discretion."

"There is, however, some thought that management is not happy with her."

"I have not heard anything of the sort," Noël said truthfully.

"Apparently, it was also Miss Tempest who found Bernard Bannister in some distress in his suite."

Noël feigned surprise. "That is news to me. But surely Bannister's distress can't have anything to do with the princess."

"That remains to be seen," Mountbatten replied.

"Does it?" Noël occupied himself finishing his brandy.

"I would be most appreciative, and I'm sure the Palace would be most thankful, if you could have a word with Miss Tempest. Discreetly, no need to say anything about our conversation."

"No need at all," Noël agreed.

"Find out what you can about what she knows, or, more to the point, doesn't know, about these incidents. Particularly if there is something about the Bannister situation she hasn't told the police."

Noël thought about the woman Priscilla had said skedaddled out of Bannister's suite; the same woman Priscilla had followed to Kensington Palace.

He asked, "You think there could be something?"

Mountbatten produced the icy smile Noël imagined had been pasted on that rugged countenance the moment he discovered Lady Mountbatten had been romancing Nehru. "See what you can find out."

"It would be my pleasure," Noël said.

"There is one other thing," Mountbatten said, withdrawing a card and a fountain pen from his inside jacket pocket.

"What's that, dear boy?" inquired Noël.

"The chap in charge of the Walsinghams, his name is Commander Peter Trueblood, seconded from the Queen's Guards, as tough a gentleman as ever wore a uniform. He served under me during the war, one of the survivors of Dieppe, in fact—Distinguished Service Order for the way he behaved on Orange Beach."

"Ah, yes, Dieppe," Noël said gravely.

Mountbatten seemed not to hear. "The point is this..." He had unscrewed the cap of his fountain pen and was writing on the back of the card. "The best thing from here on in is for you to liaise with Commander Blood."

"Commander Blood? Sounds ominous."

"Doesn't it, though? It's what everyone calls him, although possibly not to his face." He handed Noël the card. "That's his number.

Give him a ring. I really don't think there's any need for us to further discuss the matter, do you?"

"No," Noël said, "I don't suppose there is."

Mountbatten's smile was wider this time, a bit of warmth intersected the coldness of his eyes. "I do look forward to the day when I am forced to call you Sir Noël."

That would be the day, indeed, Noël thought.

CHAPTER TWENTY-THREE

Martinis for Lunch

"The Tower is over one thousand years old," Priscilla said, standing at the entrance gate to the Tower of London, desperately trying to recall the few tourist-friendly facts she had managed to pull together before meeting Eunice Kerry.

"About the same age as my son-in-law," Eunice replied with a grimace.

The day with Eunice had been, it was fair to say, a mixed success, with Priscilla constantly on edge, thinking of novel ways to please her boss's mother-in-law. Not an easy task where Eunice Kerry was concerned.

A fleeting visit to Harrod's had Eunice complaining about the prices and the state of English fashion. A trudge through the Burlington Arcade, dawdling at the boutiques, with the displays of luxury appearing to finally relax Eunice and put her in such a good mood she actually bought a Hermès bag.

When Priscilla suggested Asprey's on New Bond Street, famous for its jewellery, Eunice adamantly said, "No!" A drive down trendy Carnaby Street reignited the grump and complaints about hordes of young women in minuscule skirts, followed by a loud conclusion that Western Civilization had come to an end right there on the street. Priscilla gave silent thanks that she had chosen a longer skirt today.

Now here they were outside the fifteen-foot-thick walls of the Tower. "Built by William the Conqueror as a demonstration of his power," explained Priscilla.

"Bully for him," said Eunice.

"It's one of Britain's most iconic landmarks," Priscilla went on, warming to her knowledgeable-tour-guide role, while worrying that knowledge was about to run out. "A palace to kings and queens, a secure location for the crown jewels, as well as a prison and a place of execution and torture."

"Are they still executing and torturing?"

"Not for some time now," Priscilla said.

"Too bad. I have a few candidates for the axe."

"They used to have lions and tigers, all sorts of animals, even an elephant. Do you know what they fed him?"

"The heads of the people they executed?"

"A gallon of red wine every day. The elephant didn't last long, alas." A historic detail of which Priscilla was particularly proud.

"But I'm sure he died happy, which is something I'm not liable to do if you keep up this babble," Eunice stated impatiently.

Priscilla was heaving a quiet sigh of relief as she asked, "Don't you want to go inside the Tower?"

Eunice glumly eyed the hordes of tourists pressing through the entrance. "I'd rather be a guest at the Place of Execution." She looked at her watch. "Besides, it's almost lunchtime. I am in need of a martini."

"Am I boring you?" Priscilla asked worriedly. It was one thing to want to be away from the Tower before she was revealed to be a tour-guide fraud; it was quite another to be found boring in the eyes of Eunice.

"I know you're forced to do this, Priscilla—"

"Not at all," Priscilla protested.

"And you're doing your best. But frankly, faced with a choice between old castles, blood-soaked English history, and a martini, I'd rather have the martini."

"Where would you like to go?"

"My daughter wants to meet me for lunch at Simpson's-in-the-Strand."

"That's an excellent choice. I'll drop you off there."

"Oh, no you don't," Eunice said sternly. "You're not leaving me alone with her. You'll join us for lunch."

"But surely—"

"That's an order," Eunice stated summarily.

Amid the woody elegance of Simpson's-in-the-Strand, white-coated waiters floated unobtrusively among linen-covered tables filled with important-looking gentlemen speaking in hushed tones while carvers at the silver serving trolleys prepared the day's roast beef offering.

In an atmosphere far more comfortable dealing with the men of the world, the sober-faced maître d' guarding the entrance took one look at Priscilla and didn't appear to like what he saw. However, as soon as he spotted Eunice, his displeasure evaporated into a welcoming smile. "Mrs. Kerry, how good to see you again," the maître d' beamed. "Your daughter telephoned to say she has been slightly delayed. I will be delighted to show you to your table."

Despite Mrs. Kerry's obvious good standing, that still did not mean she and Priscilla could be seated anywhere but on the second floor. Unaccompanied women were not allowed in the main dining room.

"I need a double martini, dry, with a twist of lemon, *tout de suite*," Eunice announced as a swirl of waiters held chairs and unfurled napkins, nodding eagerly. The maître d' asked Priscilla what she would like to drink.

"Water is fine," Priscilla said.

"Nonsense," Eunice pronounced. "She will have a glass of champagne, her favourite, apparently. I cannot possibly drink alone."

The waiters led by the maître d' hurried away as if defeated by a superior force—which is what had happened. Eunice gave a sly smile. "You see, honey? I know more about you than you may think."

"Do you?" Priscilla tried not to sound surprised.

"You are single, Canadian as you informed me, and like to drink champagne."

"Correct on all three counts."

"And you like men."

"I do," Priscilla answered. "Mostly, I like men."

"Do you sleep with lots of them?"

Priscilla wasn't sure how to answer that question. "I suppose that depends on your definition of 'lots,'" she said.

"Oh, yes, and there is this thinking around the hotel that you don't quite fit in."

"I'm sorry to hear that." Priscilla was certain that the sound of her stomach twisting into a knot could be heard through the restaurant.

"Don't be," Eunice said. "I told my idiot son-in-law that if they get rid of you, I'd never step foot in the hotel again."

Priscilla managed a doubtful smile. "That's very kind, although I must say I doubt it will have much effect."

"Are you kidding?" A look of mock horror crossed Eunice's face. "Clive Banville, that old pompous goat, is absolutely terrified of me. I like you, honey, and I don't like many people. Don't worry. Your job is safe, at least while I'm around."

"Thank you, Mrs. Kerry. As a matter of fact, I like you, too."

"Sure you do. What's not to like?" The question came with a knowing wink.

The two women laughed together as their drinks arrived along with Daisee Banville, a startling vision in pale green. "Damn," Eunice murmured. "I was hoping to get a martini into me first."

Daisee was doing her best to work up a smile as the maître d' held the chair so she could be seated. "Have you ladies been having a wonderful morning?"

She did not wait for an answer but glanced up at the hovering maître d'. "Bring me sparkling water."

The maître d' nodded and said, "Yes, madam," before hurrying away.

"You're not having anything to drink?" Eunice did not sound happy.

"I never drink during the day, Mother," Daisee replied. "You know that."

"Do I? I must have forgotten."

"Tell me about your morning," Daisee said, arranging to change the subject. "What have you been up to?"

"Priscilla took me to the Tower of London where apparently they used to behead members of the establishment who had displeased the Crown. I was disappointed to learn they had closed down that part of the operation."

Daisee gave a tight smile. "Well, Mother, you'll be glad to know the Crown is very happy with this particular member of the establishment."

"I cannot tell you how thrilled I am to hear that," Eunice said dryly.

Daisee glanced around to make sure none of their pin-striped neighbours was listening before leaning forward and dropping her voice. "Now you mustn't say anything to anyone." She gave Priscilla a sharp look. "Do you understand?"

"Yes, certainly," Priscilla replied.

Eunice rolled her eyes. "What are you going to tell us? You're spying for the Russians? Don't worry. I already suspect that."

"Mother, really," Daisee said in an exasperated voice. "I'm tempted not to tell you."

"Go ahead, I doubt if anything's going to stop you, anyway."

"This is why I couldn't be with you this morning. I was meeting with...Princess *Margaret*."

Before either Priscilla or Eunice could react, a waiter arrived with their drinks. Eunice promptly gulped down half her martini. Her daughter took critical notice. "Mother, really."

"I'm so overwhelmed at the news of you and Princess Margaret," Eunice said.

"Are you ladies ready to order?" the waiter chimed in.

Daisee frowned. "Give us a few more minutes."

The waiter disappeared. Eunice drank some more while Daisee again leaned in. "Princess Margaret is having a very small and *intimate* birthday dinner party, and she'd like me to host it at the Savoy!"

Daisee paused for dramatic effect. To break the ensuing silence, Priscilla felt she had to say, "That's wonderful."

"Who gives a hoot?" added Eunice.

Daisee grimaced and sat up straight. "Well, I tell you, Clive will be over the moon—thanks to me, I might add." She again fixed a pointed look at Priscilla. "This is all very hush-hush, Miss Tempest. There is to be no publicity. Do you understand? Absolutely *no publicity*."

"I understand," Priscilla said.

"I don't understand at all," Eunice said. By now she had polished off her martini. "As soon as Margaret shows up at the hotel, everyone's going to know—and then you'll be pissed off and blame poor Priscilla."

"That's the beauty of what I'm planning," Daisee said excitedly. "Margaret has agreed to this so that she doesn't have to celebrate at that awful Kensington Palace. We will close Simpson's for the night and then bring Margaret in through the back."

"How does that get her to a dinner party at the Savoy?" Eunice asked.

"Through the *tunnel*," Daisee exclaimed.

"Tunnel? What tunnel?"

"There is a tunnel that runs between Simpson's-in-the-Strand and the Savoy. Few people know about it. We will bring her to dinner through the tunnel and no one will be the wiser."

"Seems like a lot of trouble for nothing, you ask me," Eunice said, looking around for a waiter.

"Mother, really, you just don't understand the importance of this—to me and to the hotel." Daisee was sitting back, the beginnings of a disappointed pout on her face.

"Good for you, Mrs. Banville," Priscilla said. "I'm sure it will be a spectacular dinner, and thanks to you, a real coup for the hotel. If there's anything I can do to help, please let me know."

Eunice rolled her eyes. "Priscilla, you are such a suck."

"In order to ensure everything runs smoothly," Daisee went on, "Margaret insists that I coordinate arrangements through this character I've never heard of before. She tells me he is in charge of palace security. He's the one who came up with the tunnel idea. Apparently, he's used it before."

"Interesting," Priscilla said.

Daisee dropped her voice again. "Like I say, a real character, a frightening gentleman if you ask me. Commander Peter Trueblood. Everyone calls him Commander Blood. No one to mess with, it is said. Margaret feels very safe with him."

Commander Blood? Priscilla thought. Perhaps a name to remember.

"Bring me another martini." Eunice's voice loudly cut the air as a waiter materialized. "And make it snappy," she added.

After three martinis and a slice of rare roast beef pushed around on her plate as her daughter nattered heedlessly on, a sodden Eunice at last allowed Priscilla to take her back to the Savoy and up to her suite.

"If you had a daughter like that, you'd have a drink or three, too," Eunice pronounced as Priscilla guided her toward a sofa. "Who gives a flying shit about Princess Margaret, anyway? The obsession with Royalty over here, I mean—*off with their heads*, I say!"

Once Priscilla got her settled on the sofa, Eunice immediately fell asleep. Priscilla retrieved a blanket from the closet and draped it over her. She stirred and mumbled, "You're very nice, honey. I don't give a damn about my daughter. I won't let them fire you."

Priscilla slipped away and took the lift down to the Front Hall, swiftly coming to the conclusion that if there was a takeaway from her morning with the boss's wife's mother, it was that she was closer than even she had imagined to being fired.

Not good news. *But*...and this was an important but, they had not fired her *yet*. There was still hope. Meagre hope, perhaps, but hope. Percy Hoskins might be right. With help from him, maybe she could discover what had happened to Amir Abrahim and Bernard Bannister and then she would be celebrated and her job would be safe.

Wouldn't it?

Susie had left on a couple of errands. Priscilla sat at her desk enjoying the silence. The phone for a moment was not ringing. No one wanted a free drink. The fuzz was disappearing from around her brain. She could think clearly—or what passed in her addled mind for clearly.

Commander Peter Trueblood. She couldn't stop thinking about that name.

Daisee's arrogant voice played back in her mind: *Commander Peter Trueblood. Everyone calls him Commander Blood. No one to mess with, it is said. Margaret feels very safe with him*..."

She picked up the receiver. Percy Hoskins came on the line almost as soon as she finished dialing his number. "Be still my beating heart. You have called."

"On a hunch," Priscilla interjected.

"A hunch, uh-oh." Percy didn't sound very happy.

"A name I heard. Peter Trueblood. Does it mean anything to you?"

Silence on the other end of the line.

"Commander Peter Trueblood," Priscilla added.

"I'm scratching my head here," Percy said. "I don't think it means anything. Should it?"

"Apparently he's associated with Buckingham Palace. He looks out for Princess Margaret. He's known as Commander Blood."

"Never heard of him," Percy said. "And I like to think I know everyone at Buck House."

"Will you look into it? See what you can find out about this fellow."

"What aren't you telling me?"

Plenty, when it came down to it, Priscilla thought. "Put it this way," she said aloud. "I'll know more after you help me out with this."

"I don't think you trust me," Percy said.

"I don't," Priscilla said.

"But you do love me."

"I would be out of my mind to love you."

"Aha," Percy said triumphantly. "Now I know you're in love."

Priscilla hung up the phone.

CHAPTER TWENTY-FOUR

Defence of the Realm

"What's the one about the divorced couple who end up at the same hotel with their new spouses?" asked Commander Peter Trueblood.

It was a warm day in St. James's Park, hardly a cloud in the sky, a slight breeze to break the late summer humidity. Perfect for sitting on a bench, Noël Coward reflected, watching strollers on the pathway, talking to someone he did not particularly want to talk to.

"You're probably thinking of *Private Lives*," Noël replied, trying not to show his annoyance at having one of his plays remembered in such a crass way.

"Yes, that's it," Trueblood said. "I quite liked that one."

"Very popular," Noël remarked. "A few years ago, now."

"Yes," agreed Trueblood. "You're still scribbling away, are you?"

Noël frowned "Every once in a while I manage to get something down on paper."

"Very good," Trueblood nodded. "That's excellent."

Silence. Noël listened to the birds in the nearby plane trees, taking in Trueblood out of the corner of his eye. Commander Blood was, even in sunshine, a somewhat ghoulish figure, greyish pallor, Ichabod Crane thin, eyes like pieces of coal sunk deep in their sockets, a hawklike nose doing its best to hide a pencil moustache, black hair showing beneath his Trilby. He wore the pinstripes of the career civil servant—or the paid assassin, depending on your point of view, Noël mused. Trueblood summed up was a fellow who gave the impression he worked much better at night, not comfortable once the sun was out. So possibly, Noël concluded, not so much the assassin as the vampire.

"Dickie Mountbatten suggested we meet." Trueblood broke the silence, turning the pieces of coal that were his eyes onto Noël.

"Yes, you work for the Palace, I understand," Noël offered, feeling unusually uncomfortable under Trueblood's gaze.

"Day and night, I'm afraid." Trueblood offered a weak smile. "Day and night."

"I'm not certain how much help I can be to you or to the Palace," Noël said.

"Tell me about this girlie at the Savoy. Priscilla Tempest? Do I have her name right?"

"As I tried to point out to Dickie when we spoke, I doubt if Priscilla is a threat to the British monarchy."

"Did you point that out to Dickie? Dear me. I'm afraid that message got somewhat garbled."

"I'm sorry to hear that," Noël said, longing for the cigarette that would get him through this.

"I take your point that this Tempest isn't, as you say, a threat," Trueblood said, taking his gaze away from Noël, distracted by a group of boys out on the lawn disturbing the sunbathers by insisting on kicking around a soccer ball.

"However," he continued keeping his eyes on the boys, "it's my job to investigate *potential* threats. And then, with facts in hand, arrive at a judgment one way or another."

"The Walsinghams." Noël tossed out the word, the contrarian inside him wanting to see if he could shake things up a bit.

Once again, he could hear the sound of birds. Shooed away by irate sunbathers, the boys disappeared with their soccer ball. Trueblood refocused on his bench companion. Noël thought he did so with great reluctance.

"I suppose Dickie used that term," Trueblood said in a low voice.

"As a matter of fact, he did," Noel said. "I hadn't heard it before."

"No, it's not a term I particularly like to throw around." Trueblood shifted around as though the bench had become uncomfortable for him. "I'm hoping I can persuade you to be discreet. Dickie says we can count on you."

"Yes," Noël said vaguely, thinking that people like Trueblood always believed people like him could be counted on, when in fact he could not be counted upon at all; he was the secret agent at their parties, hiding in plain sight, his true feelings about the aristocracy available on theatre stages, only for the past forty years or so.

"Basically, what it is," Trueblood went on, "I head an investigative team that looks for potential trouble and then tries to head off that trouble before it becomes detrimental to the royal family."

"Exhausting work these days," Noël said dryly.

"Keeps me on my toes," Trueblood agreed.

He continued in the lowered voice that caused Noël to lean forward in order to hear: "We are a small band of brothers, so to speak, dedicated to the Crown, naturally, but also to the values and traditions exemplified by that Crown. These are changing times. Great Britain is in great peril, thus it is left to men like ourselves to maintain as best we can the integrity of a country which, otherwise, one might argue, is falling apart."

"Well, I suppose there is that argument," Noël said, choosing his words carefully, keeping his eyes on the increased pedestrian traffic along the walkway, wishing again for a cigarette.

"Which brings us back to the state of affairs at the Savoy," Trueblood said.

"Would you mind terribly if I smoked?" Noël interjected.

"I would prefer you didn't, if you don't mind." Trueblood's gaunt face had taken on a sour expression. "My asthma, you see."

"Oh, dear me, sorry to hear that," Noël answered glumly. "You were saying?"

"I'm interested in how much our Priscilla Tempest might know about recent events and what she might say publicly about those events."

Noël made a show of clearing his throat before he said, "As I told Dickie, Priscilla had been out with this deceased individual, the notorious Amir Abrahim, the night before he was found dead. I informed Dickie that there was talk that the Princess Margaret had been spotted in the vicinity of Abrahim's suite around the time of his death."

"Quite impossible," Trueblood interrupted.

"Nevertheless, that's what the housekeeper who found the body believed. Priscilla was present when this possibility was revealed to the hotel management."

"And to whom was this revealed? Any idea?"

"In addition to Priscilla, I believe the manager, Mr. Banville, was present, as well as Major Jack O'Hara, the head of the hotel's security."

Trueblood took this in with a solemn nod. "And the police, I suppose, once they were summoned."

"I don't know about that," Noël said, truthfully.

"The Scotland Yard inspector heading the investigation, Bobby Lightfoot. Good man, Bobby. He tells me there is some suspicion our Miss Tempest could be more involved than she admits in both Abrahim's death as well as the apparent poisoning of Bernard Bannister."

Noël couldn't stifle a laugh. "I highly doubt that would be the case."

Trueblood gave no hint there was anything to laugh about. "Tell me, then," he said, "what is your assessment of this Tempest?"

"Priscilla is an intelligent young woman who likes champagne, short skirts, and men, in about that order," Noël offered. "She's a bit of a playgirl, I suppose, great fun, who thoroughly enjoys her job at the Savoy. I doubt she's going around trying to kill or poison anyone."

Yet again, Trueblood's silence allowed Noël to hear more birdsong. "I wonder if you underestimate her," Trueblood finally offered. "Apparently, she has been poking around in the company of an *Evening Standard* reporter named Percy Hoskins."

"And your concern is?" Noël asked, eyebrows elevated to their heights.

"My concern is twofold." Trueblood had raised his voice—presumably, Noël concluded, so that there was no doubt about what he was saying. "At worst she is indeed a suspect; at best she is playing amateur sleuth and snooping around in places she shouldn't be snooping, in the company of an anti-establishment reporter who has a reputation for causing trouble. Either way, I don't like it. And when I don't like something, I work very hard to straighten things out so that they are to my liking."

"And what makes you think Priscilla is playing at being some sort of sleuth?" Noël asked, somewhat taken aback by the notion of Priscilla out there snooping around to the point where it attracted Trueblood's attention.

"She is asking questions that she should not be asking. These questions have raised red flags among the people to whom I report. What's more, I learned this morning that the reporter Hoskins has been asking questions about my little operation, using a word I don't like, particularly when it comes out of the mouth of a reporter."

"I'm sorry," Noël said. "What word is that?"

"The word you used. Walsinghams," Trueblood said.

Later, when Noël reflected on what caused the sudden stab of fear that shot through him, he couldn't decide if it was the seeming merciless demeanour of this evil-looking protector of the establishment he was seated beside. Or was it the dreadful suspicion that assailed him as he left the leafy calm of St. James's Park that he had betrayed his friend Priscilla and only added to the jeopardy he was now convinced she was in?

Trouble Breathing

For the better part of a week, all was more or less quiet inside 205. Priscilla half expected—hoped?—Mark Ryde would call, but he didn't. In fact, the phone did not ring much at all.

Susie occupied herself filing her nails and talking on the phone to her mother. Priscilla had lots of time to complete the Savoy's monthly newsletter, which was sent out to the eagerly waiting local media—at least, Priscilla liked to kid herself that her victims were somewhat waiting and eager.

Thus, when Percy Hoskins ducked past Susie, still on the phone with her mother, and popped into Priscilla's office, she was almost glad to see him. If nothing else, he could briefly interrupt the monotony, even if it wasn't particularly safe to be seen in the company of the reporter who had broken news of the death at the Savoy, and who, at the best of times, was considered by the management to be an unwelcome and thoroughly irksome thorn in their sides.

"I need a drink," Percy pronounced, throwing himself onto the sofa against the far wall. "But none of that champagne crap you like to glug down."

"I don't glug champagne," Priscilla said in her best haughty voice. "One never *glugs* champagne."

"Excuse me," Percy said. "I forget that you are a woman of class and sophistication."

"Please keep it in mind from now on."

"Can I get a beer, then?"

"I'd prefer to throw you out," Priscilla said.

"No, you wouldn't. Unlike you, I haven't forgotten that we are supposedly working together. Thus, I have news of great interest."

"About Commander Blood?"

"First, a beer. It will loosen my tongue."

Priscilla pressed the waiter button, bringing about an immediate appearance by Karl. "I was beginning to think you had fallen ill," he offered in his gentle Austrian accent.

"Whatever would make you think that?" Priscilla replied.

"You have failed to summon me for nearly a week. Either you were deathly ill or perhaps dead."

"Even worse than illness or death, a misguided attempt to behave," Priscilla said.

Percy let out a snort of laughter. "Fat chance of that," he pronounced.

"That is certainly no way to act," Karl admonished with a slight smile. "You should be ashamed of yourself."

"I have to agree with you." Priscilla pointed to Percy sprawled on the sofa. "Could you bring this man a beer?"

Karl turned to Percy. "Will that be the usual, Mr. Hoskins? A Double Diamond, I believe."

"A Double Diamond, Karl," Percy said. His grin would have been at home on the Cheshire Cat.

"I must remind you not to be so welcoming, Karl," Priscilla said. "Otherwise, we will never get rid of him."

"As long as Karl keeps the Double Diamonds coming, I shall keep returning," declared Percy.

Karl took in the two combatants poised for battle and decided an exit was in order. "I will be back with Mr. Hoskins's drink," he said, making a hasty departure.

"What do you want to tell me, Percy?" Priscilla rose from her desk to close her office door.

"Okay, an update about Amir Abrahim. My sources at Scotland Yard tell me Charger Lightfoot and his minions are stumped as to what happened to him. The toxicology reports confirm the presence of trace amounts of a foreign substance, but they can't figure out what it is."

"But he was poisoned," Priscilla said, leaning against the edge of her desk.

"Definitely. Poisoned with what, though? What's more, they believe Bernie Bannister suffered the same fate."

"How is he doing?"

"Not good, but as with Abrahim, no one is willing to say anything. I've written a story for tonight's paper about this mysterious delay in the release of information about what happened to the two men. In the case of Abrahim, I'm saying the police seem to be hiding the fact that he was murdered. Which brings us to the subject of your so-called Commander Blood."

"What did you find out about him?" Priscilla asked.

"That's the interesting thing. Almost no one at the Palace wants to talk about this character. But I did a little more digging. He's ex-military, served under Mountbatten, known for his ruthlessness during the war, a staunch monarchist who apparently does work for the Palace as part of a secretive group called the Walsinghams. Exactly what kind of work Commander Blood and his Walsinghams do is not clear."

"I might have some idea," Priscilla offered.

Percy's eyes lit up. "I knew it. You've been holding out on me. What secret have you been keeping to yourself?"

"Princess Margaret is celebrating her birthday with a private dinner at the Savoy. Everyone—including me—is sworn to secrecy so you mustn't print anything, do you understand?"

Percy nodded, leaning forward intently. "Yeah, sure. But what's the point?"

"The person who is coordinating the dinner at the Palace is this Commander Trueblood."

"Okay, he's arranging a dinner for Princess Margaret." Percy leaned back, a bit deflated. "What's the big deal about that? Doesn't sound very secretive to me."

She was saved from having to answer by the return of Karl, bearing Percy's Double Diamond on his silver tray.

"Here you go, sir, as ordered," Karl said, pouring Percy's beer into a glass.

"Like I always say, a millionaire's lifestyle on a beggar's wages, certainly at the Savoy," Percy said as he accepted the glass from Karl. "Cheers."

Percy finished half the glass in a single, long gulp. "Karl, perhaps you could bring me another, like the good man you are."

"Coming right up, sir."

As soon as Karl was gone, Priscilla said, "It's a big deal if Commander Blood and his Walsinghams are working for Princess Margaret and doing more than simply arranging her birthday dinner."

"You're not suggesting that Commander Blood, and therefore the Palace, is responsible for two possible poisonings at the Savoy? Are you?" It was clear Percy was having trouble with the idea.

"I'm saying it's a possibility we should consider."

Percy drank more of his beer and said nothing. Priscilla grew impatient. "Tell me what you're thinking. Does any of this make sense or not?"

"I'm thinking about where such a possibility would take us."

"To the door of Kensington Palace," Priscilla offered.

"And the answer to the question of why someone named Commander Blood would arrange to have an international arms dealer knocked off at the Savoy Hotel."

"To protect the reputation of Amir's lover and her family," Priscilla put in.

"The lover being Princess Margaret." Percy was on his feet, pacing, his glass of beer forgotten. "That would mean your house-keeper was telling the truth," he added.

Silence as Percy kept pacing and Priscilla remained in place against the desk's edge, the two of them digesting the implications of what they had been discussing.

"Is this even a possibility?" Priscilla finally asked, half-hoping Percy would accuse her of weaving a fictional tapestry out of nothing.

"And even if it is possible," Percy went on, "I don't know that there's much we can do with it."

"What do you mean?"

Percy stopped pacing and confronted her. "What I mean is, I'm not sure the British press would have anything to do with a story that implicates the queen's sister in a possible murder."

"Wouldn't your paper be hard-pressed to ignore such a thing?"

"I don't know," Percy said. "When it comes down to it, the cop-pers are controlled by the same powerful people who control just about everything in this country and who are probably working very hard to keep the lid on this."

"So what do you think we should do?"

"Find out more," Percy said with a shrug. "We have plenty of theories and suspicions but no hard evidence. The police, and my editors for that matter, will use any excuse not to listen to us. If we've got evidence, they will have to listen—my paper, too."

"Yes, I guess that's the best thing."

"Also," Percy went on, standing close to her, his usually mock-ing face drawn into an unaccustomed expression of seriousness, "from here on out, you must be very careful."

"Funny, Millicent Holmes said the same thing."

"Let's face it, Priscilla, if we've got this right, and people con-nected to Buckingham Palace are willing to commit murder, they won't hesitate to take similar action if they find out you're involved."

"You mean they would kill me, too?"

"It's a possibility you shouldn't ignore."

Why was it, Priscilla pondered, whenever anyone threatened her life, she had the same reaction as when she feared losing her job? She had trouble breathing.

Karl appeared in the doorway. The second Double Diamond sat like a totem on his tray. "Sir!" he exclaimed to Percy in shocked disbelief. "You haven't finished your beer!"

CHAPTER TWENTY-SIX

Invitation to Ride

The new, healthy Priscilla, the Priscilla who would eat well and drink less champagne—well, a *little* less champagne—the Priscilla who would get a good night's sleep for a change, who would be undaunted by a tiny thing like unseen establishment forces potentially murdering her, that Priscilla decided to walk home so she could clear her head.

After all, the new healthy Priscilla with a keen mind not fogged by champagne could think straighter as she came along Knightsbridge toward her flat, the dying light of the day reflected in shades of gold off the brick facades, the golden London, the mythical London, the safe London—*ha!*

She was only vaguely aware of the black Mercedes-Benz pulling to a stop slightly ahead of her. She didn't really notice the car until an impressively tall and muscular man emerged, bald and dark-complexioned in a grey three-piece suit, holding the rear door open. She snapped to attention when the tall man said, "Miss Tempest. I hope you are well this evening."

Priscilla slowed, blinking, making herself refocus as the tall man added, "We'd like you to come along with us, if you'd please be so kind."

"What?" Priscilla was having trouble digesting what this stranger was saying.

"I said, we would like you to come with us."

"Who are you?" Priscilla demanded.

"I represent people who would like to have a word with you."

Priscilla frowned. "People? What people?"

"Just get into the car, please."

Priscilla glanced around. The golden street was deserted. "I am not getting into any car," she pronounced.

"No harm will come to you," the tall man said.

"Right. I hop into cars with complete strangers all the time just as long as they say, 'no harm will come to you.'"

"I should tell you I have a gun." To demonstrate the truth of his statement, the tall man opened his suit jacket enough so that she could see the shoulder holster and the stock of a pistol.

"Is that a real gun?" Priscilla asked.

"It is," agreed the tall man.

"I don't think I've ever seen a real gun before, except, you know, in movies."

"Would you please get in the car?"

"What? Otherwise you'll shoot me?"

The tall man appeared frustrated. "Please, get in the car. You will not be harmed, believe me."

"Says a man who then shows me a gun. No thanks."

Priscilla resumed her march along the street, her heart thudding so hard she thought it might burst from her chest.

Behind her, a sharp voice called, "Miss Tempest!"

Priscilla turned to see a short, portly man, well dressed, with a grey beard, emerge from the Mercedes. "Miss Tempest, I am Aziz Abrahim. I am Amir's brother. My father wishes to speak with you."

"I didn't know Amir had a brother," Priscilla said. Was that true? Had Amir said anything about a brother, let alone a brother who might show up at her doorstep?

"Would you please come with us?" Aziz said. "You have my personal guarantee you will be safe."

Priscilla came back to the car, fearful, but now curious. "Supposing I did get in your car. Where is it you intend to take me?"

"Not far," Aziz said. "Please, get in."

Priscilla gave the tall man a look as she started to duck down into the back seat. "I didn't really think you would shoot me."

The tall man smiled. "Many people have said the same thing before I shot them."

Marry Me!

The Hampstead Heath house was large. Not—Priscilla decided as the Mercedes turned through entrance gates into an adjacent drive—like a mansion in the how-could-anyone-possibly-live-there sense, but a fine three-storey structure, surrounded by hedge groves that hid a high wall.

The gate, Priscilla couldn't help but notice, was guarded by two men who, in their dark suits and ties, looked much like the tall man in the driver's seat. She wondered if the gate guards also wore shoulder holsters with guns—and bet that they did.

The tall man parked in the drive at the front of the house and then once again politely held the door while Priscilla slid out. Meanwhile, Aziz Abrahim was already striding toward the entrance. The tall man indicated that she should follow.

Inside, a wide foyer featured a winding staircase and a hallway along which she trailed the briskly moving Aziz. He entered a dimly lit great room filled with smoke coming from an individual puffing a cigarillo, sunken into an immense throne-like chair. He wore a scarf tied loosely around his neck. The expression on his brown, cratered face was contemplative. The hand holding the cigarillo was twisted and gnarled with arthritis. He added more blue smoke to the air as he studied Priscilla. No one spoke.

Annoyance soon got the better of her fear. "What's this about, then?" she demanded.

Beneath the heavy lids of the man on the throne chair, Priscilla was certain she could see the gleam of a predator sighting easy prey. "Did you sleep with my son?"

"I'm sorry?" Priscilla wasn't sure she had heard correctly.

"I asked you if you slept with my son." He brought the cigarillo slowly to his mouth, waiting for the answer Priscilla wasn't about to give him.

"Well?" The word was barked out amid a fresh stream of smoke.

"Who are you?" A question, that, to her horror, came out as a nervous squeak rather than the authoritative demand she had been attempting.

"I am Tarak Abrahim," he announced with an authority Priscilla knew she could not possibly match. "I demand to know if you slept with my son."

"Do you mean Amir?"

"He is my son, yes."

"I don't think I care to answer that question," Priscilla said.

Behind her, Aziz's voice rose angrily. "You will answer my father."

"Please," Tarak added.

"Not that it's anyone's business, but no, I never slept with your son."

"But I have it on good authority that you were in his suite when he died."

"I was in his suite, but not when he died," Priscilla asserted.

"And you did not have sex with him?" Tarak followed the question with another drag on his cigarillo.

"I already told you, no."

"Nonetheless, you agreed to marry him."

Priscilla didn't think she had heard correctly. "I'm sorry. I did what?"

"He asked you to marry him, and you said yes. That is the truth."

Priscilla vehemently shook her head. "That is most definitely *not* the truth. Is that what Amir told you?"

Aziz, who until now had remained in the background, stepped forward. "My father spoke to Amir late in the afternoon. He said he was on his way to the opera with a wonderful woman he hoped to marry."

"You have the wrong woman," Priscilla said in a much more pleading voice than she intended. "I met Amir at a caviar tasting organized by the hotel and accompanied him to the opera at Covent Garden. That was the extent of it."

"But you went to his suite with him," Aziz insisted. "You had sex with him. You said you would marry him."

"I repeat—although I shouldn't have to—I did *not* have sex with him," Priscilla said. "And I certainly never agreed to marry him."

"Then what were you doing in his suite?" Tarak demanded.

"He'd had too much to drink. I wanted to make sure he got back safely. That was all."

"Enough!" Tarak cried out. The cigarillo held daintily in his fingers, he wobbled to his feet, his face fierce. "In my family, when someone makes a promise, then the family is bound to keep that promise, no matter what. Therefore, my son Aziz will fulfill the promise made by Amir, his younger, more headstrong brother."

"I'm not sure what that means," Priscilla said.

"Aziz will marry you."

"What?" Priscilla blanched in astonishment.

Aziz was beaming happily. "It would be my honour and pleasure."

"It would not, however, be my honour or pleasure," Priscilla replied, doing her best to keep a growing panic out of her voice. "I don't want to marry anyone, least of all someone I only met tonight, who practically forced me into a car to come here."

"We insist on fulfilling the promise made by my son." Tarak noticed that the cigarillo had burned down close to his yellowed fingers. He gave a quick nod to the tall man who hurried forward to pluck it from his boss.

"I thought you might be more interested in who poisoned your son," Priscilla said.

"We know who poisoned him," Tarak asserted calmly. He gestured toward the tall man who immediately produced a fresh cigarillo and placed it in the corner of Tarak's mouth. No sooner was that done than the tall man produced a lighter to fire up the cigarillo.

Again, Priscilla was having trouble crediting what she had just heard. "What do you mean you know who poisoned him? Have you told the police? They don't seem to have any idea—in fact I'm told they're not even certain he was poisoned."

"He was most definitely poisoned," Aziz asserted, while his father blew more smoke into the already choked air.

"But how do you know?" Priscilla asked insistently.

"Our business, founded many years ago by my father, requires us, on occasion, to interact with Russian counterparts," Aziz explained. "Most specifically, on occasion we must deal with the KGB, the Russian intelligence organization. For some time, they have been quietly informing us of a remarkable toxic substance, a deadly nerve agent they have been developing. Very much a secret, known only to a few."

"Tell her what our Soviet friends call it," Tarak ordered.

"They do not yet have a proper name," asserted Aziz. "For the time being, they call it simply A-232."

"What are you saying?" Priscilla asked. "The Russians killed your son?"

"They assure us they had nothing to do with either my son or the poisoning of this British member of parliament."

"Then who?"

"We have many enemies."

"But it's the Russians who have the poison you think was used."

"I repeat, many enemies."

"As I said before," Priscilla said, "shouldn't you talk to the police about this?"

Tarak did not look at all happy with that suggestion. He glanced at his son, who had adopted an equally churlish expression. Aziz said coldly, "We do not deal with the police."

"But wouldn't that help them in the investigation of Amir's death?"

"We must talk about arrangements for the wedding." Not so much a declaration as an order.

"Are you crazy?" Almost as soon as the words were out of her mouth, Priscilla realized they were a mistake.

A wintery stillness fell across the room.

"Did she call me crazy?" Tarak's was the voice of doom breaking the silence.

"It is getting late," interjected Aziz.

"Perhaps it is a mistake to marry this woman," Tarak said. The cigarillo, now ignored, burned in his arthritic fingers. "A woman who insults her family...that is not permissible."

"Yes," agreed Priscilla, "it definitely would be a mistake. I would say a *huge* mistake."

"Let us not come to any final decisions this evening," Aziz said, transformed into the soul of diplomacy. "Now that we've had a chance to meet, let me provide Miss Tempest with a ride home."

"It's all right. I'd just as soon take a cab."

"I insist," said Aziz with equanimity.

"You will be driven home." Tarak, in voice-of-God mode, brooked no further discussion.

"Amir liked to give the impression he ran the business, Mr. Three Per Cent and all that bullshit." As he spoke in his soft voice, Aziz kept his eyes focused ahead on London's dark streets, having decided he alone should drive home his potential bride. "But in fact, he didn't have much to do with our business at all."

"The business of selling guns," Priscilla said.

Aziz allowed the hint of a smile. In the shifting shadows and light, he was, Priscilla decided, a rather handsome man for his age. She wasn't sure whether she liked the beard. Or his shortness. Or the fact that he was Amir's brother. Or that he was crazy enough to want to marry her.

"We do not sell guns. We facilitate meetings between those in the East who desire certain products that can be provided by those in the West."

"Guns," Priscilla said.

"Among other products," Aziz said.

"Like caviar?"

That made Aziz frown. "Spanish caviar. Let me tell you something. I never want to hear those words again…"

"Well, given what's happened to your brother, chances are you won't," Priscilla said.

"The caviar was Amir's very ridiculous idea." Aziz gave Priscilla a quick sideways glance. "He wanted to expand the family business. That was not going to happen, not with Spanish caviar."

"If Amir didn't run your business, does your father?"

"My father is a great man. He was wise enough to open lines of communication between the East and the West many years ago. But he is not the man he used to be."

"You run the business."

Aziz allowed more of a smile. "You will be marrying a very wealthy man."

Priscilla's laugh sounded harsher than she intended. But under the circumstances she could only try to laugh off the whole notion of marrying Aziz. "You don't want to marry me. I drink too much, stay out too late, and I have what you would probably regard as a scandalous past. Actually, come to think of it, my present isn't much better."

"I am unconcerned about that," Aziz replied in a manner that disappointingly suggested to Priscilla he was not to be deterred no matter what she told him.

"While I am not in the same playboy category as my late brother," he continued, "I nonetheless consider myself something of a man of the world."

Great, thought Priscilla. Just what I need in my life, a man of the world with a dead brother and a crazy, nicotine-addicted father.

She tried changing the subject: "Tell me about Amir. When I spoke to him, he said he was in a business where all sorts of people might kill him."

"Yes, that is certainly true." Aziz gave Priscilla another glance as though to gauge her reaction. "As my father said, we have many enemies."

"Then if the Russians didn't poison him, who do you think did?"

"That is what we're hoping the police can ascertain."

"But you said you don't want to talk to them."

"The police potentially complicate matters, no question. Our business generally works better if we stay as far away as possible from the authorities."

"But in this case..."

"All the more reason." Aziz turned the Mercedes onto Knightsbridge and as he did, he glanced at Priscilla. "However, you are a different matter."

"Me?" That caught her by surprise. "I hardly think the police are going to listen to me."

"Perhaps not, but you have friendly sources in the press, do you not?"

"I see," Priscilla said, beginning to understand what he was getting at. "Maybe you don't want to marry me so much as you would like me to be a source for you."

"I *will* marry you," Aziz asserted with a smile. "But in the meantime, yes, you may be in touch with your friends in the press."

He slowed, found a parking spot, and then wedged the Mercedes into the opening, not far from her flat. He turned to face her. "I would like to kiss you goodnight."

"I would like to know if Amir said anything about being involved with anyone other than me," Priscilla countered.

Aziz looked momentarily nonplussed. "You mean other women?"

"Anything he might have said about women before he met me. Affairs he was having."

"Other than you? No, he never spoke of other women."

"You're sure about that?" Priscilla pressed. "He was something of a playboy after all. And I had just met him."

"Why would you ask such a question?" Without waiting for an answer, he reached over to embrace her.

Priscilla held him off. "Aziz, we have just met as well. We are not serious."

"I am very serious," he murmured.

Priscilla managed to reach back and unlatch the door. "I guess I didn't tell you."

"Tell me what?"

"I never kiss a gentleman on first acquaintance."

"I thought you said you were a woman with a scandalous past."

"I'm afraid it doesn't include kissing men I've just met."

Priscilla opened the door and slid out. "Thank you for the ride."

Aziz grinned and said, "I will be in touch. You should know the most important thing about me."

"What's that?"

"I never give up!"

As Aziz drove off, Priscilla looked up beseechingly to the night heavens. She wanted to cry out, *What have I done to deserve this?*

But she resisted the impulse, thinking it best not to disturb the neighbours, and suspecting the heavens were not about to give her an answer.

CHAPTER TWENTY-EIGHT

A-232

As soon as Priscilla got into 205 the following morning—noting that Susie had yet to arrive and was, as usual, late—she telephoned Percy Hoskins. She told him what had happened and what she had learned from her encounter with the Abrahims.

"A-what?" Percy appeared to be having trouble understanding what she was telling him.

"A-232." She spoke with an authority designed to showcase what little knowledge she had. "According to Aziz Abrahim, Amir's brother, it's a deadly nerve agent developed by the KGB—that's Russian intelligence in case you didn't know."

"I know what the KGB is," Percy said irritably. "Are they saying the Russians poisoned Amir?"

"They don't think it was Russians," Priscilla amended.

"Then who?"

"The Abrahims were kind of vague about that. But they did say they want the police to find his killer."

That gave Percy pause on the other end of the line. "Okay, the Russians didn't kill Amir, but they might know who did. Is that it?"

"Something like that." Priscilla's sense of authority was quickly slipping away.

"Have they gone to the police with what they know?"

"They don't want to talk to the police," Priscilla said. "I think that's why they got me involved."

"So you can talk to them?"

"Not quite. I tell *you*, and you can write a story, quoting unnamed sources, and that story will then force a police investigation."

"That's why they kidnapped you?"

"Not the only reason. The father wants me to marry Amir's brother, Aziz."

More pausing on Percy's part. "Why would they want you to marry him?"

"Apparently Amir told his family that he had planned to marry me, and they are sworn to fulfill that promise."

"Did Amir ask you to marry him?"

"No."

"This doesn't make any sense."

"No, it doesn't. And it may not have been me Amir was talking about when he talked to his family about marrying."

"You don't mean he was thinking of marrying Princess Margaret?"

"That's what crossed my mind. Never mind that she's already married. But then Aziz didn't seem to know anything about his brother's involvement with her."

"Okay, let me get on this toxic A-232 thing."

"Can you write a story about it?"

"Definitely. Where did you leave it with the Abrahims?"

"Aziz said he would be in touch."

"Are you going to marry him?"

Priscilla decided to hold off an immediate answer, anxious to see how he'd react.

"Priscilla." Was that a touch of concern in Percy's voice? "Are you going to marry this bloke?"

"He's very rich, he says, and sort of attractive in an older-man kind of way. Maybe a trifle short for me. If I did marry him, would you be jealous?"

"I would be except you're going to marry me," Percy said with the sort of confidence guaranteed to annoy her.

"You're tall enough, I suppose," Priscilla ventured, "but you don't have any money, and you drink too much."

"However, I am irresistible."

"No, you're not. Besides, I'm not going to marry anyone."

"Ha! That's what you think."

"Goodbye, Percy," Priscilla said, hanging up as the second phone on her desk began to ring.

She took a couple of deep breaths, debating whether to answer it. When she did, she was immediately sorry.

"He wants to see you." The supercilious voice of El Sid.

"When?"

"Immediately, of course."

The line went dead. Susie appeared at the door, finally having arrived. "Anything up?" she asked.

"Mr. Banville wants to see me."

Susie's eyes grew large. "You're not going to lose your job, are you?"

"The way things are going lately, he probably wants to marry me."

CHAPTER TWENTY-NINE

No Leaks

Wondering what she could possibly have done wrong now to once again incur the general manager's wrath, Priscilla strode resolutely across the Front Hall, so preoccupied that she nearly missed Mark Ryde.

"You seem lost in thought," he observed after she was brought to a stop with a start.

"On my way to the general manager's office," Priscilla said, thinking that Mark was looking fine today in a navy sports coat and grey slacks, just the thing for a young man about London sauntering through the Savoy's Front Hall.

"Is that good or bad?" Mark adopted the insouciant smile that she had come to like.

"That's what I'm about to find out," she answered. "What brings you to the Savoy?"

"To be honest, I was hoping to run into you."

"Well, you're in luck—into me you have run. But I've only got a couple of moments."

"How about a drink later?"

"As long as you don't want to marry me," Priscilla said.

"I hadn't thought about it—"

"Good."

"—until now."

"Oh, dear." Priscilla feigned a look of horror.

"If you *do* want to marry me," Mark said thoughtfully, "I can certainly take it under consideration."

"I don't want to marry you." Did she say that a little too quickly?

"Good. That's a relief."

"Why? Are you already married?"

"No, as a matter of fact I'm not. When do you want to get married?"

"That's the point, I *don't* want to get married."

Mark laughed and said, "Let's go back to the time before we started talking about marriage—that period in both our lives when I asked you if you'd like to have a drink with me."

"I should be finished around five o'clock."

"I'll be drowning my sorrows at the Admiral Codrington, not far from you, I believe. Why don't you join me there?"

"Okay."

"And I promise not to marry you."

"Darn," Priscilla said. She made sure she smiled when she said it.

From his perch huddled at his desk, Priscilla thought El Sid looked like a smug red rat.

"You're late," he said.

"You always say that," Priscilla said.

"Because you are always late. Go straight in. He is waiting." The words, as they always seemed to, sounded sinister. Priscilla felt her stomach tightening into a familiar knot as she opened the door to Banville's office.

Today, Banville was resplendent in his morning suit, poised at his desk, his visage baked into a state of unhappiness. "Miss Tempest," he announced, as though to simultaneously remind Priscilla of her name and also the deficiencies accompanying that name. It occurred to Priscilla that she was spending far too much time with authoritarian old men displeased with her.

"Good morning, Mr. Banville. You wanted to see me?"

"Indeed, Miss Tempest. I'm curious, have you spoken yet today with Mrs. Kerry?"

"Not today, sir. Is anything wrong?"

"She is feeling abandoned, Miss Tempest."

"I'm sorry to hear that," Priscilla said. "I've been somewhat overwhelmed the past couple of days. I thought Mrs. Banville was spending time with her."

"As you have been made aware—although I must say I was dismayed to hear you were present when the revelation was made—Mrs. Banville has been preoccupied with the forthcoming celebration for HRH the Princess Margaret."

"A coup for the hotel, sir. Mrs. Banville is to be congratulated."

"Quite. However, in the meantime, we still have the problem of Mrs. Kerry. "

"If I may, sir—"

"You may not." Banville wasted no time cutting her off. "I have obtained two tickets to tonight's performance of *Hair* at the Shaftesbury Theatre. She is most anxious to see that show. You will accompany her. Is that understood?"

"Yes, it is, sir."

"Now, returning to the subject of Her Royal Highness. Buckingham Palace is very concerned about possible leaks to the press. I have assured officials that from our end there will be no leaks. Do you understand?"

"No leaks to the press, yes sir."

"I will not look kindly on any word that gets into the papers about the princess's dinner evening here at the Savoy. I will hold you personally responsible if anything gets out. Do you further understand?"

"Nothing will come out of our office," Priscilla said.

Banville gave what Priscilla could only read was a skeptical look. "Despite my best efforts to reassure everyone involved, the Palace remains anxious. To that end, you may be contacted by one of their representatives who will want to assess the situation here for himself. You should be prepared for that."

"Certainly, sir. And who is this representative?"

"A chappie I don't know but is said to be quite thorough, a Commander Peter Trueblood."

CHAPTER THIRTY

Dead!

"Percy Hoskins is on the phone, holding for you," Susie announced shortly after Priscilla got back to 205.

"Don't tell me that," Priscilla ordered. "I've already got a headache. Percy will only make it worse."

"He says it's urgent that he talk to you.".

Priscilla closed her eyes, wishing she were somewhere else— anywhere else. Maybe in the South of France with Richard Burton. Could she put up with him? She would have to.

"Priscilla!" Susie's voice cut through her reverie.

"Yes, all right," she sighed. She picked up the receiver.

"He's dead," Percy Hoskins announced.

"Who's dead?"

"Bernard Bannister. Who else?"

"When?"

"About an hour ago. I just got the news. They're saying it's heart failure, but we know differently, don't we?"

"Do we?"

"Don't say that. I just talked my editors into going with the poison angle. I'm phoning to make sure that's accurate. The attribution will be to unnamed sources—*you* being my sources."

Her other phone began to ring.

"Priscilla, are you there?" Percy asked.

"Yes. My other phone's ringing."

"You're sure about this toxic substance? A-232?"

"That's what Amir's family believes—that's what I was told."

Susie called out from her desk. "It's Mr. Banville's office..."

Priscilla closed her eyes again. She heard Percy saying, "Okay, that's what we're going with—so get ready. All hell is about to break loose."

Susie was shouting something from the other office.

"What did you say?" she demanded.

"Mr. Banville!"

"What about him?"

"He's on his way here!"

"Impossible!" Priscilla exclaimed. "I've just left him."

"I just got off the line with Mr. Stopford," Susie called out in a shrill voice. "Mr. Banville will be with us momentarily!"

Priscilla couldn't believe it. How could this be? Mr. Banville coming to her office! That had never happened before. Never! What could it possibly mean? Nothing good, that was certain.

Before she could further gather her thoughts, through her open office door she could see Susie at attention, looking like the proverbial deer caught in headlights as Banville barrelled past followed by Major O'Hara.

Priscilla barely had a chance to rise to her feet before the two men were crowding into her office. "There you are, Miss Tempest."

"Mr. Banville." Thinking, where else would I be?

"Have you heard the news?"

Major O'Hara wasn't waiting for her answer. "Bernard Bannister has died in hospital."

"Oh, dear," Priscilla managed. "I'm so sorry."

"Apparently, it was heart failure," Banville went on, "which is something of a relief in that hopefully we won't have to deal with any ridiculous rumours."

"I'm not so sure about that." The words were out of Priscilla's mouth before she realized this was the last thing either Banville or Major O'Hara wanted to hear.

"What do you mean?" Banville demanded.

"It's just that when I found him in his suite, it didn't look as though he was suffering a heart attack."

"And you are an expert on heart attacks, are you, Miss Tempest?" Major O'Hara cocked a disdainful eyebrow.

"No, of course not—"

"Then I suggest you keep your medical opinions to yourself," snapped Banville. "The authorities have announced the cause of Mr. Bannister's death, and therefore as far as we are concerned, that *is* the cause of his death." Banville focused a hard look on Priscilla. "Are we clear on that point, Miss Tempest?"

"Most definitely, sir."

"Good. Now we need you to prepare a statement, something along the lines of us sincerely regretting the death of Mr. Bannister. Our thoughts and prayers are with his family, etcetera, etcetera."

"I can certainly do that Mr. Banville, except—"

"Except what, Miss Tempest?"

"We may still face questions about what Mr. Bannister was doing in a suite at the Savoy in the first place."

Banville and Major Jack exchanged quick, unhappy glances.

"How do you propose I answer those inquiries?" Priscilla added. Why did she have a sense of her office walls closing in?

Banville cleared his throat. "You will answer by not answering at all. The Savoy does not question the reasons why our clients stay with us. Our job is to welcome them while exercising the utmost discretion."

"If I may, Mr. Banville," Major O'Hara said. "I would suggest the best course for Miss Tempest, or any of us for that matter, is to say that we have no comment. We stick with the press release that Miss Tempest creates and leave it at that."

"Yes, very good, Major. That is the best approach. You agree Miss Tempest?"

"I do agree, sir. However, there is one other thing I should mention."

Both men appeared fed up. "What is it now?" demanded Banville.

"The *Evening Standard* is about to run a story saying that Amir Abrahim died as a result of ingesting a chemical toxin secretly developed by the KGB, that's the Russian intelligence apparatus."

With those words out of her mouth, seeing the growing horror on the faces of Banville and the major, the walls weren't so much closing in as they were collapsing down on her.

"What the hell?" thundered Banville. "What the bloody hell?"

Priscilla worked to keep her voice from breaking as she plunged on. "Further, the paper will also say that despite what the authorities may be saying, Bernard Bannister was also poisoned with the same toxin."

"Toxin? You mean *poison*?" This came out of Major O'Hara as a growl.

"Yes, sir."

"Why the hell didn't you tell us this before now?" raged Major O'Hara.

"I got the call from a reporter at the *Evening Standard* moments ago," Priscilla said.

"Jesus Christ." Banville was rubbing at his temples. "Two murders at the Savoy. Good Lord!"

Major O'Hara took a deep breath and said to Priscilla, "How should we contain this, Miss Tempest?"

"My suggestion is that we follow your original inclination and say nothing. If anything, we say what is probably true, that the Savoy cannot comment on an ongoing police investigation. We are anxious to co-operate with authorities in any way we can, but otherwise we have no comment."

That drew a silence. Major O'Hara kept his eyes on Banville, who was still massaging his forehead.

"Yes," Banville said. "That is the best approach." He stopped rubbing his head and looked at Priscilla. "That will be your approach, Miss Tempest. Is that understood?"

"Absolutely, sir. Let me get right on that."

As Banville and the major started out, Priscilla allowed herself a moment of relief at having once again dodged a bullet. Then came Banville's voice, edged in tones of ice: "Miss Tempest!"

He had stopped at her office door. "Mrs. Kerry is still expecting you to escort her to the theatre this evening."

"Of course."

"And Miss Tempest, there is one other matter."

"Sir?"

"Do not for a moment think that at a later date we will not discuss your future."

"My future," Priscilla managed to gulp. "Certainly, sir."

Banville and the major blew past Susie, still at attention. Priscilla also remained on her feet, wondering how she might get in touch with Richard Burton.

CHAPTER THIRTY-ONE

Engaged

Mark Ryde was leaning against the bar reading the *Evening Standard* when Priscilla got to the Admiral Codrington. As she squeezed through the mob of five o'clock drinkers, she couldn't help but see the big black headline on the paper's front page:

MURDER AT THE SAVOY

"Did you have anything to do with this?" he asked, putting the paper aside.

"You mean have I murdered anyone at the Savoy? Not yet," Priscilla said, as he moved to make space for her at the bar.

The bartender placed a coupe de champagne in front of her. "I told him that as soon as you arrived, given what I've been reading in the paper, you would probably need a glass of champagne."

"Well, you're not wrong about that." Priscilla lifted her glass. "Cheers."

"How are you doing? Are you all right?"

"Put it this way, I'm not happy about the adverse publicity the hotel is receiving, and the fact that the police insist on viewing me as a possible suspect."

Mark looked surprised. "The police think you're a suspect? How could they possibly think that?"

"Because I found Bernard Bannister in distress and called for help."

"But you tried to help. How could that implicate you in his death?"

"You would think it wouldn't, but apparently that's not how it works. This entire situation has put me under a bit of a cloud, and made me start to question everything."

"I can imagine," Mark said.

Priscilla took a sip of her champagne, thought about it, and then said, "I told them about the woman who was in Bannister's suite at the time."

"A woman you say?" Mark's face revealed no emotion.

"She ran out of the room as soon as I arrived," Priscilla explained. She paused for effect before adding, "I got a pretty good look at her."

"Did you?" Mark's face showed nothing.

"In fact, I believe I saw her again soon after—at least I think it was her."

"Oh? Where did you see her?"

"She was in the American Bar that evening with you. Your friend who is not a girlfriend."

"I'm afraid you have me at a loss," Mark said. His expression remained determinedly blank.

"Her name is Alana Wynter, is it not?" The shot across the bow, Priscilla thought.

Mark, his expression held to neutral, nevertheless hesitated a bit too long before he said, "Yes, it is. But I'm sure you're mistaken."

"Am I?"

"I can't imagine Alana would have anything to do with the likes of Bernard Bannister."

"Are you certain you're not involved with her?" Thinking, how could he not be?

Mark allowed a tight smile. "Aha. So that's what this is about."

It's about prying a straight answer out of you, Priscilla thought. Aloud, she said, "I'm trying to confirm that Alana was the woman I saw leaving Bannister's suite."

"But you can't be certain."

"I can't be absolutely certain, no."

"Because the night you saw me in the American Bar with Alana, she had just arrived back from France," Mark explained smoothly. "I doubt she had had time to murder anyone."

"Are you sure about that?"

"About being in France? That's what she told me at any rate, and I have no reason to doubt her."

"Because you're involved with her?"

"You keep asking me that." And Mark evidently didn't like it.

"You keep dodging an answer."

"Well, this is certainly going in a different direction than I imagined." Mark's smile didn't look nearly as agreeable as it had previously. "Do you mind if I ask you a question?"

"Certainly," Priscilla said.

"How much of this have you told the police?"

What should I tell him? she thought. Thinking fast...

"I haven't told them about Alana, if that's what you're getting at."

"Because?"

"Because I want to be absolutely certain it was her."

"Alana couldn't possibly have been in that suite," Mark stated firmly.

"Because she was in France?"

"And because I know her. I know what kind of person she is."

"And just how do you know that?"

"I'm engaged to marry her," Mark said.

"Oh," was all Priscilla could manage while working hard not to look as gobsmacked as she felt.

"A friend who is not a girlfriend but the woman you plan to marry." Was she choking on the words coming out of her mouth? "What am I to make of that?"

"Well, you might ask how the woman I'm going to marry was upstairs at the Savoy potentially murdering another man." Mark had rediscovered the easy reasonableness in his voice.

"Perhaps not murdering him, but how about sleeping with him?"

"Preferable to murder, I must say," Mark replied coolly. "However, I doubt that was the case."

"But now it's my turn to say that you can't be certain."

"Like I said, Priscilla, Alana was in France when all this happened. You mistook her for someone else, that's all. It couldn't have been her."

What could she say to that except, "You might have told me you were engaged." Did she sound a bit hurt? Possibly.

"It didn't come up," Mark said. A lame excuse if there ever was one, thought Priscilla.

"You told me you are a civil servant." Spoken as though delivering a blow...

...That failed to land: "I am a civil servant." An avowal so casual, one might actually believe him, Priscilla thought.

Or maybe not. "Yes, but what kind of civil servant?"

"The kind who can't say a whole lot about being a civil servant."

To hell with this, she thought. There was far too much ducking and weaving going on for her liking. Time, she decided, to make her exit.

Exit laughing? Well, not quite. "I'd better be going. I'll be late for an appointment."

"Do you really have another appointment?"

"As a matter of fact, I do."

"Before you go," Mark placed his hand gently on her arm. "I'd like to ask a favour."

"What kind of favour?" Priscilla was looking down at that hand, debating what to do about it.

"I'd prefer you didn't give Alana's name to the police. As I keep saying, she's not involved in this, and it would only prove embarrassing if her name was linked to Bernie Bannister's death. Embarrassing for her and for the people she works for."

Priscilla removed his hand from his arm. "Who does she work for?"

"A London-based security firm."

"That doesn't mean anything," Priscilla said.

"She's executive assistant to a fellow associated with Buckingham Palace who doesn't like publicity of any sort, let alone any suggestion the person working for him is involved in a possible murder at the Savoy."

"Who is this person she works for? The same person who employs you?" Priscilla was tempted to throw out Commander Blood's name, but resisted, reluctant to give too much away, but nonetheless anxious to see how Mark responded.

The relaxed expression he had more or less managed to maintain, until now, evaporated. "Look, I've already said too much. If you could see your way clear to keeping Alana's name out of it, I would be most grateful."

"I have to be going," Priscilla said.

"Will you at least think about what I've asked you?"

"Thanks for the drink."

She couldn't decide as she left if the lingering frown on Mark's face gave her satisfaction or if it marked the end of a possible boyfriend. That was no satisfaction.

Although she had to concede, marching away from the pub, that ever thinking in terms of Mark as a boyfriend, after seeing him with Alana Wynter, was a mistake. What in fact *had* she been thinking? What she was always thinking where men were concerned. Which was not thinking at all.

She really must work to change that, she thought.

CHAPTER THIRTY-TWO

Letting Her Hair Down

Humming the title song from the musical *Hair*, Mrs. Eunice Kerry was dancing, in her suite, a drink in one hand, a cigarette in the other. Priscilla, having just arrived, watched in amazement. This was not the same grim Eunice who had gotten off a plane at Heathrow.

"I love *Hair*," Eunice announced, continuing to move her hips around.

"It only recently opened in London," Priscilla said. "For the longest time they couldn't do the show here because of these ridiculous censorship rules that have been around since the 1800s. Now they've relaxed the rules, and thus *Hair* is allowed to hang down—so to speak."

"I saw it in New York. There's some nudity but honestly, it's no big deal, and the music is great—*love* the music."

She took a long swig from her drink and swayed over to Priscilla. "How much shit are you in with my supercilious son-in-law?"

"Not as much as I might have thought," Priscilla admitted. "Your son-in-law for the moment has been distracted by the death of Bernard Bannister."

"The man always has a pickle up his ass about something. The same with my daughter. Honestly, this Princess Margaret thing, steeped in secrecy and whispered phone conversations, and now an MP murdered—if you believe what you read. Never a dull moment at the Savoy."

And Mrs. Eunice Kerry only added to the current unpredictable atmosphere, Priscilla thought. Eunice certainly had the effect of taking her mind off the death of Bernard Bannister. Not to mention the revelation by the extremely untrustworthy, as it turned out, Mark Ryde.

Eunice finished her drink and took a final drag on her cigarette before squishing it into an ashtray. Priscilla looked at her watch. "We'd better leave. We don't want to miss the curtain."

"Let me go to the powder room."

When Eunice emerged, it was as though she had been transformed. Priscilla wasn't sure exactly what she had done in there, but she was struck by how—*glamorous* she looked. And what was with that expression? Eagerness? Yes, that's what it was all right. Eunice actually appeared to be eagerly anticipating the evening. *Hair*, Priscilla thought, must be very good indeed.

"You look lovely," Priscilla said to her.

"I do look pretty damned hot, don't I? And you're a picture yourself, Priscilla. But then you always are. I suppose all kinds of men are throwing themselves at you."

"The wrong men, usually, and rather than throwing, they seem to slip up and crawl under the barbed wire when I'm not looking."

"Ah, to be young again, chased around by the wrong men."

"It gets tiring," Priscilla had to admit. "Once in a while, I do wish the right man would chase me."

"Be careful, honey. That's when you get yourself married and suddenly the right man turns into not just the wrong man, but the worst man. Take it from someone who knows."

"I'll keep it in mind," Priscilla said.

"However, tonight, I'm open to any possibility. Tonight, I'm going to be young again!"

"Two fabulous women off to the theatre," Priscilla announced.

"More or less," Eunice said enigmatically. She resumed humming *Hair* as she headed for the door.

More or less? What did *that* mean? Priscilla wondered.

Mr. Bogans was waiting with the Daimler in the Savoy Court. "Good evening, ladies," he said, holding open the rear door for them. "You both look lovely, if I may say."

"Why thank you, Bogans," Eunice said. "You certainly can say." There was a twinkle in her eyes. Where did that come from? Priscilla wondered. What was going on with Eunice? Whatever was happening, it had turned the general manager's mother-in-law into a much nicer person.

For the evening, at least.

The crowd outside the Shaftesbury Theatre, the Edwardian building dominating the corner of Shaftsbury Avenue and High Holborn, hummed with anticipation as the Daimler pulled up to the curb in front and disgorged Priscilla and Eunice. Onlookers turned expectantly, then turned away quickly as soon as they realized the two women were not celebrities.

They stood beneath the theatre's overhang, Eunice glancing around, somewhat nervous, Priscilla thought, as though looking for someone.

"Expecting company?" Priscilla asked.

Eunice merely smiled weakly and then busied herself lighting a cigarette. The crowd began to move into the theatre.

"We'd better go inside," Priscilla said.

"Wait a moment." Eunice appeared anxious, still peering around. "Let me finish my cigarette."

A short, slim young man with curly black hair and big dark eyes whose pupils appeared to be swimming in liquid, abruptly landed at Eunice's side. "Enrique," she said enthusiastically. "There you are."

"So sorry to be late," Enrique said in accented English before embracing her, kissing her cheeks. "The traffic."

Priscilla did not bother to hide her astonished expression. Who the hell was Enrique, with those large watery eyes, and why was he now wrapping his arm around Eunice's waist?

"Now Priscilla, honey," Eunice said, "I don't want you getting upset with me, but I won't be going to the theatre tonight."

"I beg your pardon?" Priscilla couldn't quite believe what she was hearing.

"I don't want any of this getting back to my daughter. You know how she is."

"But where are you going?"

Eunice turned impishly to her curly haired companion. "I don't know, Enrique. Where are we going?"

Enrique just grinned, showing dazzling white teeth. Priscilla noticed the long almost feminine lashes framing those eyes now dancing in what Priscilla could only imagine was merry anticipation.

"You will keep this to yourself, Priscilla, won't you? We went to the theatre tonight and had a marvellous time—that's the story when my daughter asks, as she surely will."

"Are you going to be all right?"

"A lot better than I would be if I had to sit through that goddamn show a second time. If I'm being honest, I did not like it when I saw it in New York. Not to worry, Enrique will take very good care of me." She hugged against him. "Won't you, Enrique?"

"That is what I am here for, to treat you like the beautiful woman you are." Accompanied by another show of white teeth.

"I wish you had told me you were going to do this, Eunice," Priscilla said. "It puts me in an awkward position."

"If I had told you, you might have tried to stop me—or worse yet, told my daughter."

Eunice stepped over and, to Priscilla's surprise, embraced her. "We all have our secrets, don't we?"

She danced away to take Enrique's arm. "Come my darling. We are off into the night."

Enrique displayed more of his spectacular white teeth, directing Eunice along the street to where a motorcycle was parked on the pavement. Enrique handed Eunice one of the two helmets mounted on the saddle. He took the second helmet for himself.

The helmeted Enrique sat astride the motorcycle and started it up. Eunice proceeded to squeeze into her helmet and then unceremoniously hiked her skirt so she could sit behind him.

Then, with a final wave from Eunice, they shot off down Shaftesbury Avenue toward Piccadilly Circus, leaving Priscilla shaking her head in dismay.

CHAPTER THIRTY-THREE

An Offer of Port

As soon as he arrived, Mark Ryde was ushered into Commander Peter Trueblood's oak-panelled office. Lit by a single desk light, Commander Blood looked more sinister than ever this evening. If there was a villain of the piece, Mark reflected, then Commander Blood definitely fit the bill.

"Sit down, Mark," Trueblood said. "I'm nursing a port, would you like one?"

"Not for me, thanks," Mark said, settling into a chair in front of Trueblood's desk.

The room fell quiet. Trueblood ignored the port at his elbow. "You've seen the *Evening Standard*?"

"I have."

"And you think what?"

"Frankly, I don't know what to think. We know the Russians have been developing some nasty toxins, but for my people it's hard to imagine this is their work."

"Then who?"

"It crossed my mind that perhaps your people, the Walsinghams, might be involved."

Instead of answering immediately, Trueblood sipped his port. "Personally, I was thinking along the lines of MI5."

"That's a bit of a stretch."

"Is it? No more of a stretch than putting it on us. You people certainly have the wherewithal to orchestrate something as nasty as this and make it look like the Soviets."

"But hardly, I would argue, the inclination."

"Let's face it, we both have motive, but perhaps we have to deal with two possibilities. One is that neither of us is responsible for the somewhat careless events that have transpired at the Savoy."

"And the other?"

"The other possibility is that one of us in this room is lying to the other."

"Whatever the case, we both have good reasons for keeping this out of the public eye," Mark said. "Which brings me to another problem."

Trueblood raised his eyebrows. "Well, neither of us needs more problems, do we?"

"It's Priscilla Tempest."

"Yes, Miss Tempest," Trueblood nodded, as though coming to the acceptance of her existence. "Her name keeps coming up. Are you not keeping an eye on her?"

"I am."

"Eyeing or seducing?" The raised eyebrows now represented accusation.

"The point being, I've learned that Priscilla somehow knows that Alana Wynter was in the suite with Bannister."

"She has Alana's name?" Off Mark's nod, Trueblood added a quiet, "Jesus Christ."

"She *thinks* she has the name." Mark doing what he considered he did best—reassuring men in authority like Trueblood. "I've managed to persuade her that Alana was out of the country and that she has mistaken Alana for someone else."

"Has she given this information to the police?" Trueblood's tone had grown tense.

"She says she hasn't, and I believe I have sowed enough doubt that for the time being, she won't."

Trueblood frowned. "This nothing young woman, this tart in a miniskirt who for some reason was able to land a job at the

Savoy—and God knows who she had to sleep with to accomplish that—this woman could endanger us all."

"I would say Alana's carelessness puts us in far greater jeopardy," Mark offered.

"We can debate that later, but for now we have my concerns about Miss Tempest to address."

"Your very conservative view of things I would suggest allows you to mischaracterize Priscilla," Mark said, choosing his words carefully.

"Am I mischaracterizing her, as you would say? I wonder." The thought seemed to add a note of distress to Trueblood's pale, haunted features. "To me she represents everything that is wrong with this country: the lack of respect for those in power, the disintegration of our values amid a cacophony of popular music and chants for...Lord above us, equality."

"And doing it all in a miniskirt."

"The short skirts I do not mind." Trueblood managed a weak smile. "It's all the rest."

"Nonetheless, these are changing times, Commander."

"And therefore, we must stand as a bulwark against those changes, particularly when they threaten the established institutions that have kept this country together for hundreds, if not thousands, of years."

"Institutions such as the monarchy?"

"The most enduring and therefore most important institution of all."

"Priscilla Tempest is not going to destroy the monarchy."

"But she can potentially cause us a great deal of trouble, if she goes to the police. I cannot take the risk and allow that to happen."

"It won't happen," Mark said.

"There is only one certain way to put a stop to her talking to the police," Trueblood said.

"Your methods will not solve our problem, Commander."

"No?" Trueblood was once again raising a doubtful eyebrow. "Then you had best prove me wrong—and be damned quick about it."

After Mark had left, Trueblood finished his port and then rose from his desk and went to a sideboard where he had stationed the decanter. He was pouring himself another glass when the rear door opened and Alana Wynter stepped into view. She looked particularly fetching this evening, Trueblood thought. He could feel the warmth of her as she came close.

"Did you hear?" he asked.

"Most of it, yes. This bloody woman has discovered my name."

"Would you like a port?"

"Is that all you have?"

"I'm afraid so."

Alana made a face. "Port." A pretty face, Trueblood thought. "You are so old-fashioned," she said.

"You and Mark, so modern."

"Mark is soft," she pronounced. "Far too modern. This Tempest woman cannot be allowed to wander freely with the knowledge she apparently has."

"You should not have been in Bannister's suite," Trueblood said.

"He called saying he wasn't feeling well. Then he started making crazy statements, saying he knew all about the Walsinghams, didn't like what he was hearing. I thought I'd better talk to him. I wasn't expecting him to die, and I certainly wasn't expecting a visitor."

"Mark will deal with this," Trueblood said.

"Mark is infatuated with this woman," Alana argued. "You'd be better off to let me," Alana said.

"I have agreed to give him more time."

"That's not something we've got a lot of," Alana said.

"Stay out of it for now, Alana," Trueblood admonished. "You will only complicate matters."

She paused and then smiled. "Anything you say, darling." Thinking that she was not going to stay out of it and she certainly was not going to wait.

CHAPTER THIRTY-FOUR

The Persuasive Gunman

Priscilla arrived at her flat from the theatre worrying about the boss who would certainly hold her responsible if anything happened to his mother-in-law. The news that she had disappeared into the night on a motorcycle with a curly haired young man with liquid eyes named Enrique, half her age, would not be well received.

It would be received very badly, in fact.

Lies would have to be told, and telling lies was not Priscilla's strong suit—although lately she was getting lots of practice.

As she got out of her cab and crossed the sidewalk, she reassured herself that Eunice was a grown woman, mature—definitely mature—and capable of taking care of herself. She appeared to have dealt with the youthful Enrique before. A London boyfriend? Hard to imagine, but then what did she know? If Eunice could do nothing else, she could constantly surprise.

She fumbled in her purse for her keys as a voice called out, "Priscilla!"

Swinging around in alarm, she saw Aziz Abrahim approach. She had been so distracted thinking about Eunice, she hadn't seen Aziz's Mercedes parked further along the street.

"What are you doing here?"

"I have been waiting for you. You keep late hours, I must say." Aziz did not look happy.

"I was at the theatre. What is it that's so important?"

"You must come with me at once," Aziz said sternly.

"I am very tired. It's been a difficult day. The only place I'm going is to bed—alone."

"My father demands your presence. He is very unhappy."

"That's too bad, Aziz. I'm not going anywhere tonight."

"Most unfortunately, he insisted I bring along a person who specializes in persuading people to do things they might not otherwise choose to do. Tonight, if necessary, this person will persuade you to come with me."

Now she saw the tall man, resplendent in his dark suit. He waved at Priscilla. "Does he have his gun with him?"

"I'm afraid he does," Aziz confirmed.

"You know, Aziz, if you're trying to court a lady, bringing along your own gunman is unlikely to be helpful."

"Please, this is most important." Aziz's eyes were pleading. "I promise. No harm will come to you."

"Everyone tells me the same thing at this time of night. *Come with me at gunpoint, Priscilla. And don't worry. No harm will come to you.*" Priscilla groaned. "All right. Let's get this over with."

The tall man drove with both hands on the wheel of the Mercedes, which somehow had the effect of calming Priscilla. As long as he kept his hands where she could see them, he wouldn't be going for his gun. Aziz had settled beside her in the back, comfortable enough so that he felt he could place his hand on her knee. He said, "There is something I must warn you about."

Priscilla summarily removed his hand. "Honestly, Aziz, what is it about men in London groping women in the back seats of their cars?"

"Do men grope you?"

"Endless numbers," Priscilla said. "So please, don't be like all those others. In the meantime, what must you warn me about?"

"It is most important that you do not reveal to my father that you are the source for the story in today's *Evening Standard*."

"But Aziz, I *am* the source for the story because *you* told me to be the source."

"I may have mentioned something about this, but I never suggested you inform the press."

"You certainly did," Priscilla said indignantly. "You're the one who said you couldn't go to the police, but if the press was informed then the police would know and your family would not be implicated."

"I don't recall saying anything of the sort," Aziz said.

"You're joking."

"I am most serious, but much more importantly, so is my father. What you must tell him, you must say that you have no idea how the story got into the paper, and that will be that. Simple, don't you think?"

No, Priscilla thought. She didn't think that at all. She was beginning to lose track of all the secrets she was supposed to keep, the lies she had to tell. Don't tell the police this, don't tell Eunice's daughter that, don't tell Aziz's father something else. Her head was spinning.

Aziz's hand returning to her knee brought Priscilla out of her reverie. "I don't want this to affect our relationship," he said.

"Aziz, there is no relationship." She removed his hand, rougher this time. "There's only a guy who has more or less kidnapped me twice now."

"I understand how you're feeling." Aziz spoke calmly. "But I am a very patient man—as you will discover as we get to know each other better."

"Aziz, we're not getting to know each other better."

"Don't be too sure about that," Aziz said.

Priscilla began to worry all over again.

CHAPTER THIRTY-FIVE

An Excellent Wife

Beyond the front gate opening to admit the Mercedes, the Hampstead home of Tarak Abrahim appeared cloaked in darkness. As before, Priscilla was ushered into the foyer with its winding staircase and from there into the great room, still dimly lit, the stale air clogged with the smell of tobacco smoke.

But this time the throne-chair was empty.

That appeared to confuse Aziz. He had stopped, gaping at the chair. Priscilla sensed the tall man looming behind her, in case, she imagined, she tried to make a run for it. Presently, she heard the sound of coughing and Tarak Abrahim hobbled into view, leaning hard on a cane. As he moved forward, he seemed not to notice the presence of the others until Aziz called out, "Father!"

At that, Tarak jerked to a halt, his head snapping up, the ruins of his face flooding with relief. "You're here," he said.

"I brought Miss Tempest as you requested," Aziz offered.

The effort needed for Tarak to turn toward his visitors seemed to tire him. He leaned even harder on the cane so as to get more comfortable while he spent time studying Priscilla. What he saw did not please him.

"You have caused me a great deal of pain," he pronounced in a gravelly voice.

"I don't see how I could have done that." Her voice came out as a croak.

"However, I have decided to forgive you," Tarak went on as though Priscilla had not spoken. "My son thinks highly of you, and so I must take his happiness into consideration."

"Very kind of you, Father," Aziz interjected.

"This is because I am essentially a kind man who desires to put his son's happiness first. Therefore, I have decided to allow the marriage to go forward—"

"Marriage? What marriage?" There was renewed panic in Priscilla's voice.

"Silence!" Tarak bellowed. He appeared to be having trouble breathing. With some effort, he straightened himself. "As I say, I will allow the marriage." His piercing gaze fell on Priscilla. "The marriage will take place at our estate at Giza, outside Cairo. You will be transported there in the morning so as to begin arrangements for the ceremony."

"This is madness," Priscilla managed to say.

Again, Tarak appeared not to hear. "In the meantime, you will be my guest here tonight."

Priscilla spoke imploringly to Aziz, "Tell your father this is impossible. I'm not going to Egypt, and I am not marrying you."

In the face of her assertions, Aziz merely shrugged. "I'm afraid my father believes you know too much, and left to your own devices you will present a continuing threat to our family." He tried for an encouraging smile that didn't quite come off. "Listen, you will have a wonderful life in Giza. You will be my wife. The riches of the world will be available to you. Any wish will be immediately granted."

"I wish to go home and forget this craziness," Priscilla said shrilly.

"Ah, yes, Priscilla, I'm afraid that is the one wish I cannot grant."

Priscilla realized that the tall man now had a friend, the taller man. Together, they crowded in, taking her arms. Priscilla tried to pull away. It was like setting out to free herself from a pair of vises.

"You may scream if you wish," Aziz said. "But it will do no good. No one outside the house will hear you."

"I wouldn't give you the satisfaction of screaming," Priscilla said.

"I knew it!" Aziz said excitedly. "You really will make an excellent wife."

Actually, Priscilla thought later, she would have screamed her bloody head off at the indignity of all this. But she never got the chance thanks to the sudden commotion that stopped everyone in their tracks, including the two thugs who were taking particular pleasure in manhandling her out of the room.

The thunderous crash from somewhere in the house brought the manhandling to an abrupt halt and saved her the need for screaming.

Distant shouted orders were punctuated by the sound of shattering glass. Pounding bootsteps grew louder, accompanied by angry cries and panicked screams. A pair of stern-looking London bobbies broke into the great room, taking in the tableau confronting them with blank amazement. Then one of the bobbies in a gruff voice demanded, "Here, what the devil is going on?"

A good question, Priscilla thought.

"This woman broke in and attacked my father!" Aziz immediately accused.

"I most certainly did not!" cried Priscilla indignantly.

"Thank goodness we were able to stop her in time! This woman is crazy! Out of her mind!"

"They kidnapped me!" Priscilla had found a necessarily loud voice.

The police officers were stopped, baffled, when a familiar figure waded into view. Detective Inspector Robert "Charger" Lightfoot reacted with the same blank expression of incredulity as his fellow officers.

"Miss Tempest!" He, too, sounded accusatory.

CHAPTER THIRTY-SIX

An Arrest Is Made

From what Priscilla could see through the smudged window in Inspector Robert Lightfoot's office at Scotland Yard, it looked as though the dawn was breaking. She tried to recall the last time she had seen the dawn or gotten a good night's sleep, and couldn't.

"Here we are again, Miss Tempest," Inspector Lightfoot was saying in a tired voice.

Priscilla had done her best at the Abrahim's Hampstead house to explain what had happened and how she came to be kidnapped and held captive. She was at pains to assure the inspector that, contrary to what Aziz was loudly proclaiming, she had not broken in to attack Tarak Abrahim, that in fact she was the victim, not the perpetrator.

Despite her explanations, she was not certain Inspector Lightfoot had believed her then and she was even less certain that he was any more convinced back at his office.

"As much as I would like to embrace your previous declaration that we arrived in the nick of time to save you from a fate worse than death—"

"Which you did, Inspector," Priscilla interjected vehemently.

"Nevertheless," Lightfoot continued, "your fate was not exactly on our radar when we arrived. Based on an article in the *Evening Standard* and information received as a result of a longtime investigation of the Abrahim family, we executed a warrant at Tarak Abrahim's residence in Hampstead. You can imagine our amazement when we discovered that you were also there."

"Not as surprised—and relieved—as I was," Priscilla said.

"You have previously explained to the attending officers, as well as to myself, how it was that you came to be there. Aziz Abrahim, you may not be surprised to learn, has a completely different story—"

"All lies," Priscilla exclaimed.

"That notwithstanding, we are inclined to acknowledge your rather strange tale—"

"It's *not* a tale, Inspector." Priscilla, even more vehement.

"—and add it to the treasure trove of dubious stories with which you have already provided us."

"I'm telling you the truth," Priscilla said insistently.

Inspector Lightfoot gave her a look that suggested he could go either way on her truth-telling. "You should be aware that based on the evidence resulting from our investigation, we have charged Tarak and his son, Aziz, with the murder of Amir Abrahim."

"That is good news, I suppose," she said, choosing her words carefully. "However, I must say, I'm somewhat confused as to why they would kill someone in their own family."

"From what we can ascertain, the murder occurred as the result of a family feud. Our information is that Amir was moving into, of all things, the caviar business. Tarak and Aziz didn't like that and decided to take the action that resulted in Amir's murder."

"What about Bernard Bannister? I guess it could be understandable that Tarak and his son might want Amir dead, but why would they harm Mr. Bannister?"

"The investigation of Mr. Bannister's death is ongoing," Inspector Lightfoot stated formally. "We have yet to file charges in that matter."

"And what about our head housekeeper who believed she saw Princess Margaret leaving Amir's suite?"

"We have interviewed Mrs. Holmes several times and have reached the conclusion that she mistook someone else for the princess."

"And the woman I saw leaving Bernard Bannister's suite?"

"What about her?"

"Have you identified her?"

"Not as yet, no. There have been suggestions that in the chaos of the moment, discovering Mr. Bannister in such a state, you may have seen something you didn't see at all."

"And how is that possible, Inspector?" Priscilla's indignant tone was back full force. "I saw a woman in the room but I didn't really see her?"

"As I say, Miss Tempest. Possibly in the chaos of the moment."

"I see." Priscilla fought to control her rising anger. "And has Millicent Holmes suffered from that same problem—seeing something that she really didn't see at all?"

"That's quite enough, Miss Tempest. Your sarcasm is noted."

"And just supposing I had a name for this woman I didn't see, then what?" Priscilla glared across the desk at Lightfoot.

"Then I would ask you for that name. Do you have it?"

Priscilla was just tired enough and angry enough that she nearly blurted out Alana Wynter's name. But a little voice deep inside told her to keep quiet. "I don't have a name—not as yet."

"Then there's nothing much we can act on, is there?" Inspector Lightfoot made a resigned gesture with his hands. "However, I do have a few more questions for you."

"I'm so tired, Inspector. Can't I just leave?"

"A couple of things and then you can go." The inspector leaned forward, his hands now clasped in front of him on the desk, his face solemn, the very picture of stolid authority. "The question has arisen as to how the press received information about this unknown toxic substance that has baffled our experts. I wonder if you might enlighten us about that."

"That's the thing, Inspector," Priscilla explained carefully. "It was Aziz who told me about A-232. The reason he did is because he and his father didn't want to deal with the police. They *asked* me to inform the press."

"And that is what you did? You didn't tell us? Instead, you informed a reporter at the *Evening Standard*?"

"Yes, but the point is, Inspector, why would they give me that information if they had killed Amir? Why would they want the police to know how they did it?"

Lightfoot leaned back in his chair, as though to dodge the question. "Miss Tempest, you should have come to us immediately." He spoke in his most disapproving police-inspector tone. "You should not have gone to the press. By taking matters into your own hands, you not only put yourself at risk, but you also, in my view, imperilled our investigation."

"I am sorry, Inspector." Priscilla decided a contrite reply was in order. "It's the part of my personality that needs improvement. I keep thinking I am doing the right thing when in fact it turns out I am doing the wrong thing entirely."

"What I can do, Miss Tempest, is advise you to strive to improve from here on in." At least he sounded a bit more sympathetic, Priscilla thought.

"I will do my best, Inspector."

Inspector Lightfoot gave her another look that suggested he had doubts about the truthfulness of that statement.

"I think we've had enough for the time being," he said, and he actually blessed her with a smile as he added, "Go home, get some rest. For what it's worth, you probably deserve it."

Yes, Priscilla thought. She certainly did.

CHAPTER THIRTY-SEVEN

Trouble!

The sun strained through the morning cloud cover, throwing flattering light on Mark Ryde and his MGB. He waved to Priscilla as she emerged from Scotland Yard. Priscilla immediately thought how terrible she must look before questioning how and why Mark had managed to be here waiting for her.

"I thought you might need a ride," he said, grinning.

"How did you know I was here?" Not certain whether to be angry that he had shown up or relieved that he was offering transportation.

"Come on, hop in," he said. "Let me drive you home, or to the hotel, if that's what you'd like."

"I've taken enough unsolicited rides for one night, thank you," Priscilla said huffily. "And you still haven't answered my question."

"Like I told you before, I'm a civil servant who knows certain things—like when a damsel is in distress and may require a ride."

"Yes, but you never tell me what kind of civil servant that is exactly, do you, Mark? Not only am I finished with unsolicited rides, I'm also tired of mystery men who won't reveal the truth about themselves."

"Tell you what. Let's take a walk by the Thames. That way I can try to answer any questions you might have. How's that?"

"I don't want to walk by the Thames," Priscilla said petulantly.

"For a few minutes and then I'll drive you wherever you want to go."

"I hate you," she said.

"No, you don't, but even if you did, you're intrigued. You want answers. And I am willing to give them to you—as best I can."

As tired as she was, she couldn't deny his logic. Or maybe it was simply that a walk with Mark Ryde wasn't such a bad idea.

Or maybe it was. She was too tired at this point to decide.

The sun continued to struggle over the day's first batch of happy tourists, crowded onto the River Thames boats floating past Mark strolling with Priscilla.

"The official name is Military Intelligence, Section 5," he explained.

"What's that?" Priscilla asked. She didn't want to look at him; didn't want to do anything to weaken what resolve she had left. She kept her eyes on the tourist boats.

"The more popular name is MI5."

"You're a *spy*?" Now Priscilla stared at him.

"Domestic intelligence," Mark explained. "We don't spy so much as we look for spies—or people deemed to be a threat to national security. We leave the international spying to those stumbling asses over at MI6."

"Turning up in front of my flat with your overheated MGB, what was that?" Mark had become more interesting than the tourist boats. She noted the bristle darkening his chin and concluded he hadn't shaved that morning. Too busy scurrying over to Scotland Yard to intercept her, she imagined.

"That was me in front of your flat with an overheated MGB," Mark said.

"Nothing else?"

"Your involvement with Amir Abrahim might have had something to do with it—that and the fact that you are rather attractive."

"*Rather* attractive? There's a compliment to set a girl's heart fluttering."

"My English reserve at work. I actually find you highly attractive."

"Too bad you're spying on me *and*, even worse, you're engaged to be married. How is Alana, anyway?"

"As far as I know, she's fine. Incidentally, we are no longer engaged."

"That was fast. One day you're going to be married, the next day you're not."

"I'm as surprised as anyone," Mark said. "But there you have it. Alana has decided to move on, and I wish her the best."

"But you're still a spy," Priscilla pointed out. "Or have you decided to give that up along with marriage?"

"Intelligence officer is much more accurate," Mark said.

"I'm never going to be sure of your motives, am I?" Or my feelings, she added silently.

Mark came to a sudden stop and turned to face her. He placed his hands on either side of her face and gently drew her to him so that he could kiss her mouth.

She told herself that she must stop him. And she *would* stop him—soon. Very soon. So very, very soon.

When he pulled away finally, she was certain her eyes were sparkling. She hated that, knowing Mark knew that he had caused the sparkling in her eyes. "What was that all about?" The words came out in a breathless explosion.

"It was about my motives—which include, at this particular moment, the desire to kiss you."

"Yes, I thought that's what it was," Priscilla said with a nod.

"Look, Priscilla, I like you—a lot, which is why I'm telling you things that I probably shouldn't tell you. I'm going to do my best to ensure no harm comes to you, but I need you to stay away from the press, and stop antagonizing the police. I don't think you've done anything wrong, but they seem to think you have."

"You're trying to seduce me into silence," Priscilla accused angrily.

"I may be trying to seduce you," Mark said. "But it has nothing to do with your silence."

Now she wasn't sure of anything. Was he finally being honest with her—the spy revealed? Or was he merely replacing one set of lies with another? Right now she was too tired and fed up to decide.

"You said you were going to drive me."

"Yes, certainly."

"Then let's go, before I get myself into even more trouble than I am in now." As she turned to start away, Mark took her arm and swung her around so that she was directly facing him.

"It may not look like it, but I'm on your side," he said. That grave look on his face was particularly appealing, she couldn't help but think. "I'm not trouble, Priscilla. Honestly, I'm not."

"Yes, you are," she said insistently. "You are most definitely trouble."

"You're wrong."

"Am I?" She was aware that the clouds had cleared and the sun was shining brightly. Out on the Thames more tourist boats appeared. There was a light morning breeze. She reached up to touch Mark's unshaven cheek. Then she kissed him. "There," she said, breathless all over again. "I'm right. You are trouble."

CHAPTER THIRTY-EIGHT

Find the Mother-In-Law!

Priscilla's sleep-deprived body told her to go home and get some rest. Priscilla's brain, not always connected to the rest of her, pushed her toward the office.

Priscilla's brain, for once, won the morning. Mark drew the MGB up to the curb further along the Strand from the Savoy.

"Don't try to kiss me," she said to him. "We are much too close to the hotel."

"The thought never crossed my mind," Mark said.

"I suppose they teach you that sort of discipline at spy headquarters."

"It's a large part of our training—how to not kiss pretty girls on London streets. Unfortunately, they neglected the part where I'm the one getting kissed."

"A momentary lapse in judgment," Priscilla declared.

"I'm sure it was," Mark said. He leaned over and kissed her.

She told herself that she should never have kissed him in the first place; she should not be allowing him to kiss her now. She finally gathered the wherewithal to pull away and unlatch the passenger door. "I still don't trust you," she announced, in case he should get the wrong idea about these kisses.

"And I'm not sure I trust you, either," he replied.

She gave him a look and then got out of the car. He leaned across the passenger seat. "I'll be in touch."

"Will you?"

He smiled and closed the door.

"You're wearing the same clothes you had on yesterday!" Nothing this day could have astonished Susie more.

"No comment," Priscilla said, falling into the chair at her desk, staring at her phones, daring one of them to ring.

"Are you all right?" Susie inquired. "You look like you were put through the wringer. What were you up to last night?"

"A typical night out for me, kidnapped and held captive by a man who wants to marry me."

Susie laughed and said, "Right!" Then, more seriously, "Have you spoken to Mrs. Banville? She's looking for you."

Eunice. *Damn!* Priscilla thought. In the chaos of the previous night, she had totally forgotten about her.

She hit the waiter button, and a couple of minutes later Karl made his welcome appearance. "Do not tell me," Karl announced. "Coffee."

"How do you know?"

"Look at you," Karl said. "What happened?"

"A guy who wants to marry Priscilla kidnapped her," Susie called.

"Ah, yes," Karl said. "Another late night in London."

"There you go," Priscilla agreed. "Coffee—and hurry."

Karl nodded curtly and was gone. Priscilla got up, ignoring Susie's wondering eyes, and closed the office door. She sat at her desk a minute and took a deep breath, thinking about her encounter with Mark Ryde.

The spy who kissed her. Or if you cared to look at it from a slightly different perspective, the spy she kissed. Either way, the last thing she needed right now was kissing spies, particularly one who left her at once breathless and suspicious. More breathless than suspicious, she had to admit.

Even so, she decided, someone who made her breathless should not also be making her suspicious.

She certainly enjoyed the kissing. She couldn't deny that. Far too much, in her estimation. But then no matter how he described his job, Mark Ryde was still a spy—and spying on her. A spy who was probably a liar and who could be kissing her because that was part of the job. That's what spies did, didn't they? They seduced young, susceptible women like herself.

After all, he wanted her to stay quiet and avoid the press. A few kisses might persuade her to do just that.

Well, she would show him. She picked up the phone.

"It's me," she announced when Percy Hoskins came on the line.

"I'm on deadline, Priscilla," Percy said curtly. "What's up?"

"Oh, nothing much," Priscilla said with affected nonchalance. "I just thought you'd like to know that Aziz Abrahim and his father, Tarak, have been arrested for the murder of Amir Abrahim,"

"What?" Percy blurted, abruptly all ears. "Jesus Christ, are you sure?"

"I just left Scotland Yard where I was interviewed yet again by Inspector Lightfoot," Priscilla said brightly. "I do believe I'm his favourite suspect."

"What's going on?" Percy commanded in a tense voice. "Why would they be talking to you again?"

"It's a long story, but for now, you must call Scotland Yard immediately."

"Hold on, let me get this straight. They think Tarak participated in the killing of his own son?"

"Inspector Lightfoot told me the murder was the result of a family feud. Personally, I don't believe it, but naturally, the inspector isn't listening to me."

"Still, it explains the A-232 doesn't it?" Percy said after allowing what Priscilla told him to sink in. "The Russians could have put them onto this deadly toxin, and they used it to knock off Amir."

"But how would they actually do that?" Priscilla asked. "They would have to have gotten the poison into the champagne delivered to Amir's suite. That seems highly unlikely. What's more, their arrest doesn't explain how Bernard Bannister ended up dead from the same substance."

Before Percy could answer, the door to Priscilla's office flew open. Daisee Banville, perfection itself except for her ugly scowl, crashed in, shouting, "Where the hell is my mother?"

"I'm going to have to call you back," Priscilla said into the phone before hanging up, gulping for air as she faced the furious Daisee.

"I'm sorry, Mrs. Banville, I was on the phone. What seems to be the problem?"

"The *problem* is my mother didn't come home last night," Daisee yelled. "What did you do with her?"

"We were at the theatre together," Priscilla said, her stomach doing another flipflop as she stalled with an approximation of the truth.

"Well, now she's not in her room!"

"Perhaps she went out early this morning."

"I was just up there, her bed hasn't been slept in," stated Daisee.

"I don't know," Priscilla said honestly. "She was all right when I left her last night." Also more or less true.

"You were responsible for her," Daisee shouted. "My husband was stupid enough to entrust her to you. This should never have been allowed to happen."

"Let me see what I can do to track her down," Priscilla said, determined to remain the picture of calm in the storm, without having the slightest idea of what she would do.

"How can this be happening?" Daisee wailed. "Margaret coming tonight and my goddamn mother disappears."

"Princess Margaret is here tonight?" That caught Priscilla off guard. "It's not her birthday yet, is it?"

Daisee shot her a horrified glance. "You're *not* to *know* that!"

"Unfortunately, you just told me."

"It's not supposed to be happening now but it *is* happening," Daisee said in a despairing voice. "I can't cope, but *must* cope. I have no choice!"

She pointed a threatening finger at Priscilla. "And you, everyone's suspicious of you. You're not to say anything to anyone. Do you understand?"

"Yes, of course. Can I do anything?"

"Find my mother—and keep your mouth *shut*!"

And with those orders delivered in no uncertain terms, Daisee was gone.

Priscilla's head began to ache. The world was against her. Evil men set out to abduct her. Scotland Yard didn't believe her. Daisee Banville was suspicious of her—and probably her husband was as well. She wanted to crawl down into a hole and stay there—except Karl had yet to show up with coffee, and the telephone was ringing again. And again. She gritted her teeth and picked up the receiver.

"Help me," Eunice said, plaintively.

No Secrets at the Savoy

Priscilla sat up straight. "Where are you?"

"I don't know, somewhere, in a phone booth. Can't you help me?" Eunice's voice contained a note Priscilla had not heard before: desperation.

"I need some idea of your location," Priscilla said.

"Wherever I am, it's not good, let me tell you," Eunice said grimly. "There's not a single luxury car in sight. Hold on a minute." She was gone for a couple of moments and then, out of breath, came back on the line. "It looks like Brick Lane. I'm in a place called Brick Lane."

"Okay, stay where you are, I'm coming for you."

"People are looking at me," Eunice said plaintively.

"You'll be all right, but stay put. I'll be there as soon as I can."

"Hurry—please! I could be murdered at any moment!"

Karl appeared with coffee. Priscilla took a couple of gulps and then called out to Susie. "Have Bogans bring the car around right now—and don't take no for an answer."

"Right-o!" Susie called back, picking up the receiver.

Priscilla finished the coffee, spent a few moments in the bathroom freshening her makeup and brushing her teeth so that she returned to a facsimile of her healthy self—not that she could recall the last time she was her healthy self—hiding as best she could the late-night, sleepless party monster she was certain she resembled.

Cecil Bogans was hunched against the Daimler as Priscilla hurried out the Savoy entrance. "We're headed for Brick Lane, and the sooner we can get there, the better," she said. "I'll ride in front with you."

"Very good, Miss Tempest," Bogans said, holding the front passenger door for her.

The traffic along the Victoria Embankment slowed them. Bogans looked impatient. "Traffic, ma'am, worse every year."

"Do your best, Bogans. We're on a mission to rescue Mrs. Banville's mother."

Bogans's aged countenance maintained the neutral expression borne of long experience unobtrusively serving the Savoy's guests—and, on occasions like this one, its employees.

"Might I enquire if Mrs. Kerry is in trouble, ma'am?"

"I hope not," Priscilla said ruefully. "I'm in enough trouble around here without losing the general manager's mother."

"I suppose you must get her back in time for the arrival of HRH the Princess Margaret."

Priscilla stole a glance at him. "How do you know about that? It's supposed to be top secret."

Priscilla saw Bogans do something she hadn't seen him do much before: smile. A rather mischievous smile at that. "There are no secrets at the Savoy, Miss Tempest. Not among the staff, anyway."

"Everyone knows about Princess Margaret?"

Bogans kept his eyes on the road.

"What about the deaths of Amir Abrahim and Bernard Bannister? What does the staff have to say about those?"

"Ah, yes, our mysterious head housekeeper."

"Millicent Holmes?"

"Well, she *says* her name is Millicent Holmes, doesn't she?"

"What do you mean? That's not her real name?"

Again, Bogans concentrated on the road. Finally, he added, "Mysterious Mrs. Holmes and her Austrian lover."

"Karl? Karl Steiner is her lover?"

"At least he *says* he is Austrian."

"Don't tell me he's not Austrian…"

This time, Bogans just shrugged. "We are all putting on a show, are we not? Masks that we wear each day to perform for our guests. None of it has anything to do with who we really are. Some of us are housekeepers who find it helpful to see princesses where there may not be any princesses. Some feel it is necessary to be good waiters in order to hide other activities. Our masks can cover up all sorts of things—except, finally, those masks slip. As I said, there are no secrets at the Savoy."

"Are you telling me that Mrs. Holmes didn't really see Princess Margaret the morning she found Amir Abrahim?"

"I am not *telling* you anything," Bogans said. "I am putting my mask back on where it has been firmly in place for the last twenty-five years in the service of the Savoy and not saying more—other than to point out that we are approaching Brick Lane."

They soon found Eunice, agitated, pacing near a red call box. Bogans pulled the Daimler up beside her and Priscilla got out.

"Where the hell have you been?" Eunice demanded.

"Are you all right?"

"Certainly, I'm all right. Why wouldn't I be?"

"When we last talked, I believe you were concerned about being murdered."

"Well, no one murdered me. In fact, people have been quite friendly—except for that bastard Enrique."

"Does he live around here?"

"Somewhere nearby. A crummy flat where, it turns out, Enrique has a wife who wasn't happy to find me in bed with her husband this morning."

"You were in bed with Enrique?" Every time Priscilla was sure nothing about Eunice could surprise her, something else surprised her.

"Where else would I be? Except when Mrs. Enrique showed up, I had to get out before I had a chance to pay him."

"You *paid* Enrique?" Yet again, where Eunice was concerned, Priscilla was having difficulty keeping the amazement out of her voice.

"Naturally, I have to pay him. You don't think the Enriques of the world are for free, do you? Although most of the time they don't come equipped with wives. Supposedly, she was away for the week, but I suspect she thought he was up to something and came back unexpectedly. What the hell, I'll send him a cheque. Come along, Priscilla, let's get out of here."

Bogans, his mask firmly in place, held the back door for Eunice. "Good morning, madam," he said as she climbed in.

"Nothing good about it yet," Eunice snarled.

Bogans merely touched the peak of his cap.

As the Daimler started back to the Savoy, Eunice, curled into the seat corner, heaved a contented sigh. "I'm dead. Was my daughter asking about me?"

"She is quite worried about you."

"Why would she be worried?"

"Apparently, she went to your suite and saw that the bed hadn't been slept in."

Eunice frowned. "You didn't say anything to her, did you?"

"I said we were at the theatre together."

"Good girl. How was the show, incidentally?"

"I don't know. I didn't stay for it."

"I see. What did you get up to?"

"I was kidnapped and then the police rescued me."

Eunice laughed. "Okay, I get it. I guess I shouldn't have asked. Never a dull moment in Swinging London, right?"

"Never," Priscilla agreed.

Eunice issued another tired sigh and stared out the window. "I wonder what my daughter wanted. She must want something. Otherwise, she would never take any interest in my comings and goings."

"It may have to do with Princess Margaret. Apparently, she's coming to the Savoy this evening."

"What?" Eunice sat upright. "Where did you hear this?"

"Your daughter told me when I got to the office."

"Good God in Heaven, she's not supposed to come tonight." Eunice leaned forward and spoke urgently to Bogans: "Driver, get your ass in gear. I need to be back at the Savoy—now!"

"On my way, madam." Priscilla caught Bogans's eye in the rear-view mirror. Unless she was mistaken, he was smiling mischievously again.

Dinner for Two

If Princess Margaret was soon to arrive at the Savoy, there was scant evidence of it in the late morning stillness of the Front Hall as Eunice strutted to reception. When Mr. Tomberry saw who was bearing down on him, he struggled to keep the look of dread off his face.

"Where is she?" Eunice demanded before Tomberry could get his mouth open.

"Where is whom, madam?" he asked archly.

"Don't play games with me," Eunice snapped. "Where is my daughter?"

"I believe she is arranging things in Suite 501," Tomberry answered in his coldest voice.

Without another word, Eunice steamed toward the lifts, Priscilla trailing. "Don't dawdle, girl!" Eunice barked.

On the lift, she grimaced and issued one of the sighs Priscilla had grown accustomed to. "Prepare yourself for fireworks. Hopefully, with you there, the incoming fire will be reduced."

When the lift reached the fifth floor, Priscilla followed Eunice to Suite 501. She knocked and a moment later, Karl Steiner opened the door. "Madam," he said formally, stepping aside so that Eunice could steam forward.

"Mother!" Daisee Banville shrieked, as she careened in from the bedroom, her face scrunched with anger. "Where the devil have you been?"

Priscilla saw that the sitting room had been decorated with dramatic flower arrangements bursting with colour from the hotel's florists. A linen-covered dining table was set for two with the finest Royal Worcester bone china.

"Why don't we concentrate on what's going to happen this evening?" Eunice answered, smartly dodging her daughter's accusatory tone.

Daisee was not to be deterred. "I know what you're up to, Mother. Don't think for a moment I don't." She shot Priscilla an angry glance. "And I hold *you* responsible. You will hear from my husband about this in light of your carelessness."

"Leave Priscilla alone," Eunice admonished. "She hasn't done anything wrong. If you want to be upset with someone, be upset with me."

"I *am* upset with you, Mother."

"Good, because unlike Priscilla here, I don't have to give a shit about what you think."

"Mother, honestly. And on a day like this when I'm being driven crazy ensuring everything is in order for tonight."

"Let's get out of here," Eunice said to Priscilla. "I need a shower and some sleep."

"Mother, I will need your help today." Daisee trained another fierce look at Priscilla. "And you too. I may need you as well."

"I'll be glad to assist in any way I can," Priscilla said.

Out in the hall, Eunice rolled her eyes. "Forgive my daughter. And don't worry, I'll make sure you don't get into any trouble. Daisee's under a lot of pressure so she lashes out, particularly at people like yourself who have to stand there and take it."

Priscilla restrained herself from observing that the daughter had learned a few lessons from her mother. Instead, she said, "It doesn't look like it's going to be much of a birthday celebration."

"Priscilla, don't you get it? There is no *birthday* celebration." Eunice was shaking her head in dismay. "It's not even Margaret's birthday. That's why there is all this secrecy. That's why Daisee is so paranoid that word of this will get out to the press."

"Then what is this?" Priscilla asked, now knowing full well what it probably was.

"It's dinner for two!" Eunice practically hissed out the words, leaning into Priscilla. "Margaret and—"

"And who?"

"Who knows?" Eunice reared back, considering the question. "That is the mystery, isn't it? I don't think even Daisee knows." She grinned impishly. "But then all will be revealed this evening, won't it?"

Susie, as usual, was in a state of near-panic when Priscilla got back to 205. All the telephones were ringing away. "The phones are going crazy, everyone's looking for you," Susie said, saucer-eyed.

"Me?"

"They've arrested a couple of people for the murder at the Savoy and every reporter on Fleet Street seems to want some sort of comment. I don't know what to tell them."

"Susie, for heaven's sake, we say what we always say."

Susie made a face. "Remind me what that is, exactly."

"You say that the Savoy can't comment on an ongoing police investigation."

"Good, I like that." Susie looked relieved. Priscilla refrained from making a sarcastic crack. She loved Susie dearly, but sometimes...

Her thought was interrupted by the renewed ringing of the phone. Priscilla cast Susie a look. She quickly picked up the receiver. Priscilla heard her say, "I'm sorry but the Savoy cannot comment on an ongoing police investigation."

That's more like it, Priscilla thought. She yawned, shaking off the exhaustion she was feeling, and pressed the waiter button. Plenty of coffee was needed if she ever hoped to get through the day.

Five minutes later, Karl arrived with the rescue coffee. "I guessed it would be either coffee or champagne. I took a chance on coffee."

"Champagne would be wonderful, except it's too early."

"Thus, I chose wisely," Karl said, setting down a cup and saucer along with a silver creamer. When he started away, Priscilla had a sudden thought and called to him. He turned around. "Yes, Miss Tempest?"

"Can I ask you something?"

"Certainly." Karl's smile had turned somewhat artificial.

"It's just that you're in here all the time, and you're so terrific, but I don't know much about you."

"Those who serve at the Savoy, serve quietly." The smile was held in place, but the light had gone out of his eyes.

"You're from Austria, are you not?"

Karl hesitated before he said, "I spent time there, yes."

"In Vienna?"

"Salzburg. At the Hotel Goldener Hirsch."

"But you are Austrian?"

"Indeed, madam. However, my father travelled a great deal. I actually grew up outside Moscow."

"How long have you worked at the Savoy?"

"A number of years now. Really, Miss Tempest, I am most uncomfortable with these questions." Karl's tone had turned cold and formal.

"I'm sorry, Karl, I didn't mean to be forward."

"That's fine. Will there be anything else?"

"Tell me, how's Mrs. Holmes doing? I ask because I just heard the police have made arrests in the death of the gentleman she found in his suite."

"Mrs. Holmes has left the hotel," Karl said stiffly.

"Left the hotel? You mean she's quit?"

"That is my understanding, yes."

"She wasn't fired, was she?"

"Not as far as I know."

"Is she okay? Have you spoken to her?"

The smile was gone. Karl looked beleaguered, very unusual for someone Priscilla had thought to be the essence of Savoy composure. "I have not spoken to Mrs. Holmes. If there is nothing else, please, I have other duties that need my attention this morning."

"Yes, sure, Karl," Priscilla said apologetically. "I didn't mean to hold you up."

Karl, his body rigid, left the office, giving the impression he had just been grilled by the Gestapo. Priscilla sat pondering the unexpected news that Millicent Holmes had quit. Why would she have done that?

Priscilla called to Susie. "Supposing I wanted information on hotel employees, where would I get it?"

Susie got up from her desk and came to the doorway, looking uncertain. "Why would you want something like that?"

"Maybe I'm just a snoop, I don't know," Priscilla replied. "How could I find out?"

"I believe there's a fellow in the basement that looks after that sort of thing," Susie said.

"Do me a favour, will you? See what you can find out."

CHAPTER FORTY-ONE

Break and Enter

As she locked her car, Alana Wynter was already regretting the black leather tapered trousers she had chosen to wear. Judging by the looks of the male passersby, they were drawing too much attention on a day when she wished not to draw any attention.

There wasn't much she could do about it now, she thought as she lifted her bag to her shoulder and walked along Knightsbridge until she reached 37–39, the address where they had told her Priscilla Tempest lived. Alana wasn't certain why they were treating this woman with such kid gloves; the reluctance to act was putting everything at risk and certainly no one was more at risk than she.

Let's find out who this woman is, and how she lives, Alana thought. After that, she could decide what to do about her.

Somewhat to her surprise, she found the front door unlocked. She went up the stairs to Priscilla's flat—or the flat she had been told was Priscilla's. Alana rapped on the door a couple of times, and then, reassured there really was no one inside, she went to work on the mortice lock with a tension wrench and a pick.

When the lock was sprung, Alana opened the door into the sort of cramped, chaotic flat occupied by single young women all over London. Clothes were scattered everywhere; the small fridge in the kitchen was empty except for a half bottle of Stoli vodka and an unopened split of Dom Perignon. In the bedroom, more clothes spilled out of an open armoire and were scattered across an unmade bed. The bathroom was, as expected, a mess of creams, cleansers and combs, lipstick tubes, eye shadow. A hairdryer dangled on the end of a cord from a towel rack.

Alana returned to the sitting room, looking for evidence of a life outside of work. There was a photograph on a side table, an older couple, smiling at the camera with mountains in the background. Priscilla's parents?

Alana had wanted some idea of who she was dealing with, so having a look inside Priscilla Tempest's flat seemed worth the risk. A long-limbed London tart fortunate enough to work at the Savoy who knew more than she was supposed to know. That was enough as it turned out. No use making any more of it than that. Except, the tart had seen her in Bernie Bannister's suite. The tart knew her name. The tart would have to be dealt with.

She heard movement from outside the flat. She froze as someone worked on the door. Was Priscilla Tempest returning home unexpectedly? Good, Alana thought. She could be taken care of right now. Alana drew the Enfield revolver from her shoulder bag. She would use a pillow to muffle the sound of the gunshot.

The door swung open.

When Alana saw who it was, she lowered the revolver and relaxed. "Fancy meeting you," she said.

"What? Were you planning on shooting me?"

"Not you."

"Priscilla?"

Alana smiled slightly as she put the gun away. "Let's say it crossed my mind."

"You should not be in here, Alana," he said.

"You didn't follow me here, did you?"

"Let's say I don't trust you," he said. "Something like this makes things bad for all of us."

"Or is it 'could make things bad for *you*,'" Alana countered. "After all, I know so much about you, don't I?"

"You do, unfortunately." He started toward her.

"But not to worry, darling. Your nasty secrets are safe with me."

"How could I ever think otherwise?" he smiled. "It's all right. We've got time. She won't be back for a while."

That familiar glint was in his eye. She allowed him to draw closer and take her in his arms. They kissed for a while and then she pulled away, turning her back to him, beginning to undo the leather slacks.

As she did this, he withdrew one of the knives from the block on the counter.

"I love you in leather," he said as he came toward her.

She knew she shouldn't have worn them, she thought, as she turned to him.

Stood Up, Broken-Hearted

The telephones had gone silent, Susie had left, and Priscilla was at her desk, thinking she really should go home and get some sleep. At the same time what was left of her adrenalin pumped away and that, along with innate curiosity about who exactly Princess Margaret might be entertaining upstairs, kept her more or less awake.

The sound of the telephone was a jarring screech, startling her. She grabbed the receiver.

"Get up here," ordered the tense voice of Eunice Kerry.

"Everything all right?" Priscilla asked.

"Just get up here."

The clerk on duty at the reception desk looked worried as Priscilla entered the lift. "Have you heard anything?" Priscilla called.

"Complaints about the noise in 501," the clerk said. "Shall I go up?"

"It's all right," Priscilla said. "I'll take care of it."

"Good luck," the clerk said.

As soon as Priscilla got off the lift, she could hear the sound of someone singing—off-key.

The door to suite 501 was ajar. From the other side, the singing had become louder, a warbling version of "Anything Goes." Priscilla rapped softly. Almost immediately the door opened wider and an unsmiling Eunice said, "Get in here."

Daisee Banville was sobbing quietly on a sofa. Nearby, the dining table remained neatly laid out, untouched, awaiting missing guests, the candles in their silver tapers having burned down to a forlorn flicker. Swaying and singing in the middle of the room, a lit cigarette in one hand, a tumbler of scotch in the other, was the munchkin-sized Princess Margaret, barefoot, dressed in a knee-length black cocktail dress.

She stopped singing when she saw Priscilla, her eyes bright and glistening, the smile crooked. "Ah, yes, very good, a new arrival. Reinforcements as I destroy Cole Porter and lament the state of things.

"What about it, you?" she asked Priscilla. "Would you like a drink? I have Famous Grouse scotch. I only drink Famous Grouse. I guzzle Famous Grouse. Particularly on a night like this."

"I'm fine, Your Highness, thank you," Priscilla said.

"Call me ma'am. Jesus Christ! Doesn't everyone know? You call me *ma'am*!"

"Yes, ma'am."

"Priscilla works for the hotel," Eunice said carefully as Daisee continued her weeping on the sofa. "I asked her here in case she can be of assistance."

"She could have a drink, that would be of assistance."

"Priscilla," Eunice said quietly, "why don't you take my daughter downstairs and see to it she gets a ride home? That would be a great help."

"I don't want to go home," Daisee wailed.

"Daisee, it's time to go home. Someone from the Palace is coming for Her Royal Highness and—"

"Call me ma'am!" yelled Princess Margaret.

Priscilla saw that the princess had somehow attached a box of matches to the bottom of her tumbler. She fumbled with the matchbox, spilling scotch, finally managing to light another cigarette.

Waving the lit cigarette, she stumbled and fell to the sofa beside Daisee, wrapping a comforting arm around her weeping friend. "Don't worry about it, my dear. It's all thoroughly buggered. Everything. The world. The men in the world. All of it."

Daisee only cried harder. Eunice leaned into Priscilla and hissed, "Get my daughter out of here."

Priscilla nodded and went over to the phone and dialed the front desk. A moment later she was connected to Bogans. "Where are you?" she asked.

"Not so far away, madam," Bogans said. He sounded wide awake. "Is there a problem?"

"I need you to take Mrs. Banville home."

"Be right there, madam."

Priscilla hung up the phone and turned to Eunice. "A car is on the way."

"Get Daisee downstairs. I'll handle the princess until someone from the Palace arrives."

Princess Margaret had begun another discordant croon, "Night and Day" this time, sung with her arm still around Daisee.

"You're so sweet," Daisee said, falling against the princess.

Priscilla leaned down and said, "Mrs. Banville, I have a car waiting downstairs. Would you like to come with me?"

Daisee looked cross. "Who the hell do you think you are?"

Princess Margaret stopped singing and looked at Priscilla with narrowed eyes. "I know her. She's the one who won't drink with me. You should immediately have her sacked!"

"Daisee, it's time to go home," Eunice said to her daughter in a level voice. "Your husband will be worried about you. Go along with Priscilla."

"My husband," Daisee moaned. "That old fart."

But she allowed Priscilla to disentangle her from the princess and lift her to her feet. "Goodbye, Margaret," Daisee sobbed. "I love you."

"Call me ma'am—and sod off!" the princess replied.

Priscilla managed to get Daisee into the lift and that pretty much brought a halt to her tears. She sank against the wall as they rode down, mumbling, "You're an awful person. The princess wants you fired. My husband will fire you."

"Yes, ma'am," Priscilla replied. "I'm sure he will." Marvelling that whatever the crisis, there was always someone around anxious to be rid of her.

Thankfully, Bogans was waiting by the Savoy Hill entrance when Priscilla came out with Daisee. Bogans did not threaten to fire her. Instead, he held the back door open. Daisee was another matter. "My husband is going to dismiss this woman because of the way she's treated me this evening," Daisee told Bogans in a slurred voice. "I think you should know that."

"Thank you, madam," Bogans replied courteously.

He gave Priscilla a quick look but otherwise showed no emotion as he helped Daisee into the rear. "You're fired, too," she announced to Bogans. "Manhandling me! How dare you! Fire the lot of you!"

As soon as Bogans got her inside the car, Daisee threw back her head and fell into a deep sleep.

"You know where to go?" Priscilla said to Bogans as he closed the rear door.

"I do," Bogans said. He touched the tip of his cap. "I'll see her safe home, Miss Tempest. Not to worry."

As the Daimler drove off, Priscilla hurried back inside the hotel and rode the lift to the fifth floor. As she reached the suite, the door opened and out lurched Princess Margaret, waving a cigarette and leaning hard against the tall, handsome frame of Mark Ryde.

"I will never, ever forgive you for being so late," the Princess was saying to him.

"I'm so sorry, ma'am."

"You are such a prick, you know that? A right prick."

"Indeed, ma'am," Mark said.

They both came to an abrupt stop when they saw Priscilla, who was working to keep her jaw from dropping more than it already had. Princess Margaret regarded her with narrowed eyes full of suspicion. "I remember you," she said to Priscilla. "You're the awful person who wouldn't drink Famous Grouse with me. You will be sacked!"

"Yes, ma'am," Priscilla said.

Mark had recovered enough to say, "I'm escorting the princess home."

"Very good," Priscilla said.

Mark loomed over the diminutive princess as he navigated her along to the lift. "You really are a prick to stand me up like that," Priscilla heard the princess saying.

"Yes, ma'am," Mark replied.

At least he addresses her properly, Priscilla thought.

CHAPTER FORTY-THREE

Knife Out

The cab driver's determination to apprise Priscilla of his views on the American involvement in the Vietnam War kept her from dozing off on the ride home.

She resisted the temptation to tell him about the real problems of the world: kidnapping arms dealers, drunken princesses, a chorus of critics insisting she soon would be terminated, and—most worrisome—handsome, duplicitous men who turned out to be spies who would stand up Princess Margaret for dinner.

Now *those* were real problems, she thought as she paid the driver and started into her flat. For the time being, though, she would set all that aside in favour of finally getting a good night's sleep. She was feeling very old as she unlocked the door and heard the low moan.

Moan?

Who would be moaning in her flat? Was she hearing things?

A single light from the kitchen pierced the darkness. As she crossed the sitting room, more sounds, the moaning reduced to a whimper. She definitely was not hearing things.

Alana Wynter, clad in leather slacks Priscilla immediately envied, was propped awkwardly on a kitchen chair, her long legs splayed, holding her stomach trying to stop the flow of blood in the place where one of the flat's kitchen knives protruded. Ashen-faced, she looked up as Priscilla let out a gasp that was a combination of shock and horror.

Alana responded by jerking up on the chair and then with a loud, painful cry, falling forward.

Priscilla reached out to catch her. Instead, she found herself grasping the knife handle as Alana sank to the floor. The knife came out in her hand.

Horrified, Priscilla held the knife, blood dripping onto her clothes, blood everywhere. This couldn't be happening to her, she thought. This *could not* be happening.

She stared uncomprehendingly at Alana Wynter's leather-clad body on the floor in front of her—indisputable evidence that it *was* happening.

"Let me explain what I'm having difficulty with," Chief Inspector Robert Lightfoot said to Priscilla.

Priscilla, insensate, detached from the world, could not be sure how much time had passed. She was vaguely aware of Lightfoot with her in a police van on the street outside her flat. The rear door was partially open, allowing a uniformed female officer to hover close by.

Priscilla tried to focus. "What are you having difficulty with, Inspector?" She was so tired, and puzzled as to how the inspector could possibly have a problem.

"With the fact that a woman you now say was in Bernard Bannister's suite—a woman you previously had refused to name—is then found dead in your flat with a knife belonging to you sticking out of her. You are then found by attending officers standing over the deceased covered in her blood."

"You're having trouble with that?" Priscilla asked. "Why should you be having trouble?"

"I find myself struggling with the urge to conclude that you employed your kitchen knife in order to stab Miss Wynter when you arrived home and discovered her in your flat."

Priscilla could only stare at the inspector in slack-mouthed disbelief. Then, in a voice barely above a hoarse whisper, she said, "As I have repeated many times to the other officers, when I got home from work, Miss Wynter was in my kitchen with the knife sticking out of her. I have no idea how she got in, nor can I fathom what she was doing there."

Lightfoot appeared unmoved by her explanation. "If you didn't stab her, then who do you suppose did?"

"I have absolutely no idea. I'm as mystified as you."

"The deceased used the lockpicks we found in her purse to gain access to your flat. We can therefore put this unfortunate episode down to a case of self-defence, but you must stop lying and tell me."

"I am so exhausted, Inspector. I haven't slept forever and I haven't killed anyone."

"For now, Miss Tempest, I'm afraid I'm going to have to ask you to come with us to Scotland Yard."

"Am I under arrest?" Words she never thought she would hear herself say.

In response, Lightfoot rose to his feet. Priscilla noticed that his head was touching the roof of the van so that he had to bow slightly in order to say, "You will come with us. You have the right to remain silent, but anything you do say will be taken down and may be used in evidence."

The gravity of her predicament began to sink in. She was a murder suspect! *Impossible!* How could this be?

Inspector Lightfoot turned and pushed the van door open further. The female police officer tensed as though preparing in case Priscilla made a break for it. "Let's step out, shall we Miss Tempest?"

She followed him onto the street, into the warmth of the night, the quiet sounds of police officers moving in and out of her building, the neighbours in various states of nightdress, possibly confirming long-standing suspicions that she was up to no good—the sort of no good that eventually brings the police. Everyone looked sombre and accusatory, having already found her guilty of a murder she didn't commit. A single face shone out of the crowd, familiar and sympathetic. The unshaven Percy Hoskins, as close as she was probably ever going to get to a knight in shining armour, in the uncertain light looked even shaggier and more unkempt than ever.

"Good evening, Inspector," Percy said in an unexpectedly merry voice.

"What are you doing here, Hoskins?" Lightfoot, who never looked less than unhappy, appeared downright angry.

"Inspector, I'm investigating a potential scandal involving Miss Alana Wynter and her relationship with the Honourable Bernard Bannister, the well-known Conservative member of parliament."

Lightfoot looked taken aback. "I have no comment at this time," he answered formally.

"But I have plenty of comment to make," said Priscilla, losing her whispery hoarseness and speaking up.

"That's enough, Miss Tempest," retorted Lightfoot irritably. "You are only getting yourself into more trouble."

"Am I? You know what? I don't think I am."

"Come now, Inspector," Percy joined in, "I have it on good authority that it may be Miss Wynter who was murdered at this address tonight. Is that true?"

"No comment," Lightfoot snapped.

"It *was* Alana Wynter," Priscilla confirmed, making sure she could be heard.

"Miss Tempest!" Lightfoot, appalled by her blurted revelation.

Priscilla was undeterred. "Inspector, no matter what you think, I believe Alana was murdered in order to keep her quiet about her affair with Mr. Bannister," she plunged on. "What do you say to that?"

"Yes, Inspector," Percy said. "In light of what Miss Tempest is alleging, surely you must have a comment."

"I have none," Lightfoot muttered, glancing uneasily around as though to see who might be listening.

"Well, you might want to say something about the possibility that I am being framed for Miss Wynter's murder," Priscilla said.

"Preposterous," Lightfoot sputtered.

"Based on what Miss Tempest has revealed to me," Percy said, "I must advise that I will prepare a story suggesting Miss Tempest is in fact being charged for a crime she did not commit, but which would aid in the coverup surrounding the deaths of Bernard Bannister and now Alana Wynter."

"There has been *no* attempt at a coverup," Inspector Lightfoot sputtered indignantly.

"Then I suggest you immediately free Miss Tempest and allow me to take her away, thus removing one allegation of misconduct that would have been part of what is already a damning story for the next edition of the *Evening Standard*."

Inspector Lightfoot gave every indication he was about to explode. Then his sense of survival kicked in and he took a breath, gritted his teeth, and turned to Priscilla. "You are free to go, Miss Tempest, but keep in mind you may be required to answer further questions."

"Just make sure you don't question her without her solicitor present," Percy said.

"Get out of here, Hoskins," growled Inspector Lightfoot. "I'm sick of the sight of the two of you."

Percy took Priscilla by the arm and guided her through the onlookers who were still hanging about. Priscilla slowed. "I can't go anywhere," she protested plaintively. "I'm covered in blood and all my clothes are in my flat."

"They're not going to let you into your place tonight," Percy said. "Let's get you away from here before Charger changes his mind. We'll figure out the rest later."

"That's another thing, I've nowhere to go."

"Yes, you do."

"Where?"

Percy grinned. Priscilla thought, Uh-oh.

CHAPTER FORTY-FOUR

Shenanigans Is a Canadian Word

Percy's ground-floor Camden Town flat in North London was much neater than Priscilla expected considering he was male and single and in the newspaper business. Certainly, it was a whole lot tidier than her place.

And anyway, she was zombie-like with exhaustion, beyond caring about how neat Percy was or wasn't. He had an efficient shower with good pressure that allowed her to wash the blood off her naked body. And that was something she never thought she'd have to worry about—the problem of washing a murder victim's blood off one's body.

Once that was accomplished, she stepped out of the shower, dried herself using the surprisingly fluffy towel Percy had provided, and then struggled into an oversize T-shirt with the profile of a lion's head on it—the logo of the Great Britain National Rugby League Team. Finally, she put on the silk housecoat adorned with a curling dragon that he had bought in Hong Kong for a girlfriend who had gone from his life by the time he returned to London.

That was his story, anyhow.

She padded into the sitting room, taking note of the shelves full of history books—the five volumes of Winston Churchill's Second World War histories stuck out—the John Coltrane jazz album playing quietly on what looked like an expensive phonograph, and suddenly she felt more relaxed than she had in weeks. Exhausted as well, she had to admit.

Percy in shirtsleeves appeared from the kitchen. "I'm brewing tea, would you like some?"

Priscilla made a face. "I shouldn't have been allowed into the country, I hate tea."

"Something stronger, then?"

"A glass of water would work wonders."

By the time Percy returned she had sprawled on the sofa, having trouble keeping her eyes open. She sat up and gratefully gulped down the water. "I suppose I should thank you for coming to my rescue," she said, handing him back the glass.

"Not a bad idea," Percy allowed. "I do believe Charger was about to throw you into the clink."

"I could have handled it," Priscilla said.

"Sure, it looked like you had the situation under control." Percy sounded as though that was the last thing he believed.

"Still," Priscilla said, "it does raise the question: How did you know to come to my rescue?"

"I didn't, not at first," he said, sitting beside her. "As I keep saying, I've got friends in high places and low—including sources at Scotland Yard who know I've been working on the Bannister death and thought I should know that someone rumoured to be associated with him had turned up dead in a Knightsbridge flat. You can imagine my surprise when I got to the address I'd been given and discovered it was your flat and that you were able to confirm what I only suspected."

"That it was Alana Wynter."

"I know what you told the police, but do you have any real idea what she might have been doing in your place?"

"There's more I haven't told you—or the police for that matter," Priscilla answered after thinking about it for a minute.

"Bloody hell, Priscilla," Percy said in exasperation, "you're always saying that."

"Because otherwise I'm afraid you're going to print what I tell you and get me in more trouble than I'm already in."

"I'm not going to print anything—not yet, anyway. What is it you've kept from me this time?"

"There is a man named Mark Ryde," Priscilla explained, being careful about how she told Percy about Mark. "Initially, Mark told me he was a civil servant. But now it turns out he works for MI5, or he says he does. He also told me he was engaged to Alana Wynter, and that's why it couldn't have been her I saw in Mr. Bannister's suite. He talked me out of giving her name to the police—or to the press—because, he says, she was in France at the time I found Bannister."

"But you don't believe him."

"Now he tells me they are no longer engaged. Honestly, I don't know what to believe at this point."

"Okay, so Alana might have broken into to your flat to find out more about you."

"Yes, I suppose so."

"Could this MI5 guy have followed her to your flat?"

"And then killed her? Why would he do that?"

"Maybe to keep her quiet," Percy suggested.

"That's another thing. It turns out Mark was supposed to have dinner with Princess Margaret at the Savoy earlier tonight. But he missed the dinner and then showed up very late to take her home."

Percy's eyes had brightened. "Late because he was busy murdering his ex-fiancée at your place."

"Alana Wynter in the suite with Bernard Bannister. Alana Wynter with Mark Ryde. Alana Wynter knifed by Mark Ryde who then meets up with Princess Margaret. It all more or less fits together—kind of fits together."

"And takes us along the Yellow Brick Road that leads straight to Buckingham Palace," Percy offered.

"Yes, it does," Priscilla agreed.

"Is this Mark Ryde from MI5 Princess Margaret's lover?"

"He could be," Priscilla said, not wanting to believe it to be true. But then after seeing the two of them together, suspicions were naturally raised.

"What about you?" Percy tried unsuccessfully to make the question sound nonchalant. "Have you slept with this guy too?"

"Why does everyone always ask me that? Who have you slept with?"

"I haven't slept with you," Percy replied.

"What does that mean? Are you trying to sleep with me?" Not certain, sitting there in his flat, wearing an old girlfriend's silk robe, whether she should be pleased—or scared.

"The thought never crossed my mind." The denial sounded anything but sincere. The wry smile didn't help.

"Good. I'm far too worn-out for any shenanigans tonight."

"Shenanigans. What is that? A Canadian word?"

"A word used the world over to describe what we're not going to get up to." Priscilla, by now stretched out on the sofa, was even more aware of her vulnerability. Or was it availability?

"Because you're not interested?" Percy pressed.

"I wouldn't go so far as to say that," Priscilla replied cautiously.

"You're much more interested in Mark Ryde, I suppose."

"He's engaged—was engaged—and possibly shagging Princess Margaret."

"And don't forget murdering his fiancée."

"Ex-fiancée." And on top of that, a liar, Priscilla silently added. Although, she had to concede, being a possible killer was doubtless worse than being a known liar.

A little worse.

"Not the sort of bloke I'd have anything to do with if I were you," Percy was saying. "I'm a much more attractive prospect."

"Because you haven't knocked off your ex-fiancée?"

"Because I don't have a fiancée to knock off."

"I've been considering it," Priscilla said.

"Considering what?"

"The possibility of kissing you."

"And what have you decided?"

"That you can kiss me," she said, sitting up on her elbows. "But that's it. Only a kiss. Nothing more."

"That's enough," Percy said.

He leaned down to kiss her. She kissed him back. Telling herself not to think about Mark Ryde kissing her. Trying not to compare the kisses. She interrupted the kissing to say, "I don't want you printing anything I just told you, not yet."

"If I agree to that, can I kiss you some more?"

"That's blackmail."

"It is."

"As long as you don't print anything."

"Promise."

Priscilla lay back on the sofa and they resumed. Not bad at all, she thought, although she was unsure who had won the Kissing Priscilla sweepstakes. The kisses of both men had pluses and no detectable minuses. From the other room came the sound of the tea kettle reaching a boil.

"Saved by the tea kettle," Priscilla said, her voice muffled against his lips.

That failed to stop him. She sighed and rejoined the fray. The tea kettle continued to make discordant noises. Percy issued an impatient grunt and then rose to go into the kitchen.

By the time he returned with his tea, Priscilla was fast asleep.

There would be no shenanigans tonight.

CHAPTER FORTY-FIVE

Morning Has Broken

Priscilla came out of a deep sleep, curled beneath a duvet on Percy Hoskins's sofa. She sat up groggily, noticing that she was still in Percy's silk robe, then seeing the note pinned to the duvet. *"Off to work. Coffee in the kitchen. Call me. P."*

If Percy were any kind of gentleman, Priscilla thought, he would have offered his bed, while he took the sofa. Ah, well, Percy wasn't much of a hero, but he would have to do. And, she had to admit as she proceeded barefoot into the kitchen, he was not a bad kisser. As good a kisser as Mark Ryde? Coming to any conclusions would require more research. This wasn't the sort of thing about which one rushed to judgment.

Further, Priscilla had to admit, he made a not-bad cup of coffee. Another checkmark in Percy's plus column. Mark Ryde had not made her coffee or saved her from a jail cell. Mark Ryde had lied to her while Percy, well, Percy had more or less told the truth, despite the fact that until now, she had more or less *not* told him the truth.

There was a phone on the counter. She breathed a silent sigh of relief when Susie for once was on time and immediately answered.

"Are you all right?" Susie blurted. "I'm hearing all sorts of crazy things."

"I'm fine, but I need you to get over to Marks & Spencer at Marble Arch and buy some clothes for me."

"*Clothes?*" Susie, as she often did lately, sounded as though she couldn't believe what she was hearing.

"You know my size. I need underwear—"

"You don't have *underwear?*" Susie now sounded shocked.

"Susie, just listen without the usual hysterical comment. Underwear. A decent dress and a jacket. My shoes should be all right. Once you've done that, I want you to bring the clothes to the address I'm going to give you. I need you to do this immediately. And nothing beige!"

"Nothing beige, jolly good," Susie said. "I'm on my way."

"And if anyone asks, tell them I'm running late but I'm coming into the office."

"I should say that Mr. Banville has been looking for you." Susie's voice now filled with concern.

"I'll deal with him once I'm at 205. Now, please, get moving."

"I'm on my way," Susie said.

When a crisis did occur, Susie did move quickly and fairly efficiently, Priscilla conceded once she had hung up the phone. Sipping the coffee, she wandered about the flat, checking out the alcove where Percy had set up a desk and an electric typewriter, which was surrounded by crumpled pieces of paper, a well-thumbed copy of *The Sun Also Rises* nearby. A budding British Hemingway right here in Camden Town.

She finished her coffee and went into the narrow bathroom, showered for a second time beneath the lukewarm spray, and reused the fluffy towel from the night before.

By the time she figured out how to make herself a second pot of coffee, the doorbell was ringing. "Come in, it's open," Priscilla called, expecting Susie.

Only it wasn't Susie.

In the doorway, Mark Ryde said, "Good morning, mind if I come in?" Impeccably tailored, dropping by on his way to that *Esquire* magazine photo shoot. His red silk tie was formed in a perfect Windsor knot worn with the perfectly spread white collar. He even smelled good, Priscilla thought, as she confronted him, kind of woodsy and very masculine.

He stopped in the midst of the sitting room, raising his head to sniff the air. "That smells like coffee."

Fighting to recover from the shock of his presence, she asked, "What are you doing here?"

Mark arranged to be preoccupied with taking in his surroundings. Today he was nicely shaved, she noticed. His skin shone with health. "Not a bad flat, actually. I should ask which of your lovers lives here."

Priscilla, angry, astonished—intrigued? No, she told herself. She could not possibly be intrigued. Deeply suspicious would be much wiser.

"Doesn't matter." Mark's gaze fell on her, along with that insouciant, I-know-it-all smile that she was beginning to find not so much sexy as annoying. "I already know. The questionable Percy Hoskins of the *Evening Standard*. Consorting with the enemy, Priscilla, not a good idea."

"I repeat." Priscilla, standing her ground as best she could. "What are you doing here?"

"Possibly keeping you alive, if you care to know the truth." He shrugged. "I don't suppose I could trouble you for a cup of coffee? I haven't had mine yet this morning."

"It's in the kitchen." She gestured in that direction.

She watched him as he entered the kitchen and went through the cupboards until he found a cup. "You want any?" he called out.

Priscilla shook her head. Mark concentrated on lifting the carafe from the warming plate and pouring coffee into his cup.

"You must know about Alana Wynter," Priscilla said as he returned to the sitting room armed with the coffee cup.

For a moment, he didn't answer, taking time to sip his coffee. He made a face. "Not very good," he announced.

"Answer me," Priscilla said angrily. "Do you know about Alana Wynter?"

He placed the cup on an end table with a final disdainful glance. "Sadly, yes. That's why I tracked you down."

"Because you think I killed her? Or because you did?"

"Don't be ridiculous." Mark gave her an unbelieving look. "Why would I kill her—or why would you, for that matter?"

"Scotland Yard certainly thinks I had something to do with it. As for you, maybe you wanted to keep her quiet."

"I have no reason to keep Alana quiet, and even if I did, I wouldn't murder her at your flat."

"You might if you wanted the police to think I did it."

"But I don't want the police to think any such thing." Mark sounded entirely reasonable.

"And how did you find me? Or should I not be asking my favourite spy those kinds of questions?"

"I suppose I should remind you I'm not really a spy."

"I'm not sure what you are. But somehow you managed to find me."

"By putting two and two together, I suppose. You left with the estimable Hoskins. It wasn't hard to find his address. Thus, here I am."

"But you were at my flat," Priscilla accused.

Mark hesitated before he said, "Yes," quietly. "I got word that Alana was in trouble. I arrived as you were leaving with Hoskins."

"That must have been after you returned your lover to Kensington Palace."

"The princess is not my lover." Mark appeared amused by the idea.

"You know what? I find that hard to believe—I find everything you tell me hard to believe."

"Part of my job is to keep the princess out of trouble," he explained. "That's what I was doing when you saw me with her. I am currently trying to do the same for you, incidentally."

"Are you? Well, for your information, you're not doing a great job."

"Listen to me, Priscilla. Whether you want to believe me or not, I am on your side." So much confidence this morning, she thought; so enormously sure of himself. How could she not believe him?

Except...

"What about Alana? Whose side was she on?"

"I have no idea why she was at your flat," he answered. "She wasn't supposed to go near you."

"The police say she had tools for picking locks. That's how she got in."

Mark dodged a response with another question: "Who else might have come in? Do you have any idea? A boyfriend? Someone like that?"

Priscilla thought briefly of Aziz Abrahim and his father, Tarak. They might fit the bill, but the police had those two in custody. She shook her head. "I stopped dating murderous boyfriends several years ago." Which was somewhat true. There had been one or two since she wasn't quite so certain about.

"Let me ask you the same question," Priscilla went on. "Who would want to kill Alana and do it where I live?"

Before Mark had to answer, the doorbell rang twice and the next thing Susie was bursting through the door, loaded down with big shopping bags. She stopped dead when she saw Mark with Priscilla. "Sorry—"

"It's all right," Mark said, "I was just leaving." He turned to Priscilla. "As to the answer to your question, I simply don't know—but I intend to find out." He gave her a quick smile. "I'll be in touch."

"You always say that."

"Because it's true." Accompanied by another smile meant as reassurance: *You can believe me.*

Except she couldn't.

"If I were you, I wouldn't drink the coffee," he said to Susie. "It's terrible." Then he ducked out the door.

As soon as he was gone, Susie dropped the bags, her eyes growing large with recognition.

"My God," she breathed.

"What is it, Susie?"

"This flat."

"What about it?"

"It's where Percy lives."

It was Priscilla's turn to gape. "How do you know that?"

Susie's eyes grew even larger. "Oh, my *God*!" she moaned.

CHAPTER FORTY-SIX

The Price of Love

Navigating her Mini Cooper through rush-hour London traffic, Susie kept her eyes straight ahead, hands tightly gripped on the steering wheel, seemingly determined not to say anything.

Susie being Susie, however, the state of silence could not last long.

"The clothes I got for you, they're all right?"

"They're fine, Susie. Thanks." The Marks & Spencer black-and-white checked skirt and matching jacket combination wasn't quite her taste, but it would do.

"I hope I found things that were your style."

"You did, Susie." Well, she tried, Priscilla thought.

"That gentleman with you at the flat," she ventured.

"What about him?"

"That wasn't Percy." Susie, nervously probing.

"No, it wasn't." Priscilla, unwilling to give away anything she didn't have to.

"But it's Percy's flat."

"Yes, it is."

Susie seemed to grip the wheel tighter. "Look, I'm so sorry," she said in a small voice. "I had no idea the two of you, you and Percy, I mean—"

"There is no me and Percy, Susie. For reasons that will soon become obvious, I needed a place to crash last night. Percy was there to provide his sofa. That's all there was to it. And no, in case you're wondering, I didn't sleep with the fellow you saw at the flat, either."

"He came into the office a while ago," Susie said.

"Yes, he did."

"I guess that's all I need to know, right?"

Priscilla gave a sharp nod. "Right."

"Listen, about Percy..." The voice had gotten smaller.

"Susie, it doesn't matter. I don't want to know."

"Just so you understand that nothing—well, nothing *much* happened," Susie went on. "It was one night... We'd both had too much to drink."

"Curious how many nights gone wrong generally begin with the words, 'We had too much to drink.'"

"I feel sick about this," Susie said.

"Don't. Besides, in an hour or so I might be out on the street anyway," Priscilla added in a resigned voice.

"Oh, God," groaned Susie, a declaration Priscilla had grown all too used to.

"Well," Priscilla said, looking down at her new outfit, "at least I'll be properly dressed."

Except for one, the messages piled on Priscilla's desk were all from El Sid, demanding her presence before Mr. Banville—*immediately*.

The phone call that did not originate from El Sid had come from H.L. Higgins at the Staff Manager's Office.

Priscilla interrupted Susie in the process of lighting the day's first cigarette. "What's this from the staff manager's office?"

"You wanted to know about employees." Susie interrupted herself to blow smoke into the air. "Harry Higgins oversees employee records. He knows where the bodies are buried. I told him to call you."

"Okay, thanks."

"I should warn you, though."

"What?"

"Harry knows where the bodies are, but from what I could get out of him, he's not likely to tell anyone."

She would deal with Harry Higgins later, Priscilla decided. For now, there was no escaping the Place of Execution.

As she crossed the Front Hall, she was joined by a scowling Major Jack O'Hara. Priscilla thought it might be nice on occasion if one of the senior members of the hotel's staff blessed her with a smile that at least implied she wasn't about to be canned.

However, that was not to happen today.

"They've been calling for you all morning," Major O'Hara reported sternly.

"I had some problems at home I had to deal with," Priscilla said.

"If you can call a dead body in your flat, 'a problem,'" the major said.

"Then you know," Priscilla said, her stomach sinking.

"It is my business to know," he said with great authority as they entered Banville's outer office.

They were immediately confronted by the glowering face of El Sid. Yet again, Priscilla was overwhelmed with the stomach-tightening, heart-dropping feeling she imagined accused witches experienced in the eighteenth century upon seeing straw being placed around the stake.

"We've been looking for you all morning," hissed El Sid.

Inside, Banville was on his feet, a sure sign, in Priscilla's view, that he was agitated, although when he saw his two visitors, his face actually appeared to flood with relief. "There you are," Banville pronounced.

"I found Miss Tempest in the Front Hall," Major Jack announced, as though he had solved a crime.

"Yes, Miss Tempest, here you are, finally. We have a rather awkward situation requiring a great deal of discretion that you may be able to help us out with."

244

A situation like a dead body in the press officer's flat? Priscilla wondered.

Banville was asking, "Are you familiar with a fellow named Enrique Ramos?"

For a moment the name didn't register. Then Priscilla blanched. *Enrique?* Eunice's lover? *Enrique* the gigolo with the white teeth and big watery eyes?

"Should I be familiar with this gentleman?"

"Let's not dilly-dally around, Miss Tempest," Banville said impatiently. "I know your first inclination is to protect Mrs. Kerry and that's all well and good. But right now, I need you to be honest with us. Do you know this man?"

"Only that he went off with Mrs. Kerry," Priscilla said.

"And when was this?"

"The night we attended the theatre."

"This is when the two of you saw *Hair*?"

"Mrs. Kerry didn't attend the performance, sir."

"What the devil did she do?" Banville looked grimmer.

"She left with Enrique."

"She left with him?" Banville looked baffled. "What do you mean, '*left* with him?'"

"They went off together on a motorbike."

"A motorbike? My mother-in-law? And you allowed her to do this?"

"I didn't have a great deal of say in the matter. Mrs. Kerry is a woman who certainly knows her own mind. Why? Has something happened to her?"

"I received a call from this Ramos character earlier this morning. He reported to me that he had spent the night at his flat with my mother-in-law. He further reported that he had taken photographs of their encounter."

"The bugger," growled Major Jack.

"Precisely," agreed Banville. "This man Ramos is demanding twenty-five thousand pounds in return for the photographs—and his silence. Otherwise, he plans to go to the *News of the World* with the story—'*I Slept with Savoy Manager's Mother-In-Law*'—that sort of nonsense."

"Blackmail!" pronounced Major O'Hara. "No other damned word for it!"

"I'm afraid so." Banville directed his gaze at Priscilla. "What Major O'Hara is suggesting is that we find out where this Ramos fellow lives, visit him, and see if we can't get the photos back."

"And not pay him?" Priscilla asked.

"Major O'Hara informs me that in his experience, blackmailers such as Ramos do not easily give up photographic evidence. The major argues that the twenty-five thousand pounds is just the beginning of the payments he will demand." He gave the major a sharp look. "Isn't that correct, Major?"

"As you rightly observe, sir, that is my experience."

"Now, Miss Tempest, I imagine after my mother's assignation, she had to somehow return to the hotel."

"That's right, sir. She called me and I picked her up and brought her back here."

"Yes, that's what I was hoping you'd say. And where did you meet her?"

"At a call box in Brick Lane, in Bethnal Green."

"The East End!" Major O'Hara made it sound as though there could be no greater horror than to be found in the East End of London.

"Mr. Banville," Priscilla said, "could you not ask Mrs. Kerry and perhaps get more information from her?"

Banville looked even more horrified than the major. "My heavens, no! Neither Mrs. Kerry nor my wife must know anything about this. My wife in particular. No, we must handle this ourselves with utmost delicacy."

"I understand, sir," Priscilla said.

"Do you think you would recognize this Ramos character if you saw him again?"

"He was a young man, Spanish I believe, quite small with curly black hair."

"Damnable foreigner!" Another explosion of horror from Major O'Hara.

"What do you expect?" stated Banville. "A decent English gentleman would never have slept with my mother-in-law in the first place, let alone carried on like this."

"What about it, Miss Tempest? Do you have any idea where we can find this chappie?" Major O'Hara's tone suggested Priscilla might be hiding Enrique under her desk.

"When I picked her up, Mrs. Kerry said Enrique lived nearby, but that was the extent of it."

"Nearby, eh?" Banville addressed Priscilla. "That narrows it down a bit, I suppose. Here's what I want you to do, Miss Tempest—accompany Major O'Hara to the Brick Lane area and see if you can find out where this foreign fellow lives."

"We can certainly do that, sir, although I must say, I'm not sure how effective that would be."

"At the moment, Miss Tempest, we have little choice. Correct, Major?"

"I'm afraid so," Major O'Hara concurred.

"I suppose we could locate the call box and go from there," Priscilla said. "We have to assume that Mrs. Kerry wouldn't have walked very far from where she spent the night."

"We'll drive there straight away, find the call box in question," Major O'Hara said in his best I'm-taking-over voice. "That is, if Miss Tempest is available."

"Of course," Priscilla said.

"Good enough, off you go, the two of you—and good luck," Banville said.

"We'll do our best, sir," advised Major O'Hara.

As Priscilla and Major O'Hara turned to leave, Banville called out "By the way, Miss Tempest..."

Priscilla stopped and turned.

"Given recent events which I understand from the major you may be involved in, do not think that we will not be discussing your current situation at a later date. Is that understood?"

"Understood, sir."

One step away from the Place of Execution, Priscilla reflected, then two steps back.

CHAPTER FORTY-SEVEN

Find Enrique!

"Bloody needle in a haystack," groused Major O'Hara as he steered his Ford Anglia through the London traffic. "Bloody waste of time, if you ask me."

Priscilla had not asked Major O'Hara, but that didn't seem to matter to him. Unprovoked, he offered a steady stream of opinions, interrupted every so often by a cry of despair at the shortcomings of the drivers in the various cars and lorries he encountered as he navigated into the city's East End. Not the major's favourite destination, as he was only too willing to make clear to Priscilla.

"Bloody East End," he went on, "filling up with foreigners and malcontents—tossers just like this villain Enrique."

"Not to mention a few working people as well," Priscilla managed to get in, feeling that as a member of the working classes herself, she should try to put in a supportive word or two.

"Bloody hell! Look at this bugger in the lorry. Blocking the damn traffic." Major O'Hara angrily smacked his horn.

"Let me ask you something, Major," Priscilla said, distracting him from the ills of London traffic.

"Yes, what is it?" he demanded impatiently.

"In your capacity as head of the Savoy's security—"

"Keeps me busy, that's for damned certain!"

"Yes, I guess it does. But you must have to deal constantly with the hotel's employees."

"Employees?" Major O'Hara made it sound as though he was unfamiliar with the species. "Why should I have to deal with the employees?"

"You know, ensuring that the hotel hires the right people, that sort of thing."

"Of course the Savoy hires the right sort of people. The Savoy is the world's finest hotel. Only the best people apply. Those chappies in charge of hiring, that fellow Harry Higgins, his sort, they keep an eye on things. Lord knows I've enough to deal with, what with our guests and the scoundrels, male and female, who attempt to prey upon them. Not to mention your lot, the so-called celebrities who think they can raise holy hell whenever they feel like it."

"Do you have any idea why Millicent Holmes left the hotel?"

Major O'Hara gave her a sharp sideways glance. "Why would you ask a question like that?"

"I only recently learned that Mrs. Holmes had quit. I wondered why, that's all."

"Under a bit of a cloud, I suspect, what with telling those lies about HRH the Princess Margaret."

"Was she lying do you think?"

"Absolutely lying," Major O'Hara pronounced.

"Why would she do that, I wonder. Why would she lie?"

"Who knows what goes through the minds of some of these people. You know she's not really English?"

"No?"

"Russian, I'm told. In confidence, mind. A Russian background of some sort. And if I know anything, it is that you cannot trust the damn Russians."

"Do you mind if I ask how you discovered Mrs. Holmes's background?"

"Shouldn't really yammer on about this sort of thing." Major O'Hara had puffed himself up as he drove. "But the intelligence comes from an unimpeachable source, fellow I've been dealing with at Buck House. Mysterious bloke, but highly efficient. You know what they call him?"

"Fascinating," enthused Priscilla. "What do they call him?"

"Commander Blood. Name's actually Trueblood. How do you like that for a nickname?"

"Scary," said Priscilla.

"And believe me, when you meet the commander, there is something about him that immediately makes you think, this gentleman is in charge, this gentleman is not to be messed with."

"My goodness, Major," Priscilla said. "You really are moving in rarefied circles."

"All part of the job, Miss Tempest. Contacts cultivated over the years."

"Did you speak to this Commander Blood about Mrs. Holmes?"

The major nodded quickly. "He made a convincing case against Mrs. Holmes, let me tell you. If she hadn't quit when she did, I would have urged Mr. Banville to fire her, no doubt about that."

When they reached Brick Lane, Priscilla had little trouble finding the call box where she had picked up Eunice Kerry. It stood outlined in a burst of sunshine lighting the bright red of its cast-iron surface, reflecting off dusty window panels. Major O'Hara parked down the street and they walked back to stand in front of it, as though somehow expecting Enrique to magically appear.

He didn't.

Major O'Hara shuffled impatiently. "Now what?"

Now what, indeed, Priscilla thought. They couldn't very well stand here forever hoping Enrique might show. As much as she hated to agree with Major O'Hara, searching Bethnal Green was like looking for a needle in a haystack.

"He's got to be close by," Priscilla said. "Why don't we split up? You've an idea of what he looks like. Walk up toward Bethnal Green Road, see if you can spot him. Meanwhile, I'll check out Allen Gardens, and then start south toward Whitechapel."

"Waste of time," Major O'Hara grumbled. "If I were Banville, I'd tell this tosser to sod off and be done with it. I doubt the newspapers would be interested in the story, anyway."

Priscilla thought of Percy Hoskins and what he might do when confronted with a story like this. Given recent events at the Savoy, Percy and reporters at other papers might well have a field day with it.

"Let's give it a try, anyway," Priscilla suggested. "We can say we've done something, even if we don't find him."

"Very well," Major O'Hara said with a roll of his eyes.

"We meet back here in one hour, how's that?"

"I'm going north, you're going south, is that it?"

"Exactly."

"Short swarthy bugger with curly black hair, right?"

"Handsome, but short, big eyes."

"Could be half the blokes on the street."

"Do your best, Major," Priscilla said encouragingly.

And off he went, huffing loudly, leaving Priscilla shaking her head at his antics. Inside the protective confines of the Savoy, dealing with the rich and aristocratic, he was the tough-as-nails security chief; outside, rubbing shoulders with the lower classes, Priscilla decided, Major O'Hara turned into a petulant baby.

She spent far too much time wandering across the open green space of Allen Gardens. There weren't many people in the park at this time of day and none of them remotely resembled Enrique. The more she thought about it, the less certain she was that Enrique would be the type to spend a lot of time here. She glanced at her watch, discovering to her horror that she had to meet Major O'Hara in less than half an hour.

Angry with herself for wasting so much time, she exited the gardens, starting to cross the street when she came to an abrupt stop. No, she told herself, it could not possibly be.

Yet unless she was totally mistaken, there was someone at the call box on the far side of the street who looked an awful lot like Enrique Ramos.

She stood there gawking, hardly able to credit what she was seeing. But sure enough, it was Enrique—gigolo, lover for a night to Eunice Kerry, blackmailer—emerging from the call box, an expression on his handsome face of enormous satisfaction.

He started walking briskly north on Brick Lane, Priscilla following. He hurried along, as though late for an appointment, ducking into a busy street market. That made it easier for Priscilla to blend in with the crowd as she trailed him. She felt a surge of adrenalin, Miss Marple on the case, although she doubted Miss Marple would lower herself to actually follow someone. Tailing people—wasn't that what it was called?—seemed more the province of American private detectives.

Enrique abruptly ducked off the market street. She picked up her pace, turning a corner in time to see him go up steps halfway down the block and disappear. Priscilla hurried along to the building that Enrique had gone into. A set of steps led up to the entrance and a recessed door in shadow. Priscilla went up and tried the latch. The door creaked open.

A narrow staircase became lost in the darkness of the interior hall. From somewhere above her, Priscilla could hear the sound of music and over that, faint laughter. Priscilla hesitated, debating whether she should go back and find Major O'Hara, but deciding that would take too long. She removed her shoes and started up the stairs.

A woman's tinkling laugh grew more distinct as she reached the top. Was her heart in her mouth? Actually, it wasn't, but she was thankful for the romantic orchestral strings swirling along the corridor, masking the sound of a heartbeat she otherwise was certain could be heard blocks away.

Priscilla proceeded along to a closed door. The music came from inside, now accompanied by a woman's satisfied gasp. Enrique at work? At the end of the corridor, an open door led into an office with a desk pushed against the wall. The desk was covered with copies of London tabloids, all featuring recent events at the Savoy. She shifted the papers around. Underneath she found a manila envelope full of 8 × 10 photographs. The photos were badly lit, apparently shot from beyond a bed. A lover who looked like Enrique was on top of a woman who looked like—it was impossible to identify for certain who it was.

From the other room came a loud moan of pleasure. Priscilla turned around to an open closet where a camera was mounted on a tripod facing a small window. Priscilla entered the closet and peered through the window into a bedroom where Enrique was co-starring in a live-action version of what was memorialized in the photographs. This time, Enrique was on the bottom. A woman with her back to the camera moved on top of him.

Well, well, Priscilla thought, here was Enrique the blackmailing scumbag hard at work.

The camera was an Empire Scout. She unscrewed it from its tripod, and then snapped open the back and removed the film inside. Priscilla re-entered the office and quietly went through desk drawers, finding negatives that she added to the photographs. She lifted an empty metal wastebasket off the floor and placed it on the desktop and then dropped the roll of film from the Empire Scout as well as the photographs and negatives into it. Enrique had helpfully stored matches beside a pack of cigarettes in the top drawer. She struck a match and dropped it into the wastebasket. She did the same with a second and third match. Flames whooshed up from the wastebasket as the photos and the negatives caught fire. Priscilla leaned against the wall and waited.

The noises in the other room reached a crescendo, highlighted by Enrique's confused cries as he either climaxed or realized the room next door was on fire—or both.

It did not take him long to burst into view, naked, showing a mixture of stunned horror and rage. When he saw Priscilla, the horror and the rage were replaced with astonishment. "What the hell do you think you're doing?"

"I'm burning the photos and the negatives you are using to blackmail Mrs. Kerry," Priscilla answered in a level voice.

"You crazy bitch!" he yelled, moving threateningly toward her.

"I'd be careful, Enrique," Priscilla warned. "I'm here with Savoy security people. They know where I am and are prepared to call the police."

That brought him to a stop.

"You don't want the police involved, do you Enrique?"

Before Enrique had a chance to answer, a woman entered, a towel wrapped around her otherwise nude body.

"What's going on?" Daisee Banville demanded.

Priscilla to the Rescue!

Daisee recognized Priscilla through the enveloping smoke and cried out, her hand shooting to her mouth in alarm. She reeled out of the room. Enrique sprang after her. "Daisee," he called, "Daisee, please, let me explain..."

Priscilla wondered how he was going to do that as she followed them into the hall. Daisee leaned against the wall, holding onto her towel while she choked back tears and desperately searched Enrique's eyes.

"What are you doing? What is this? What's happening?"

"This terrible, insane woman broke in here and started a fire, making crazy accusations that are all lies."

"Mrs. Banville," Priscilla was trying to explain, "this man Enrique Ramos— "

"Enrique?" Daisee's eyes flashed angrily through her tears. "You said your name was Ricardo."

"Ricardo is my middle name," Enrique offered lamely.

"I doubt whether Enrique is his real name, either," Priscilla said. "Whatever it is, this gentleman was blackmailing your mother— "

"My *mother*?" Daisee, thunderstruck. "You *slept* with my *mother*?"

"He took photos of her that he threatened to make public unless your husband paid him off. There's a camera and a one-way mirror in the office beside his bedroom, making me think he planned to do the same to you."

"You *bastard!*" The towel dropped as Daisee threw her impressive body against Enrique, pounding at his face with her fists.

Enrique fought back, getting hold of her wrists and twisting her down on the floor.

Priscilla leapt in, pushing him away. "Touch her again," she cried out, "and so help me I'll go to the police and you will go to jail."

Enrique, breathing hard, settled somewhat. "You will not involve the police." He spoke with a confidence she hadn't expected.

"Mrs. Banville, please get dressed," Priscilla said, keeping her eyes on Enrique.

Daisee struggled to her feet and with a final sob disappeared into the bedroom.

"You're right," Priscilla said to Enrique. The police won't be involved—unless you continue to threaten either Mr. Banville or his wife and mother-in-law."

"You're a goddamn bitch, you know that?"

"A first-class bitch who knows where you live and where to send the police if there's any more trouble."

As the air filled with the acrid smell of burning plastic, Daisee came out of the bedroom, dressed. She ignored both Enrique and Priscilla, pushing past down the stairs.

Priscilla went after her, pausing long enough to put on her shoes before exiting onto the street. It had begun to rain lightly as Priscilla looked around for Daisee. She spotted her at the curb down the block, a forlorn figure caught in the light from oncoming traffic. Priscilla started toward her, calling out. Daisee did not answer.

"Are you all right?" Priscilla asked as she came abreast of Daisee.

"Get away from me," she snarled. "I don't want to be near you." She held her head high, the rain and tears making her mascara run down her cheeks, her damp hair flattened unattractively against her head. If ever there was an orphan sadly in the storm, it was Daisee Banville.

Priscilla felt as though she had been walloped in the stomach. "I only wanted to help—"

"I don't *need* your help," Daisee snapped. "Why couldn't you leave well enough alone?"

"He was blackmailing your mother—" Priscilla started to say.

"He wasn't going to blackmail anyone," Daisee interrupted angrily. "I could have handled him. Now I suppose you're going to tell my husband and my marriage is over—thanks to you."

"I'm not going to say anything to Mr. Banville," Priscilla said.

"But you'll know, won't you? Every time you see me, you'll remember what happened—you'll know."

"It doesn't make any difference," Priscilla said.

"Yes, it does. You're the help. And I am most definitely not the help. I am your better. You shouldn't *know*."

The two women stood staring at each other, Priscilla thinking, She's going to walk away from this, and I won't have said anything. In the midst of my silence, she makes her escape.

Except, she decided, Daisee was not going to get off so easy.

"You know what?" Priscilla said to her. "Maybe we're both nothing more than the help when it comes down to it."

"What are you talking about?"

"I'm talking about Princess Margaret. After all, what are you to her but the help?"

"That bitch." Daisee's voice turned nasty. "All the times I've come to her rescue. She insisted she had to see that bloody awful Amir Abrahim. She ought not to have had anything to do with him. What is it about men you should never go near but you somehow end up with them?"

"A very good question," Priscilla said ruefully.

"Margaret couldn't have gotten into the hotel without me."

"But she didn't actually see Amir..."

Daisee shook her head. "The bastard never answered the door. It would all have been fine if the bloody housekeeper hadn't seen her—but then no one believes the help, do they?"

A cab pulled over to the curb. Daisee went to it. She was about to get in when she turned to Priscilla.

"Maybe you're right. Maybe we are both no more than the help. But here's the thing."

"What's that?" Priscilla said.

"I'm the help that survives." She practically spat out the words: "You're not going to."

Daisee got in and closed the door. The cab pulled away, leaving Priscilla standing alone in the rain, once again having trouble breathing.

Out of the Rain

Still fuming from her encounter with Daisee and Enrique—
or Ricardo, depending on who he was entertaining—Priscilla
trudged through the rain back to the red call box where all the
trouble seemed to have started. The street was deserted. There
was no sign of Major O'Hara. He had probably given up on her.
She would never hear the end of it.

She stepped into the call box to get out of the rain, feeling very
sorry for herself. Depending on who you talked to lately, she was
the help, a murder suspect, or—and there was no other readily
available word for it—a tart.

Or possibly a combination of all three.

The tart and the murder suspect she could deal with. But the
help? Well, yes, when it came right down to it, what could she say.
Still, a thank you might have been in order since she did save what
she had to concede was Daisee's trim, attention-grabbing ass, and
probably her marriage as well.

Priscilla's flat remained a crime scene so she couldn't go there,
and no way was she going back to the two-faced Percy Hoskins.
There was, however, Percy's amour, or his one-night stand,
depending on one's perspective.

To her immense relief, Susie Gore-Langton came on the line
after a couple of rings.

"Susie, it's me," Priscilla announced. "I need a place to stay tonight."

"You want to stay *here*?" Susie made it sound as though the
prospect was unimaginable.

"It's only for tonight," Priscilla said.

"Well, I guess so. I mean—"

"I'm on my way. Shouldn't be long. Get rid of whoever it is you're entertaining."

Priscilla hung up before Susie could object. She stayed in the phone box for a good thirty minutes more until the rain finally let up and a life-saving taxi appeared.

Even so, she arrived at Susie's mews on Kenway Road in Earl's Court looking and feeling like a drowned rat. "I'll have you know I wasn't *entertaining* anyone," Susie, already in blue-flannel pyjamas, stated defensively as soon as she let Priscilla into her tiny flat. Unlike the chaos of Priscilla's place, Susie's flat was surprisingly neat. The sitting room was a lemony yellow with white trim. There was a chintz sofa and matching chintz curtains. The antique furniture had been provided by Susie's mother.

"Your discipline is admirable, bravo," Priscilla said, stepping over to warm herself at the gas fireplace near the sofa. "And, incidentally, thank you. It's very kind of you to take me in at such short notice."

"You must get out of those clothes," Susie said in motherly fashion. "You'll catch your death of cold. Would you like something? I know you don't like tea. Coffee?"

"Something stronger would be in order," Priscilla said.

"I'm afraid I don't have anything like that. I make it a practice never to drink when I'm alone at home."

"Again, wonderful discipline. Good for you."

"And if you must know," Susie stated defensively, "most nights I sit here worried about what you're up to, pretty certain we're both about to lose our jobs—and incidentally, do you mind if I ask what you've been doing in order to get yourself into this state?"

"You don't want to know," Priscilla said, turning away from the fire, "otherwise, you'll definitely be on the phone looking for your next job."

"Oh, God," Susie said. "What a nightmare! It looks like I'm going to have to marry Harry Higgins."

"Harry Higgins?" Priscilla looked puzzled as she shrugged out of her wet jacket.

"I told you about him. H.L. Higgins at the Staff Manager's Office. Harry. He has a bit of crush on me it turns out." Susie nodded sagely. "I'll bet if I asked him, he'd marry me and take me away from all this."

"Do you want to marry him?"

"I don't want to marry anyone." Susie smiled wanly at Priscilla. "But the way you're carrying on, I might not have a choice."

Priscilla was lost in thought. Susie began to look concerned. "Uh-oh," she said. "I can hear the wheels turning. That's not good. What are you thinking, Priscilla?"

"Let me ask you this: Does Harry go to lunch?"

Suspicion clouded Susie's face. "Not sure why you ask, but I don't believe Harry ever goes anywhere. He never leaves his little cave in the basement. The guardian of the records and all that."

"Supposing," Priscilla offered, "you ask him to lunch tomorrow?"

The question only increased Susie's level of suspicion. "Why would I do that?" she asked carefully.

"Because you're absolutely infatuated with Harry and want to get to know him better."

"But I don't."

"Yes, you do, Susie, yes you absolutely do—at least for tomorrow."

"A nightmare," Susie groaned, "we're going to get fired. I just know it."

CHAPTER FIFTY

Harry for Lunch

"After we located said telephone box, Miss Tempest then went off on her own and despite clearly agreeing to meet back there in exactly one hour, I never saw her again," Major Jack O'Hara angrily related first thing the next morning as he and Priscilla appeared at the Place of Execution before the stony-faced Clive Banville.

"I stood around the call box in the rain for a long time waiting for her to reappear," Major O'Hara continued. "Then, finally, I gave up and went home."

"What about it, Miss Tempest?" The accusatory tone in Banville's voice could not be missed.

"First of all, my apologies to Major O'Hara," Priscilla said, hoping that neither man would notice she was wearing the same checked skirt-and-jacket outfit she had worn the day before, more or less dried out in front of Susie's gas fire. She hoped further that they would fail to observe that she'd had to make do with Susie's limited makeup choices before the two of them had taken a cab into work.

"By the time I finished with Enrique Ramos it was late. I returned to the call box but the major had long since departed."

"Wait a minute," Banville said, his stone face now clouding with uncertainty. "You encountered this chap Ramos?"

"I did, sir."

"What the hell!" Major O'Hara thundered in unhappy disbelief.

"What happened?" commanded Banville.

"I confronted Mr. Ramos—who also goes by the name Ricardo, incidentally—in his Shoreditch flat, obtained the photographs and negatives from him, destroyed them, and advised him that if he ever came near Mrs. Kerry again or threatened this hotel, we would summon the police."

"You *destroyed* the photographs?" Major O'Hara sounded as though he could not believe what he was hearing.

"Mr. Ramos, Enrique, was not happy about it, but yes, the photos and negatives have been burned. They will no longer be a problem."

An uneasy silence descended. Banville and Major O'Hara traded quick glances. Banville cleared his throat. "Yes, well, good work, Miss Tempest. I believe this turn of events has taken Major O'Hara and I somewhat by surprise."

"If that is what in fact happened," put in Major O'Hara.

Banville gave him a pointed glance. "You doubt Miss Tempest's veracity?"

"No, no, of course not. But I suppose time will tell whether or not we have heard the last of this Ramos—or whatever the devil he calls himself."

Banville cleared his throat again before he addressed Priscilla. "I've discussed the situation this morning with Mrs. Banville, and we've decided that it's best to cut short Mrs. Kerry's visit and return her to New York."

"That's unfortunate, sir," Priscilla said, realizing she was actually somewhat disappointed.

"It's better for everyone to put this sorry incident behind us," Banville went on. "Therefore, Miss Tempest, you will see to it that Mrs. Kerry gets safely to the airport this afternoon."

"Very good, sir," Priscilla said.

Major O'Hara followed her out of the office, past a scowling El Sid who appeared disappointed that upon leaving the Place of Execution, against all odds, Priscilla still had her head on her shoulders. When they reached the Front Hall, Major O'Hara took her suddenly by the arm and guided her to one side.

"Do not think I am unaware of what you're up to, Miss Tempest."

Nonplussed, Priscilla managed to say, "What is it you think I'm up to, Major?"

"Attempting to undermine me, make me look a fool."

"Are you serious? Why would I do that?"

"To secure your tenuous position here at the Savoy through lies and deceit. I find it impossible to believe that, as soon as we split up, you somehow encountered this Ramos and he happily gave up the photographs. My suspicion is that it did not happen. And if it did, it's because the two of you are in cahoots."

"Cahoots? You think I'm in *cahoots* with Enrique Ramos?"

"Deny it all you want, Miss Tempest, but I will continue to entertain that possibility and will investigate accordingly. I am, you will now discover, a formidable adversary."

The major marched away, striding majestically, displaying the full grandeur of the English gentleman and former military man off to preserve the Empire.

Prick, Priscilla thought angrily as she watched him go.

Still steaming, she went back to 205 and the saucer-eyed Susie. "Do you still have a job?"

"Until I get Mrs. Kerry to the airport. After that, I'm not so sure."

"Oh, God," Susie said.

Karl entered with coffee. "I thought you might need some," Susie said.

"I also brought you a croissant," Karl added.

"Right, eating," Priscilla said. "That's what normal people sometimes do, if I remember correctly. I'd almost forgotten about it."

Karl was pouring coffee before Priscilla noticed the black-and-blue puffiness around his left eye and cheekbone. "Are you all right, Karl? It looks as though you ran into a door."

"What is it they say here?" He smiled slightly. "You should see the other guy? Yes, that is it. You should see the other guy."

Karl finished pouring the coffee and turned to leave. His limp was only too evident. She sat chewing contemplatively on her croissant. The secrets of the Savoy, she mused. Wives and mothers misbehaving with East End gigolos, close-mouthed Austrian waiters with unexplained black eyes and limps.

Susie drew her out of her reverie. "He'll do it," she said excitedly.

"Who?" Priscilla brushed crumbs off her lap and made herself refocus.

"Harry. He'll have lunch with me."

"Good. What time?"

"Noon, I suppose. He's going to meet me here. Very excited he is, too."

"Don't meet him here. Meet him in his office—and make sure he doesn't lock the door when you leave."

"How am I going to do that?"

"Employ your considerable wiles."

"Oh, what a nightmare," Susie moaned. "Where am I going to find wiles on such short notice?"

A few minutes after noon, Priscilla watched as Susie, holding onto the arm of the bespectacled, rather gangly Harry Higgins, allowed him to lead her across the Front Hall and out the main entrance; the happy couple on their way to an intimate lunch.

Actually, Priscilla thought as she headed for the lift, Harry wasn't bad looking. Maybe Susie should marry him, given that her boss's future looked pretty bleak. For her part, she had decided she would marry Major Jack O'Hara. That would certainly fix his wagon. If she was to lead a life of misery, Major O'Hara could damn well share it with her.

Reaching the basement, she went along a narrow corridor until she found the office of the Staff Manager. She tried the door. It was locked.

Damn!

Priscilla stood wondering what to do next when one of the cleaning staff came along, carrying a mop and pail. Priscilla fought to remember the woman's name. Jane?

"Hello there, Jane," she said to the woman.

"Janice," the woman replied.

"Sorry, Janice, of course. Listen, I'm supposed to pick up some files Mr. Banville has requested from Harry and now he's gone to lunch. You don't happen to have a key, do you?"

"Certainly, ma'am," Jane said.

She put down the pail and mop and then produced a key ring with a cluster of keys hanging from it. She chose one and used it to unlock the door.

"There you go," Janice said. "Just close the door when you're finished. I'll lock it later."

"Many thanks," Priscilla said.

She entered the darkened interior, closed the door behind her, and flipped the wall switch. The harsh overhead lights illuminated a couple of metal desks and rows of metal shelves lined with file folders. A history of hotel employees dating back to—when? Surely not all the way back to 1889 when D'Oyly Carte opened the hotel? Did they even keep employee records in those days? Did those early stars of the Savoy, César Ritz and Georges Auguste Escoffier, have to fill out employment applications? And what happened when they were booted out of the hotel after they were accused of various illegal activities? Were their transgressions noted on their employment records?

As she moved along the shelves, Priscilla was searching for someone a little more contemporary. What the record would show was anyone's guess, but maybe a secret that would either justify her suspicions or show her that they were unwarranted and the hunch she was entertaining was all wrong.

She tracked along the shelves until she found the files under H. There it was, Millicent Holmes. Priscilla pulled the file off the shelf just as she heard the office door open.

CHAPTER FIFTY-ONE

Locked In!

Priscilla froze, the file folder in her hands. She heard a voice say, "Sorry about this; they're just for reading, but without them I'll be at a loss with the menu."

"I'd be happy to read the menu for you, Harry, not to worry." Susie sounded nervous, probably suspecting Priscilla was still in the office.

"Won't take a moment," Harry said.

Priscilla could see a desk at the end of the aisle, silently praying that it wasn't Harry's desk.

"Good thing I came back, actually. I was sure I locked the office, but it looks like I didn't."

Harry came into view. Priscilla stood still. All Harry had to do was glance in the wrong direction and the game was up.

She watched as he rummaged around in a desk drawer. "Ah, here we are." He swung around holding up rimless glasses like a trophy he had won.

"We should be going," Priscilla heard Susie say. "I don't have all that much time for lunch."

"With you straight on," Harry said, clutching at the glasses as he went out of sight. A moment later, Priscilla heard the door close and a lock turn.

She waited another minute or so and then opened the file she was holding. It contained a single piece of notepaper with words in neat block letters: SEE PETROVA, IRINA.

What did that mean? Millicent Holmes wasn't Millicent; she was really Irina Petrova?

Bogans's words came back to her. *"Ah, yes, our mysterious head house-keeper...Well, she says her name is Millicent Holmes, doesn't she?"*

She moved around to another row of shelves and found the files under P. There was no sign of a file for someone named Irina Petrova. She looked again. Nothing. No Irina.

On a whim she went around to look for the file on Karl Steiner. There was one for him. In addition to the Hotel Goldener Hirsch in Salzburg, Karl had also been employed for a couple of years at the Hotel Adlon in East Berlin. No spouse was listed. His London address was 183 Southwark Bridge Road, south of the Thames.

Priscilla replaced Karl's file and went to the door and turned the knob. Nothing moved. Harry had locked her in his office—ensuring that as soon as he came back from lunch, her life at the Savoy was over.

There was a phone on the desk. Priscilla went to it, debating about who she could call for help. Major O'Hara was certainly out of the question. Wouldn't he love to find her in a locked office she should never have been in in the first place. Percy? But how could he get here in time and who would ever give him a house key?

Then it struck her—the inconceivable madness of an idea that could never work. But what choice did she have?

Priscilla picked up the receiver and asked for Eunice's suite. It took six rings but finally she answered, impatiently demanding to know who was on the line.

"It's Priscilla," Priscilla said.

"Where are you? I've got to get to the airport."

"Okay, here's the thing. I'm downstairs in a basement office. I'm in trouble and you're the only one who can help me."

"Me? What the hell can I do?" demanded Eunice.

"You can get a key and come down here and unlock the door—but you must do it very quickly."

"Can't you get the front desk to help you?"

"No, I can't, Mrs. Kerry."

"How am I going to get a key?"

"I need you to figure that out, and I need you to do it quickly. I'm in the staff manager's office."

The silence on the phone was followed by a resigned sigh. "You really are nuts, aren't you?"

"Mrs. Kerry, please..."

"All right," she said. "Let me see what I can do."

Barely ten minutes later, there was a knock on the door and Eunice's voice calling, "Priscilla? Are you in there?"

Priscilla hurried to the door. "I'm here. Have you got a key?"

"Hold on."

Priscilla could hear a key being inserted into the lock and then another and then another after that. Eunice swore and then tried a fourth key that didn't work. Finally, on the fifth try, the door opened and there was Eunice clutching a ring of keys, startled when Priscilla embraced her. "You're a lifesaver!"

Eunice pulled back in alarm. "Careful, you're going to ruin my makeup."

"How did you get a key so fast?"

"How else? I went to my totally distracted son-in-law, told him I had left my sunglasses in a basement office while I was touring around the hotel. Told him I didn't want to disturb the help. He, as I suspected he would, didn't want to hear about it and just tossed me a set of house keys. What the hell are you doing down here, anyway?"

"Put it this way," Priscilla said as they left the office. "We both have secrets that we need to trust each other with."

She took the keys from Eunice and made sure the door was locked.

"Speaking of secrets," Eunice said, "I can't get hold of Enrique to tell him I'm leaving."

"Maybe that's just as well."

Eunice shrugged. "I don't know. I like Enrique. I mean, I realize he's a for-hire gigolo, and I can barely understand a word he says, but he is somewhat charming. And once he gets me into bed…"

She finished the sentence with a smile.

As they came into the Front Hall, Priscilla spotted Harry Higgins strolling back from lunch. He was wearing, she couldn't help but notice, a silly grin.

"Actually, he's kind of sweet," Susie said when Priscilla got back to 205. "What's more, he paid for lunch."

"A man who buys you lunch. You can't ask for much more than that," Priscilla opined.

Susie allowed her voice to drop. "But I nearly had a heart attack when he insisted on going back for his reading glasses. Did you find what you're looking for?"

"Not really," Priscilla said. "The file I was looking for is missing."

"Harry says things are pretty loosey-goosey around here. He says the management believes—rightly, I suppose—that this is the finest hotel in Europe, therefore they only attract the best people. But Harry says he sometimes wonders about that."

Such as a woman named Irina Petrova who changed her name to Millicent Holmes, Priscilla thought.

The jangling of her telephone made her jump. Lordy she was jittery. This sense of impending doom arriving with every phone call. Except, to her relief, not this one.

"It's Buck's Fizz time," announced the merry voice of Noël Coward.

"There you are Noël, thank goodness," Priscilla said with relief.

"Well, my dear, I have arrived back from Sardinia after the hell that has been the experience of shooting *Boom!* A word of advice: Never go to Sardinia. Or never go to Sardinia with the Burtons."

"Was it that terrible?"

"Elizabeth and Richard appear to think shooting a movie is nothing more than another opportunity to have drinks and decide where to go for lunch, interspersed by an occasional appearance in front of a camera. I love them dearly, I do, but how they carry on. If they're drunk, they're fighting; if they're sober, they're fighting. Every so often they stop fighting and announce their undying love and passion for one another. Then they're back to fighting. Poor Joe Losey, the director, he's being driven crazy. I fear there will be very little boom in *Boom!*"

"Are you finished shooting?"

"Alas, no. Back to the salt mines in a couple of weeks. I must say, I'm quite brilliant in it, not that it's going to make much difference. But enough of my travails, how have you been, my dear?"

"I may lose my job at any moment, and a dead body turned up in my flat for which the police suspect I'm responsible. Otherwise, I'm fine."

"Honestly, Priscilla, you are so melodramatic. Dead bodies, you say? Well, then, it's all the more important we get together for a drink."

"I have to go to the airport. But can we meet in the American Bar at seven?"

"I'll have a Buck's Fizz waiting for you. Perhaps two. You may need them. You see, I have a terrible confession to make."

CHAPTER FIFTY-TWO

Farewell Tears

"I feel like I should stay so I can protect you," Eunice said to Priscilla as Mr. Bogans drove them to Heathrow. Even though the sky was overcast, Eunice was wearing dark glasses that made her look a bit like Jackie Kennedy.

"That's very kind of you," Priscilla replied. "But I'll be all right." Wondering if she would be.

"I hope so," Eunice replied. She removed the dark glasses to focus on Priscilla, and Jackie disappeared. "But listen to me. It's not easy for you around this joint, I know that. You're a young woman fighting to survive in a male world. You need someone like me to watch your back."

"For us to watch each other's backs," Priscilla amended.

Eunice allowed a rueful smile. "I have to admit that when I'm in London, I do seem to have a spectacular ability to get myself into hot water. It probably has something to do with this unnatural urge I have to piss off my daughter. I'm sure Daisee is relieved to see the end of me."

"Well, for what it's worth, Mrs. Kerry, I'm going to miss you."

To her surprise, Eunice reached over and squeezed Priscilla's hand. "I can't believe I'm saying this," Eunice said with a shake of her head, "but I'm probably going to miss you, too, honey—for a little while, anyway."

The two women laughed. Eunice looked down at her hand still holding onto Priscilla's and immediately took it away. "What the hell am I doing?"

"I'm sure it was a momentary lapse," ventured Priscilla.

"For God's sake, don't tell my daughter," Eunice said with a smile.

When they arrived at Heathrow, Bogans arranged to take care of the luggage, while Priscilla walked Eunice toward Pan Am's first-class check-in. Eunice came to a stop on the concourse and turned to her. Eunice still held the sunglasses so that Priscilla could see the intensity in her eyes. "Some advice from an old lady—make that *older* lady."

"Certainly," said Priscilla, not sure what was coming.

"Watch yourself, okay? I mean it. I told you before that I like you, Priscilla, but I like you even better now that we've spent time together, protected one another. You're like the daughter I certainly don't have—intelligent, resourceful, but a little reckless as well."

"I'm happy you feel that way," Priscilla said, feeling the emotion welling up in her. "Although perhaps not the reckless part," she added with a smile.

"That's the part that worries me," Eunice said fiercely. "I don't know what you were up to getting locked in that office earlier, but be careful. They've already got their eye on you, particularly my daughter. Watch yourself around Daisee. She's no friend of yours."

"I'm sorry Daisee feels that way," Priscilla said diplomatically.

"No, you're not," Eunice asserted. "You'd probably like to wring her neck. I know I would, except she's my daughter and your employer's wife, so I guess we have no option but to let her live."

They laughed together again and quite suddenly tears sprang into Eunice's eyes. "I don't know what's wrong with me," she hid the tears with the sunglasses and Jackie O was back. "I'm becoming emotional; I don't do emotion."

But then Priscilla was in tears, and the two women were hugging one another. "Thank goodness I'm going back to New York," Eunice said tearfully. "They don't allow crying in New York. But they go in for worrying big time, so I'm definitely going to worry about you."

"I will be fine, promise," Priscilla said in a choked voice.

"I hope so, honey," Eunice said with great emotion, "I truly hope so."

"A tearful farewell is it?" Bogans asked when he saw Priscilla's tear-stained face. There was a hint of irony in his voice.

"Can you believe it?" Priscilla said, using a tissue to dab at her reddened eyes.

"Mrs. Kerry caused quite a stir around here, that's for certain." This time, Bogans managed to retain a fairly neutral expression.

"More secrets of the Savoy, Mr. Bogans?"

"Remember what I told you previously, Miss Tempest. There are no secrets at the Savoy."

By now they were back in the Daimler, Bogans starting up the motor. "What about Karl Steiner?" asked Priscilla.

Bogans was occupied easing the car into the traffic exiting the airport, but he managed a glance at Priscilla. "Karl? What about him?"

"How he got that black eye."

"If I were to comment on that, perhaps I would say something like it was the result of a domestic crisis."

"But what kind of domestic crisis?"

Bogans concentrated on the traffic to the point where Priscilla began to doubt he would respond. Then: "If I were to answer a question like that, perhaps I would say something to the effect that Mrs. Holmes's husband has discovered that she and Karl are doing things together they should not be doing. Her husband is Ukrainian, a breed not known, apparently, for taking lightly the news of a wife's infidelity."

"I see," Priscilla said. "Mrs. Holmes, who is actually Irina Petrova."

"I would have to agree that is the case," Bogans said after another pause.

"And what is her husband's name?"

"I believe it's Grégoire."

"Grégoire Balandin, the chap who supplies the Savoy's caviar?"

"Put it this way," Bogans amended. "Grégoire works for the people who do. And you don't get to work for those people because you are a nice guy."

"Then can I assume Grégoire is not a nice guy?"

"He is particularly not a nice guy—just ask Karl."

Maybe I will, thought Priscilla.

CHAPTER FIFTY-THREE

True Confessions

Noël Coward was already in place at his regular corner table when Priscilla arrived in the American Bar.

"There you are, my dear." His deeply tanned face lit up as she approached. "As promised, I've ordered you a Buck's Fizz."

"I've missed you, Noël," Priscilla said, seating herself next to him. "I haven't had an excuse to drink a Buck's Fizz since you left."

"Oh, dear," Noël said. "In that case, I shan't ever leave you again."

"Finally, a man I can trust," Priscilla said.

"Indubitably," replied Noël.

"Indubitably," repeated Priscilla as her drink arrived. "It's so seldom you hear the word, let alone trust any man who uses it."

They toasted each other, followed by an atypical silence from Noël as he busied himself inserting a cigarette into its ivory holder.

"You said something about a confession," prompted Priscilla.

Noël frowned at the cigarette holder. "You know, I constantly hang onto this thing, and someone observed recently that I use it as a prop, something I can wield as I fight across the stage of life." He looked away contemplatively, and sighed. "I wonder."

He picked up his drink and turned to Priscilla with another heavy sigh. "But yes, a confession. I'm afraid it has to do with the subject of trust." He paused so a waiter could dash over to light the cigarette. "Thank you," Noël said. "You're so very kind."

"There, you see?" he said after taking a drag and blowing smoke into the air. "Sometimes it's more than a mere prop. Sometimes,

I actually need a cigarette." He exhaled another long smoke trail. "You know I adore you, Priscilla, ever since I stumbled into your office looking for a pen—and you handed me your fountain pen."

"Warning you to be careful of the nib," Priscilla added.

"I was immediately in love," Noël grinned.

"Me, too," Priscilla agreed.

Noël became serious. The cigarette holder was set across an ashtray, the Buck's Fizz forgotten. "All the more reason why what I am about to tell you has me feeling absolutely dreadful. I'm afraid I have betrayed you, Priscilla, and there is simply no excuse for my actions."

"How would you ever do that?" Priscilla was sitting up. A confession of betrayal from Noël was the last thing she had been expecting.

"A while back, I met with an old friend, Dickie Mountbatten." Noël spoke as though giving testimony. "I then proceeded to give him information that you in confidence revealed to me about recent events at the Savoy. In turn, once I told him what I knew, Dickie put me in touch with a man named Peter Trueblood. Commander Peter Trueblood to be more precise.

"Commander Blood, as he is known, heads a secretive group of agents dubbed the Walsinghams. These agents are dedicated to keeping the royal family safe. Their primary function, as far as I can make out, is to head off any potential scandal. They fly very much under the radar, principally because their methods in the performance of their duties are sometimes extreme and skirt the boundaries of the law. As a result of what I told Commander Blood, I believe that whatever difficulties you have encountered lately, he may well be responsible for them. This is my fault, and I'm so very sorry."

Noël stopped. He picked up his drink and took a long sip. "There you go, my dear. Confession time. Sadly. I am most ashamed."

"Thank you for telling me this," Priscilla said slowly, not quite sure how to react.

"It may be small consolation to know that they wanted me to press you for more information. Thankfully, I was able to run off to Sardinia to babysit the Burtons and thus it was easy for me to keep my big mouth shut and not tell them anything else."

"Because you didn't know anything else."

"Precisely," Noël said with a smile. "I am less a threat to anyone when I have absolutely nothing to say."

"At one time," Priscilla offered, "I was certain this group was involved in the deaths of Amir Abrahim and Bernard Bannister."

"Heavens," Noël said. "If you suspect they're involved in that sort of thing, it's no wonder Blood and his boys have been on you."

"Now, though, I'm not quite so certain."

"You have other suspects in mind?"

"I do."

"Do you care to confide who they might be?" Noël asked.

Priscilla considered this, still uncertain about how she should react. "Please don't be offended, Noël," she said finally, "but for now, you are the last person I should confide in."

"No offence taken," Noël said softly. The cigarette holder was once again elegantly held between his fingers—the needed prop in place.

As Priscilla hoped, when she got back to 205, Susie had left for the day.

She sat at her desk, reviewing her encounter with Noël Coward, trying to convince herself that she had not really been betrayed by her friend, putting aside the hurt feelings she had to admit she was experiencing, deciding she would deal with friendship and betrayal, not to mention immense disappointment, later. Right now, there were more pressing issues to come to terms with.

She pressed the waiter button.

It took Karl an unusual ten minutes before he appeared. "Apologies," he said. "I was just about to leave. What can I get for you, Miss Tempest?"

Priscilla rose from her desk and went over and shut the door. She turned to Karl. "Sit down, Karl. I'd like to talk to you."

Karl's face was a mask. "I really don't have a lot of time. Are you sure there is nothing I can get you?"

"We can talk here or I can go to the police and talk to them about Millicent Holmes, or should I say Irina Petrova."

The mask slipped a bit. Karl took the seat in front of Priscilla's desk. His body had tensed.

"Tell me about that black eye," Priscilla said.

"Why would you want to know about that?" he asked nervously.

"I'm interested in the man who hit you, Mrs. Holmes's husband, Grégoire Balandin."

"What makes you think I know anything at all?" Karl had become even more tense.

"Because you've been having an affair with Mrs. Holmes."

"This is not a subject I wish to discuss with you." Karl started to rise.

"Like I said, Karl, we can talk or you can leave and I go to the police. It's up to you."

Karl hesitated before falling back into the chair. He looked tired. "What can I tell you? A vicious bastard, this man. He beats Millicent and keeps her a virtual prisoner. I have been trying to convince her to leave him. He let me know in no uncertain terms as to how he feels about that—but that is how Grégoire always reacts when he wants people to know how he feels."

"You knew him before?"

"From the Hotel Adlon in East Berlin." The blinking of Karl's eyes was the only emotion he showed. "Most of the original hotel was destroyed during the war. But afterward, the East German authorities allowed the surviving building to remain open.

Grégoire used to stay with us from time to time. No one knew for sure, but it was suspected that he worked for the Soviets. It was said that if they required dirty work, Grégoire was the man for it. Everyone was frightened of him."

"Then he showed up in London."

Karl nodded slightly. "By now I am employed here at the Savoy. A wonderful position, one I love, and that changed my life. Then one day out of the blue, Grégoire appeared at the hotel. He informed me that he knew certain details about my earlier life in Berlin, details I would not wish my employers to know about. In return for his silence, he demanded I help get his wife employment at the hotel."

"Mrs. Holmes, who is really Irina Petrova."

"I provided the needed recommendation and she was hired. Ironically, Millicent turned out to be a very good worker and soon was promoted to head housekeeper. At the same time, I got to know her. Things led to other things, and now we have fallen in love."

"Does Grégoire really import caviar?"

Karl considered this briefly and then shrugged. "Apparently. But you can be certain that is not the only reason he is in London."

"What would be another reason?"

"The same as it has always been with him—accomplishing whatever his masters back in Moscow order."

"If I wanted to find Grégoire, where would I look?"

"You do not want to find him," Karl said decisively.

"But if I did."

"I overheard Millicent on the phone once, giving an address, I'm not sure if it's any use."

"What is that address?"

"You are insane, Priscilla," Karl said. A touch of anguish had entered his voice. "You should not do this. You should stay as far away as you can."

"Tell me," Priscilla persisted.

CHAPTER FIFTY-FOUR

Shots in the Dark

Set in grim shadows overlooking the Thames, the Victorian brick building at the end of a gravel drive appeared deserted. Behind the building, Priscilla could make out a series of houseboats moored against the embankment adjacent to a towpath running alongside the river. Further along, a big freighter was cast in light, shrouded by giant cranes poking into a velvet sky.

Now what? she thought, shivering a bit as she stood outside the building. This was the address all right, but the place appeared deserted. Either Karl had misheard the address or he had lied. Deciding she had better make sure, Priscilla took a deep breath and then went up the steps to the double entrance doors, the glass in them caked with dust. She tried the latch and found it locked. She peered inside through the grime but could see nothing except the outline of a staircase.

Returning to the drive, Priscilla decided this was a stupid idea. She had to be out of her mind, wasting time playing amateur detective. Wasting her life, for that matter.

From one of the houseboats, soft music drifted on the night breeze. Maybe someone living there might know of Grégoire. Having run out of options and beginning to think she had no future anyway and therefore nothing to lose, Priscilla allowed herself to be drawn down a gentle slope. She reached the end where the houseboat was moored, its cabin illuminated, the music louder. Beyond the houseboat, the Thames was a black smudge.

Priscilla thought about it a moment and then climbed onto the deck. The sound of a distant foghorn made her shiver as she crept along to the cabin. Through a porthole she could view part of a sitting room cast in lamplight, apparently deserted. Priscilla continued to a hatchway. The music had come to an end. She ducked through the hatchway and went down into the cabin.

Millicent Holmes was asleep, her tiny body folded into an armchair, as though trying to disappear from sight. Nearby, a table contained a three-quarters-empty bottle of vodka. A phonograph, its arm moving back and forth against the end of the record she had been playing. Priscilla lifted the arm back in place and then went over to the chair.

"Mrs. Holmes? Millicent?" Priscilla shook her gently.

For a time, Millicent didn't respond, then, abruptly, her head jerked around and she made smacking sounds with her lips. Her eyes opened and then widened in alarm as she recognized the person who had awoken her.

"Miss Tempest? Is that you?" The words came out slowly.

"Yes, Mrs. Holmes."

"What are you doing here?" A weak, confused voice.

"I was worried about you," Priscilla stated solicitously. "I came to make sure you're okay."

"You were worried about me?" The idea seemed to frighten her. "Why would you worry...about *me*?"

"I believe you're in great danger—because of what you saw and what you did."

"No idea what you're talking about," Millicent whispered. She was sitting up in the armchair now, eyes bleary, fingers stroking her temple. "Took some pills, don't feel well..."

"Let me help you, please," Priscilla said. "I know you saw Princess Margaret that morning. They know, too. But what were you doing in Amir Abrahim's suite in the first place? Were you there to make sure he was dead?"

Millicent looked around uncomprehendingly, struggling with the fact of Priscilla's presence. She moved her head back and forth, shifting her body around. That's when Priscilla noticed the polished steel of the pistol tucked into the seat cushion against the side of the chair.

"You can't be here," Millicent said in a groggy voice, her words coming with difficulty. "He is coming back..."

"Who's coming back?" Priscilla asked. "Grégoire? Your husband?"

Millicent had become even more fearful, shaking her head. "Not only my husband...him..."

"Who? Who do you mean?"

"If they find you here, they will..." she couldn't finish the sentence. "You must leave."

"Please, come with me. I want to get you to safety so you can tell the police what really happened."

"Can't go to...the police...they protect him..."

"Who do they protect, Mrs. Holmes?"

"Please..."

"I'm going to take you away from here, okay?"

"You're mad...it's all madness..."

Millicent's protestations seemed to exhaust her. She sank back against the chair but didn't resist when Priscilla lifted her upright and then struggled to raise her into a standing position. Priscilla was holding onto her as best she could to keep her from falling, when she heard the hatchway open.

At the sound, Millicent's eyes fluttered open. She gasped, "No..."

A large man with a black beard who looked as if he had been carved out of granite shot through the hatchway.

Grégoire Balandin's bulk seemed to overwhelm the cabin. If there was a man who only needed to make an appearance in order to instill fear, Priscilla thought, Grégoire certainly filled that role.

"What the...what is going on here?" he bellowed.

His face shone with aggressive light, the predator recognizing the prey. "Bitch from the Savoy..."

"We promoted beluga caviar together, Grégoire. Don't you remember?" Faced with Grégoire's massive presence, Priscilla's voice sounded unnaturally high and loud. Not at all the way she wanted to sound.

"Jesus Christ," Grégoire boomed. "What do you think you are doing?"

"I'm taking Millicent with me," Priscilla said, mustering a show of bravery she certainly wasn't feeling. "If you know what's best, you won't stop us."

Grégoire responded with a roar of anger, charging forward, backhanding Priscilla, sending her into the armchair. Millicent sank to the floor, crying out.

The room around her was spinning wildly. Priscilla felt her mouth fill with blood. Something hard and metallic pressed against her thigh—the pistol.

"Grégoire, don't," Millicent called out pleadingly.

That was the cue for Grégoire to utter another savage howl of rage. He leaned down and jerked Priscilla out of the chair with as much difficulty as it would take anyone else to pick up a book.

Priscilla vaguely heard Millicent crying, "Grégoire! Don't do it!"

He wasn't listening, proceeding instead to raise Priscilla high and then heave her across the cabin. She hit the bulkhead hard and fell onto a sideboard before tumbling to the floor. Blood from a gash in her forehead blurred her view of Grégoire lumbering toward her.

"Not only a bitch...a stupid bitch."

"They know where I am," Priscilla managed to stammer. "They are coming for you."

"Stupid bitch and a bad liar," Grégoire grunted.

He lunged.

The sound of the gunshot reverberated through the cabin. Grégoire stopped, his expression abruptly perplexed, as though he had heard something but wasn't quite sure what.

He began a turn to investigate when there was a second gunshot. His face went blank and he collapsed to the floor, enabling Priscilla to see Millicent holding the pistol she had just fired twice.

Priscilla stared numbly at Grégoire's body. Millicent, sobbing, lowered the weapon. Priscilla took deep breaths, trying not to hyperventilate, every part of her body aching. She brushed at the blood running down her forehead, telling herself that yes, that was a dead body on the floor in front of her, a man who might otherwise have killed her. Right now, though, she must stay strong, ignore the blood, and help Millicent—the tiny housekeeper who had just shot her husband.

"Come along," Priscilla directed as quietly as she could manage. "We have to get out of here."

Priscilla put her arm around Millicent. With the pistol still in her hand, she allowed Priscilla to guide her around Grégoire's body, through the cabin, and then up the stairway. As they came onto the deck, a thunderclap rattled the night. Together, they got off the boat and moved slowly along the towpath, Priscilla limping from the pain in her leg. The wind was picking up. Millicent mumbled something Priscilla didn't catch. She drew the woman to a stop. "What is it, Mrs. Holmes? What are you saying?"

Millicent's eyes were far away. "Grégoire and him," she mumbled.

"What? I don't understand."

"...Didn't know...no idea what...what he was doing...no idea... but I did it..." Her words were coming out with excruciating slowness, so softly that Priscilla had to lean close to catch what she was saying over the howl of the wind.

"Are you talking about Grégoire?" Priscilla asked.

Millicent nodded.

"I'm guessing he poisoned the champagne. But how? How did he do it?"

"A syringe, he had a syringe..."

"And what? He used the syringe to inject the toxin through the cork?"

Millicent nodded slightly. "Knew how to handle it... knew what to do..."

Millicent pulled away from Priscilla and stumbled forward. Priscilla had no choice but to follow her as the other woman started up the embankment, a small ghostlike figure, her black hair having come loose, blowing wildly around her.

The wind grew in strength. There was more thunder and rain in the air. The deserted brick pile at the crest of the embankment looked particularly forbidding in the light cast by what was left of the moon. It framed Mark Ryde as he seemed to materialize out of the shadows, fighting to rearrange his mystified face into a neutral expression, but ready as always for the photo shoot.

"Him..." Millicent announced haltingly. "That's how Grégoire knew what to do..."

"Priscilla," Mark said brightly, forcing a thin smile. "You do turn up in the most unexpected places."

"I could say the same about you, Mark." Priscilla couldn't help thinking that he was the much better actor. His portrayal of the cool, resourceful spy far outmatched her amateur attempts at calmness.

"You're bleeding," he observed. "We'll get that taken care of. It looks as though I've once again arrived just in time to save you."

Millicent, glaring angrily, pointed a shaky finger. "Him... KGB... he did this... he is responsible..."

Mark shrugged off the accusation. "As usual at about this time in the evening, you have become a drunken fool, Millicent, babbling nonsense..."

Millicent shook her head intently. "He told us Amir Abrahim would destroy the market for caviar; he convinced my husband." Hate, anger, desperation, whatever was driving her at this point had the effect of making her much more coherent. "He convinced my husband...and my husband had his methods when it came to convincing me."

"Ridiculous," Mark said, maintaining his equilibrium. "Why would I want to kill anyone over caviar?"

"Not caviar for you...for you, guns," Millicent retorted. "You stop Abrahim selling guns in the East, then the Soviets control the market."

"I must admit, Millicent does have a point," Mark allowed. "Without admitting to anything, it would make sense to be rid of the inefficient Amir and his family so as to open the way for the right kind of people—people who actually know what they are doing—to take advantage of that very lucrative and growing market."

"And you represent the right kind of people, do you, Mark?" Priscilla asked.

"It's fair to say there are advantages when it comes to playing off a number of parties in these affairs."

"What about Bernard Bannister? Why would you kill him?"

"Alana's occasional lover. I suppose if one were to admit to something like that, it would have to do with jealousy...that and a growing fear Bannister was saying too much about certain activities it would be better not to say anything about. Unfortunately, his death alerted Alana and fuelled her suspicions. Again, if one were of a mind to admit anything, one could say it became necessary to silence those suspicions. Most unfortunate—*if* that is what happened."

"Which you did after she broke into my flat."

"You are supposing I'm the culprit." Mark was holding tight to his unflappability, on the surface at least. "That's not necessarily the case," he added.

"I think it is." Priscilla, giving up her previous mere suspicion in favour of the certainty she now felt. "It worked out very well for you, killing Alana and then getting away in time to meet Princess Margaret and escort her home. That left me to find Alana's body and stand accused of the murder you committed."

"Be serious, Priscilla," Mark said with a dismissive wave of his hand. "In the end, they were never going to charge you. Alana was going to kill you. I saved you again—against my better judgment, I might add."

Millicent began to cry, sudden wails of despair as her hand rose in the moonlight and Priscilla saw too late that the gleam of steel meant she still had the pistol.

"Bastard," Millicent shouted. Mark jerked back as she turned the pistol in his direction, her face flaring with rage.

Priscilla cried, "No!" as she threw herself at Millicent, knocking her to the ground. Down on her hands and knees, Priscilla scrambled frantically to retrieve the pistol that had fallen from Millicent's hand. She found it on the gravel, vaguely thinking that it was fine that she had the weapon but had no idea how to use it. Nonetheless, as she rose, she bluffed it out, aiming the pistol clasped in her jittery hands at Mark.

He remained preternaturally unruffled. "What are you going to do, Priscilla? Are you going to shoot me?"

Priscilla tried to hold the gun steady as she kept it trained on him. Millicent, sobbing, remained on the ground.

"You know what?" Mark continued in that damnably steady voice. "I don't think you are."

"You're wrong about me." He *was* wrong, she told herself. He had gotten everything about her wrong.

"I don't think I am."

"I want you to stay where you are," she ordered in what was supposed to be a strong voice. Except it didn't sound very strong. Why should it? She wasn't strong. She was no good at this. No good at all against someone as untroubled in her presence as Mark Ryde.

As though to underscore what she was thinking, he turned and started walking away along the gravel drive.

"Mark Ryde!" she shouted after him.

But he kept walking. No hurry. As though someone threatened him with a gun all the time. And maybe he did have plenty of experience with that. Or he knew her. Knew she wouldn't shoot. That she was weak—and a coward to boot.

It began to rain; the wind blew fiercely against her so that she had to spread her legs, bracing herself. The pistol trembled in her hands. She thought about pulling the trigger. She could do this. He was a killer getting away. She could stop him.

She yelled, more of a howl of rage than anything. There were tears in her eyes.

But then he was gone in the rainy darkness and it was too late to do what she probably could never have done anyway, weak as she was. Exhaling loudly, she dropped the pistol.

"He would have killed us," Millicent said, rising shakily from the ground. "He would have killed us both..."

Save for Millicent's continued sobs, a silence fell across a world that seemed to have come to a stop as the moon lost itself behind heavy clouds and the rain fell hard. Priscilla looked down at herself, covered in her own blood, the blood in her mouth. Was Millicent right? Would Mark have murdered her? Maybe. Or perhaps he had tried to save her after all, but in the end it hadn't worked.

She had to save herself.

CHAPTER FIFTY-FIVE

Loose Ends

The Front Hall was busy as always, filled with the endlessly fascinating choreography of the rich and the privileged coming and going, so well upholstered, so comfortable in their roles, so confident in their bearing. To Priscilla, watching the parade unfold as she plodded miserably toward the general manager's office, everyone looked so happy as they checked in to be pampered by a staff of fifteen hundred charged with fulfilling their every whim. They would be making reservations for dinner in the Grill after the opera or enjoying the cabaret revue at the Restaurant, eager for the Scottish smoked salmon, the canvasback duck, the little-neck clams, or arranging to meet friends for an afternoon aperitif within the elegant confines of the American Bar.

Life at the Savoy would go on as it always had in its luxurious bubble, far away from the world's cares and conflicts. There would be no pause to acknowledge the forlorn miniskirted figure starting up the stairs, on her way to—what? As she had explained to Susie, given the events that had lately unfolded, possibly a life in prison. But first, prior to placing her in chains, there would be the ritual sacking—necessary, she assumed, for the good of the Savoy's reputation.

As she walked toward what was in all probability her doom, Priscilla thought about the day when she might look forward to the same happiness as the rich the hotel so eagerly served. Could it be achieved, simply by checking into the Savoy? Priscilla had her doubts. Or perhaps it might be delivered to her via a courier who at the same time would take away lingering dark memories, including but not limited to the image of Mark Ryde confidently walking away into a night full of rain. Her standing there bleeding, soaked to the bone, unable to stop him. Thus far, however, no one had removed the darkness to clear the way for her happiness. Gloom and doom, she thought mournfully. That's what she had to look forward to. Not to mention unemployment.

"Go right in," El Sid said in a voice like the death knell of a church bell.

Priscilla paused at Banville's door, swallowed hard, and then turned the knob and stepped to her doom.

Clive Banville, standing near one of the big windows shedding uncertain light, jerked around as Priscilla entered. A tall, rail-thin gentleman with an executioner's face stood with him.

"Ah, there you are, Miss Tempest." Banville spoke in a voice that, surprisingly, did not sound unfriendly, given the circumstances. "How are we doing?"

"Recovering, sir," was the best Priscilla could come up with.

"Yes, a slight gash on the forehead, I see. Looks as though it's healing nicely, though."

"It is, sir, thanks."

"Given what you've been through, I must say you look well. And here you are back at work, toughing it out, right?"

"Absolutely, sir."

"I've invited you here today because I'd like you to meet Commander Peter Trueblood."

Commander Trueblood rather solemnly shook Priscilla's hand. "Good morning, Miss Tempest." Nothing about it being a pleasure to meet her, Priscilla noted. But here she was, finally in the presence of the notorious Commander Blood.

"Commander Trueblood is here because he would like to have a word with you," Banville said. He nodded at the commander. "I'll leave you to it."

Banville slipped out of the office, shutting the door behind him, leaving Priscilla and Trueblood briefly shrouded in awkward silence.

"Please, won't you take a seat, Miss Tempest?" Trueblood indicated a set of sofas and chairs on the far side of the office, a no woman's land Priscilla had never before been asked to occupy.

"If it's all the same to you, Commander, I'd just as soon stand," Priscilla said. On wobbly legs, she thought to herself, making an effort to manage a heartbeat the intensity of which she feared might shatter glass—or, more worrisome, alert Commander Blood to her nervousness.

"Very well, Miss Tempest," the commander said. "I should tell you that—"

"I know who you are, Commander. You head the Walsinghams."

That gave Trueblood pause. "That is not a name that am I particularly fond of, but nonetheless—"

"You probably don't like being referred to as Commander Blood, either," Priscilla interjected. With nothing to lose at this point, she thought.

Trueblood managed a weak smile. "Now you are trying to antagonize me, Miss Tempest, and I must tell you, that is not necessary."

"Isn't it?"

"It won't be possible to do so publicly, but if anything, Buckingham Palace owes you a debt of thanks."

"It does?" Priscilla could hardly believe what she was hearing.

"If it wasn't for you discovering the truth of the murders here at the Savoy, accusations and suspicions might have continued to endlessly hang over the royal family."

"Yes," Priscilla hastily agreed, beginning to realize that the axe she imagined poised over her neck might not fall after all. She continued, gaining more confidence: "It seems Scotland Yard was far more interested in protecting that family than it was in even admitting there had been a murder. What's more, Millicent Holmes was telling the truth about seeing Princess Margaret outside Amir Abrahim's suite. You people knew she had been having an affair with Amir, and you, Commander, had obviously threatened him and therefore he actually believed he might be killed."

"Totally ridiculous," Commander Trueblood said.

"Nonetheless, that's what he believed—and he believed it enough to tell me the night I was with him that he feared for his life."

Trueblood stepped back a couple of paces as though to get a better look at Priscilla. "It's obvious you are no fool, Miss Tempest, and if anything, the police and your employers have vastly under-estimated you."

"I believe that you now know the true identity of Mark Ryde," Priscilla plunged on, "that he was in fact working for the KGB and that it was he who orchestrated the death of Amir Abrahim and Bernard Bannister. You also know that he was responsible for the murder of Alana Wynter, who worked for you, as one of the Walsinghams. He as much as admitted it to me. Nevertheless, you allow a cloud of suspicion to hang over me so that I continue to fear that at any moment I might be arrested and charged with her murder."

"As a matter of fact, that's why I wished to meet with you today," Commander Trueblood smoothly countered. "I've been in touch with DCI Robert Lightfoot at Scotland Yard, and he has agreed with my assessment that no charges should be brought against you."

"I appreciate that," Priscilla said with a combination of shock and relief. Powerful men with hard, unforgiving faces had no choice but to actually listen to her. Quite astounding, she thought.

"However," Priscilla continued, "that still leaves open the question of what has happened to the man we both know to be responsible for Alana's murder. Mark Ryde seems to have disappeared into thin air."

Priscilla had a sense of Trueblood on the defensive as he replied stiffly, "Given the circumstances, the government has decided to evoke the Official Secrets Act in the matter, which means—"

"It means," Priscilla interrupted, "you have effectively muzzled any further investigation of her murder, not to mention the true identity of Mr. Ryde."

"A manhunt is underway across Europe for Ryde. He will be brought to justice in due course."

"Unless he is safely back in Moscow which, I suspect, is where he is," Priscilla said.

"Be that as it may, Mrs. Holmes—or Irina Petrova, to use her real name—has co-operated with Inspector Lightfoot and provided him with a full confession. It was her husband who poisoned Amir Abrahim, not because he was any threat to the monarchy or because he was threatening to import Payusnaya caviar from Spain, although it may have been dressed up to look like that."

Again, Priscilla felt confident enough to go on the attack: "Mrs. Holmes told me the real reason for the murder was the Russians deciding to get rid of a bothersome competitor in the international arms trade," she maintained. "Mark Ryde enlisted Grégoire Balandin to help him with the poisoning and thus ensure that competition was eliminated."

"Naturally, I cannot confirm your suppositions, Miss Tempest—"

"You don't have to," Priscilla interjected.

"However," Trueblood continued, on firmer ground now, "I am able to report that the toxic chemical employed is called simply A-232.

"I know that," Priscilla countered. "In fact, it's now been reported in the press."

"Suspected, yes, but now confirmed," Trueblood replied defensively. "It is produced at a site near Moscow, Krasnoarmeysk by name. My friends at MI5 tell me the Russian secret police, the KGB, is involved. In liquid form, a tiny amount of it can be inserted into a bottle of, say, champagne via a syringe."

"Which is how Grégoire was able to poison Amir."

"Precisely. It's totally lethal. Death comes fairly quickly and there is no apparent cause. The team of Mark Ryde and Grégoire Balandin came very close to getting away with their crimes."

"What about Mrs. Holmes?"

"The police and MI5 are still attempting to ascertain her involvement in this affair."

"What you've just told me. Is that the official explanation?"

"It is the explanation."

"I see," said Priscilla. "And what about Bernard Bannister?"

"The coroner has ascertained that Mr. Bannister died of heart failure. There were no signs of any toxins in his body."

"Otherwise, it might look as though a jealous KGB agent poisoned him," Priscilla said.

"As far as Scotland Yard is concerned, Mark Ryde was not involved. The matter is closed."

"None of this is satisfactory from my point of view," Priscilla said. Immediately she had a sense that she may have pushed Trueblood a step or two beyond what he was willing to put up with.

"What is or is not satisfactory to you, Miss Tempest, is of little concern," he said huffily. "This is what it is." Then he softened a bit. "If it is any consolation, I've had a chat with Mr. Banville to let him know how grateful Buckingham Palace is for your assistance. He assures me that you have his full support, and he is looking forward to you continuing with your employment here at the Savoy's press office."

"In other words," Priscilla said, swallowing her growing anger, "I can keep my job if I keep my mouth shut."

"You keep your job," Trueblood replied. "Along with it, I would imagine, comes a requirement for the discretion necessary in order to maintain this hotel's dignity and reputation."

Trueblood started to turn away. "You haven't heard the last of me," Priscilla said.

"Oh, I think I have, Miss Tempest."

"Don't bet on it."

"Have a good day, Miss Tempest."

Was there just the slightest hint of concern on Commander Blood's haunted face as he left?

Priscilla liked to think there was.

Kissed

"Do you still have a job?" Susie's wide eyes were full of desperate hope as Priscilla returned to 205.

Priscilla made a show of looking around and then leaning over Susie's desk to whisper in her ear. "We are still employed—at least until the end of the day. For now, the nightmare has passed."

Susie looked relieved. "Thank goodness!" Then her face became serious again. "But the nightmare will return. It's only a matter of time, I'm sure. Incidentally, speaking of nightmares, Percy Hoskins has been calling for you."

"What does he want now?"

"He told me to tell you to meet him at the usual place at one o'clock. Would you care to know what I think?"

"Not if it has to do with Percy."

"I think he's in love with you."

Priscilla arranged to look unmoved. "I highly doubt Percy is in love with anyone but himself."

"One o'clock," Susie said. "Whatever the usual place is."

Too bad, Priscilla thought. The usual place or not, she wasn't going. She was through having anything to do with the likes of Percy Hoskins—or men in general, after what she had been through.

Definitely. That was the end of it. No question in her mind...

"I'm not here," Priscilla said as she seated herself beside Percy in the Victoria Embankment Gardens. "I just happen to be passing by," she added.

Percy kept his eyes fixed on Henry Fawcett's bronze head and said nothing. Priscilla couldn't help after a time giving him a sideways glance, noting that today he had chosen to run a razor around his chin. A comb had found its way through his unruly hair.

"I'm mounting a campaign to have his memorial removed," Percy said finally.

"Did you hear me?" Priscilla asked insistently. "I'm not here. It's just that I was passing by."

Percy ignored her. "He was such a good man, Henry. That's why I want him taken away. He was too good for this awful world. I don't want him to see all the bad stuff that's happening around him."

"May I remind you that Henry was blind and therefore can't see a darned thing," Priscilla offered, settling back against the bench. The sun was out. The sunbathers were back, and, despite herself, she did feel quite comfortable seated beside Percy.

"Ah, yes, wouldn't you know," Percy said sadly. "The last good man was a blind man. The irony is insufferable." Percy gazed up at the memorial. "Sorry, Henry. I'll leave you right where you are. Just be thankful you can't see a damned thing."

"You sound very down," Priscilla said with much more sympathy than she intended.

"That's because the woman I adore has been through hell recently, and while I've longed to tell her that she's a bit of a heroine and that she shouldn't let any of this get to her because she did the right thing when so many others didn't, I am unable to do so because she does not return my calls."

"I'll have a talk with Susie. She's been busy lately, but she's now feeling better and I'm sure she'll call."

"Ha ha," said Percy mirthlessly. "You know bloody damn well you're the one I adore—not to mention the woman I've been calling."

"Susie thinks you're in love with me." Blame Susie, Priscilla thought, safer that way.

"I'm not so sure I would go *that* far."

"No? How far would you go?"

"For the time being, I would stop at 'adore.' Until you start to return my calls."

"I've been busy lately." To say the least, Priscilla thought.

"So I'm told. According to my sources at Scotland Yard, Charger Lightfoot couldn't wait to have you for murder. Then suddenly the word came down from on high that you weren't to be charged. What happened?"

"Well, for one thing, I didn't kill anyone. That helped."

"Yes, but innocence never stopped our brave boys at New Scotland Yard."

"The fact is, I can't say anything."

"No, why not?"

She lowered her voice to a whisper and leaned into him. "The Official Secrets Act."

"You're not serious."

"I am. But there's nothing to stop you."

"Yes, unfortunately, there is."

"You're kidding," Priscilla said. "What would be stopping you?"

"Powerful people acting powerfully, helped along by my editors, only too anxious to please their betters."

"I'm so sorry, Percy."

"Hey, you're all right, and from what I've been able to learn, you made the grey, powerful lads who run things face the fact that there was murder at the Savoy, and then you found the real killer. Not bad for a kid working in the press office."

"I'm not a kid, Percy." His ability to always slip under her skin was quite remarkable.

"I apologize," Percy corrected. "An infinitely attractive, intelligent young woman working in the press office."

"That's better, although I'm not sure solving a murder at the Savoy does me much good, except for the time being I do still have a job."

"And I'm not finished yet," Percy said. "I'm working on ways to get more of what happened into the paper. We'll see."

"As long as you leave me out of it," Priscilla said. "I'm in more than enough trouble as it is. Of course, as soon as I say that, I manage to get myself into even more trouble."

"Tell you what. I'll keep your name out of the paper as long as you agree to have dinner with me."

"You're blackmailing me again."

"I wouldn't call it blackmail, exactly."

"No? What would you call it?"

"I'd say it was more like asking you for a date."

Priscilla got to her feet. "Let me think about it."

Percy stood to face her. "Don't think too long."

He kissed her deeply on the mouth. She finally made herself pull away. "That's the second time you've kissed me," she said.

"You're counting," he said.

"I am."

"And don't you think it was even better this time?"

"I'm not sure."

"No?"

"Possibly, I need more convincing."

This time she kissed him—and she took her time about it, knowing that the blind Henry Fawcett couldn't see what she was up to.

CHAPTER FIFTY-SEVEN

Undying Love!

The telephone was ringing as Priscilla re-entered 205. But then the telephone was always ringing at the press office, everyone calling for attention. Susie was nowhere in sight. Priscilla was not in the mood for dealing with anyone. However, her inbred professionalism kicked in and she finally picked up the receiver.

"Buck's Fizz time, my darling!" Noël Coward's voice on the phone sounded sweet and plaintive. "That is if you'll still have anything to do with me," he added.

Priscilla couldn't help but smile. "Are you at the American Bar?"

"Waiting for you, my one and only."

"I'll be right there," said Priscilla.

The bar was packed as usual for the cocktail hour. Once again there was excitement in the air that could only mean one thing: Elizabeth Taylor and Richard Burton, both darkly tanned from the Sardinian sun, had returned to the Savoy to hold court along with Noël Coward.

He bounced to his feet to give Priscilla a relieved hug. "So good to see you," he said, sounding unusually sincere. "You remember Elizabeth and Richard, of course. The happy couple have made their escape from Sardinia for a few days of rest and recreation."

Elizabeth offered her hand and a welcoming smile. "Good to see you again, Priscilla. Noël tells me you've had a difficult time lately."

"Difficult time?" chimed in Richard. "I'll tell you what a difficult time is, standing at a cliff edge in a howling wind wearing a long black robe, muttering inane Tennessee Williams dialogue, questioning what you've done with your life."

"If you think *Boom!* is bad, my darling," Elizabeth said, "I'll set up a screening of *The Robe*. You surely remember it's the one where you go to Heaven with Jean Simmons because you both believe in Jesus. But then given what the two of you were up to with each other, Jesus had nothing to do with the beatific shine on your faces."

"Ah, my sweet, then allow me to counter with *Butterfield 8* in which you play a whore, so fetching in your slip. But no trip to Heaven for you."

"Richard and Elizabeth, alas, got a head start on the Buck's Fizzes," Noël explained, seating Priscilla. A waiter promptly placed a champagne flute in front of her.

"Just in time," Priscilla said, lifting her glass.

Richard looked dazzled as he leaned over to inspect her more closely. "Damn, you're a beauty. A gamine-like beauty, I would say. Wasted here at the Savoy, I'd wager. Why haven't we met before?"

"You idiot," Elizabeth said, "don't you remember? You swore undying love for this woman. You were going to leave me and run off with her."

"I intend to do precisely that," Richard asserted. He gave Priscilla a blearily loving look. "Pack your bags, my darling. I'll meet you in the lobby and off we go."

"Good riddance," said Elizabeth.

"You'll miss me, pet," Richard said to Elizabeth. "But it's too late, I'm off to a happy life with—"

He paused and then said, "You must tell me your name, my darling."

Everyone laughed and the warmth of the late afternoon chatter inside the Savoy American Bar rose up around them.

Our Guests at the Savoy

Following his London appearance in *Rigoletto*, Signor Luciano Pavarotti went on to great international fame. The King of the Tenors, as he became known, sold over one hundred million records. His last public performance came in 2006 when he performed "Nessun dorma" at the Winter Olympics in Turin. He died of pancreatic cancer in 2007 at the age of 71.

Although his movie career effectively came to an end in 1972 after making fifty-four features, Mr. Leslie Townes (Bob) Hope remained America's most beloved comedian throughout the 1970s despite his controversial support of US involvement in Vietnam. Mr. Hope's NBC television specials were huge ratings hits, and he continued to relentlessly tour overseas, entertaining American troops. He made his last television appearance in 1996 and then, with his eyesight failing, announced in 1997 that he was retiring from public life. He died of pneumonia in 2003 at the age of 100.

Noël Coward finally received his knighthood in 1970. Although Sir Noël had given up writing plays and musicals by then, his fame was at an all-time high thanks to revues and revivals of his most popular works. The *New Statesman* dubbed him "the grand old man of British drama." However, within a few years, he was beset by various health and memory issues. He died of heart failure in 1973 at his home in Jamaica at the age of 73.

As Miss Elizabeth Taylor and Mr. Richard Burton suspected, *Boom!* was a colossal failure, both critically and commercially, when it was briefly released. Although Mr. Burton enjoyed a few more commercial successes (*Where Eagles Dare, Anne of the Thousand Days, The Wild Geese*), the couple's box office potency faded after *Boom!* The Battling Burtons, as they became known, divorced in 1974, remarried sixteen months later, and then divorced again in 1976. Mr. Burton suffered a heart attack and died in 1984 at his home in Céligny, Switzerland, aged 58. At the age of 79, Miss Taylor, after fighting numerous illnesses and by now a billionaire—thanks not to the movies but to her signature perfume called White Diamonds—finally succumbed to congestive heart failure in Los Angeles in 2011.

Although HRH the Princess Margaret married Mr. Anthony Armstrong-Jones (who later became the Earl of Snowdon) in 1960, it wasn't long before reports began to filter out about her various affairs (Lord Snowdon's as well). Her lovers supposedly included Mr. Mick Jagger, Mr. Peter Sellers, Mr. David Niven, and Mr. Warren Beatty as well as the less-known Mr. Roddy Llewellyn. She and Lord Snowdon finally divorced in 1978. A heavy smoker and drinker, HRH the Princess Margaret suffered a stroke in 2002 and three days later was dead at the age of 71.

Lord Louis Mountbatten's association with the Walsinghams at Buckingham Palace in 1968 was not the only intrigue in which he found himself involved. That same year, it was alleged Lord Mountbatten took part in a plot to overthrow the troubled Labour government of Mr. Harold Wilson. Supposedly, the Queen herself had to intervene to put a stop to Lord Mountbatten's participation. In 1979, at the age of 79, he was killed when the Irish Republican Army exploded a bomb in his fishing boat as it left the dock at the Irish village of Mullaghmore.

The search for the Soviet double agent, Mark Ryde, continued across several continents. However, authorities so far have failed in their efforts to run him down. Privately, agents at both MI5 and MI6 confess that Mr. Ryde escaped back to Moscow into the welcoming arms of his KGB masters. However, they continue to be on the lookout, fearing they have not heard the last of him. Incidentally, according to knowledgeable sources, Princess Margaret was never informed that she had been having an affair with a Russian spy.

From her Park Avenue apartment in New York, Mrs. Eunice Kerry continued to gleefully upset her daughter, Daisee, with suggestions she might soon return to London. So far, Mrs. Kerry has not made good on those threats, possibly because she has been kept busy with a handsome young Italian named Antonio, who says he is a model. Mrs. Kerry has chosen to believe him and not ask a lot of questions, including why it is that Antonio can't pay his own rent.

As for Miss Priscilla Tempest, it is fair to report that the management at the Savoy continues to cast a suspect eye as far as she is concerned. Also, perhaps not surprisingly, Miss Tempest's love life remains the subject of gossip and raised eyebrows. Apparently, there could be further adventures available for the recounting were they not, for the moment, subject to the restrictions outlined in Britain's Official Secrets Act. So far, it must be said in her favour, she has managed to stay out of prison, faint praise for anyone else, but a notable accomplishment for Miss Tempest.

Acknowledgements

Of the many joys writing *Death at the Savoy*, the best has been the way it enabled the two of us to rekindle a friendship that began on the set of a movie called *Black Christmas* way back in the 1970s. It was a delight not only reconnecting again but also discovering that we are darn good collaborators when it comes to conjuring all sorts of murder and mystery at one of the world's finest and most famous hotels.

In order to properly do this, Pru drew on the memories of old friends who rallied around to ensure we got the details right (well, more or less right). Thanks to Susie Grandfield who not only covered for Pru during the champagne-filled years at the Savoy Press Office (1968 to 1973) but who, fifty years later, endured endless questions to supply crucial details that helped shape this novel.

The late great hotelier, Michael Bentley, also came to our aid, drawing memories from a career that spanned assistant manager at the Savoy, assistant general manager at Claridge's and the Ritz Hotel, and lastly, ambassador for the Mandarin Hotel, all in London.

John Iversen, who trained at the Savoy and documented those unique years in his memoir, *Inn Jokes*, provided invaluable anecdotes from behind the scenes. John moved on to manage the Savoy-owned Lancaster hotel in Paris. He was so detail oriented, he rearranged bouquets of flowers while inspecting the foyer and dining areas. He was assistant manager at the world-famous Reid's Hotel in Madeira and later general manager of the Sandy Lane Hotel, the luxury resort in Barbados.

Recalled Pru: "Both Michael and John were my dear friends who ensured I experienced the best of everything, as only world class hotels provided it in those happy days gone by."

Thanks also to Victor Emery for sharing memories of his years at the Savoy and for giving us the right name for the Savoy limos— the Daimler.

And there really was a Percy Hoskins, famous back in the day as Fleet Street's ace crime reporter, often described as Scotland Yard's Dr. Watson. His presence in the novel is a quiet salute to an old friend, long gone.

In bringing Death at the Savoy to life, we were immeasurably aided by editors and readers stationed on two continents: in London, England; Vancouver, BC; and Milton, Ontario. The team at West-End Books, first reader Katherine Lenhoff in Milton, editors Ray Bennett in London, and James Bryan Simpson in Campbellville did their usual yeoman work pulling the manuscript into shape so that it could be shown to the world. The insightful suggestions and corrections from editors Pam Robertson and Jonathan Dore made for a much better book.

Many thanks to everyone at Douglas & McIntyre for embracing the work and making us feel we had found a good home for our novel.

And finally, many, many thanks to our agent Bill Hanna. Bill and Ron have been friends for many years. Their adventures together chasing publishers in Toronto, Los Angeles, Italy, and Germany would...well, they'd make a novel! Undaunted, unstoppable, the whirling dervish of literary agents, Bill believed in our book from the beginning and never gave up on it or us.

About the Authors

Prudence Emery was born in Nanaimo, educated in Vancouver, and lived in London, UK, and Toronto, ON, before moving to Victoria, BC. She has worked as the press and public relations officer at the prestigious Savoy Hotel, mingling with celebrities and politicians such as Canada's past Prime Minister Pierre Elliot Trudeau and actor Marlene Dietrich. She has worked on more than a hundred film productions and is the author of the best-selling memoir *Nanaimo Girl* (Cormorant Books, 2020).

Ron Base is a former newspaper and magazine journalist and movie critic. His works include twenty novels, two novellas, and four nonfiction books. He has been published in the United States, Canada, and Great Britain. He has written screenplays and worked with legendary filmmakers such as John Borman (*Deliverance*) and Roland Joffe (*The Killing Fields*). Currently, Base divides his time between Milton, ON, and Fort Myers, FL.

More Trouble for Priscilla?
This time it's absolutely scandalous!
Read an excerpt from Priscilla Tempest's next gripping adventure

SCANDAL AT THE SAVOY

They know!

As she made her way past the Front Hall, down the stairs to the Restaurant, Priscilla was certain everyone could hear the loud panicked thump of her heart as they noted her pale clammy skin. A sickly young woman with great legs and bad judgment, born to screw up her life.

But if management did know, then why would Major Jack O'Hara call her to the Cabaret? Why would she not simply be drummed out in General Manager Clive Banville's office, the Place of Execution where her misdeeds ordinarily would be punished?

But this was Canada's prime minister, for heaven's sake! Mr. Banville would want to stay as far away from scandal as possible. Therefore, Major O'Hara would conduct the inquisition in a place where he was certain not to be disturbed at this time of the day—*the bandstand!*

Reaching the deserted Restaurant, Priscilla crossed the dance floor. In the evening the floor rose on a hydraulic lift to become the Cabaret's stage. Major O'Hara bolted suddenly from behind the bandstand, giving her a start. He looked grim, the way executioners tended to look as they were about to spring into action. All he lacked was the axe with which to take off her head.

"Miss Tempest, there you are. Come with me."

"Please," Priscilla began, "I would just like to—"

"No questions," Major O'Hara snapped. "Follow me and do as you are told."

Major O'Hara performed a perfect parade-square about-face as befitted an ex-military man and marched off, Priscilla hurrying after him, not certain what to make of this.

They entered a narrow hallway flanked by cubicle-like dressing rooms. Clive Banville came out of the end dressing room, his face grey and drawn. "Miss Tempest," he said in a choked voice. "I'm afraid we are going to need your assistance this morning."

"Yes, of course, sir," Priscilla said, not quite believing what she was hearing.

"This is a most unfortunate duty—"

Oh, shit, Priscilla thought. Maybe she wasn't finding it so hard after all. Here it comes, the axe droppiwng...

"—inside, please..." Banville indicated the dressing room he had just exited.

Priscilla paused, wondering what any of this had to do with being fired. "I'm not certain—"

"Miss Tempest, please!" O'Hara stated angrily. "Do as you are asked."

Banville moved aside to allow her to enter.

"Make sure you do not touch anything," warned Major O'Hara.

Priscilla pushed the door open further and stepped into the dressing room. The light from the hallway illuminated the body crumpled against a makeup table, its mirror outlined in light bulbs. Skye Kane was still in costume from the night before, her long showgirl's legs stretched out at odd angles. Her lavish red hair was dishevelled, her mascara smeared. She stared with glassy, unseeing eyes at a world she would never see again.

Priscilla's hand shot to her mouth too late to stifle a loud gasp. Major O'Hara had moved directly behind her. "Can you identify this person?" he asked in his crisp military voice.

"Skye Kane," Priscilla managed to say, hardly able to breathe.

"Then you know her?"

"Yes. She's one of the Savoy dancers in Diana Dors's show."

Major O'Hara directed her back out into the hallway, where Banville waited anxiously. "Well?"

"A showgirl," O'Hara reported. "One of our dancers. Skye Kane by name. Is that correct, Miss Tempest?"

Priscilla nodded.

"How well did you know this person?" Banville gave her a sharp look that assured her that knowing a dead person at the Savoy was not a good thing.

"Not well," Priscilla said. "I've gotten to know her the last few weeks since Miss Dors opened here. The two of them are— were—friends."

Banville closed his eyes. His mouth tightened. "Damnation," he said. "I don't suppose this is some sort of accident."

Major O'Hara considered the possibility before shaking his head. "Doubtful," he stated. "I'm no expert but there is a slight blue discoloration on Miss Kane's neck."

"What does that mean?"

"It could mean a lack of oxygen, which would indicate that she was strangled to death."

"Oh, God," Banville groaned. "More scandal at the Savoy." He opened his eyes again. "As if we don't have enough trouble with Miss Dors."

He sighed. "How shall we handle this?"

"We must not delay further calling in the police," Major O'Hara said. "Otherwise it begins to look suspicious."

"Why would it look suspicious?" Banville sounded suddenly angry.

"It might appear as though we're trying to cover something up."

"We have a dead showgirl in a dressing room at the Savoy. How the devil could we cover that up?"

For a moment nobody said anything. The three of them stood awkwardly together, the hallway seeming to press in on them.

"Very well," Banville said in a resigned voice. "Call them in. Call the damned police!"

"Skye was one of the eight Savoy dancers who open and close the show," Diana Dors was explaining.

With her white-blond hair, flawless makeup, a voluptuous figure this morning hidden beneath a black trench coat, even under these terrible circumstances Diana managed to personify the movie sex symbol the former Diana Fluck had worked so hard to become. A pale goddess surrounded by a mob of plainclothes detectives.

"What happened last night after the show?" Priscilla recognized the stolid copper's face, the piercing eyes and firm jaw of Detective Chief Inspector Robert "Charger" Lightfoot.

"What happened is what usually happens," Diana answered. "We all get out of our costumes, tell each other lies about how good the show was, and then go home and fall dead tired into bed."

"And last night how did Miss Kane seem?"

"I talked briefly with her before the show. She seemed fine," Diana said.

She spotted Priscilla and broke away from the detectives to embrace her. Around them the Restaurant had filled with uniformed bobbies. "Oh, God," Diana cried, holding tight to Priscilla. "Isn't this the most horrible, awful thing imaginable?"

"It's dreadful," Priscilla said consolingly. "Do you have any idea what happened?"

Diana dropped her voice to speak into Priscilla's ear. "The police are saying Skye was murdered—*murdered!* Can you believe it. And, and—"

Her words were lost in a flood of tears.

"What? What is it, Diana?"

"They want to know where I went after the show. Can you imagine?" She embraced Priscilla again, her tears damp on her face as she whispered, "I know who did this. I know—"

"Who?" Priscilla asked.

But then Inspector Lightfoot was hovering, offering a large white handkerchief that might have been mistaken for a flag of surrender—but to what? The charms of Diana Dors? It wouldn't surprise Priscilla in the slightest.

"Are you going to be all right, Miss Dors?" Lightfoot asked solicitously.

"Yes, yes, I'm fine, Inspector, thank you," Diana said using the handkerchief to carefully wipe at her tears so as not to disturb the makeup. "This has been a terrible, terrible shock, as you can imagine..."

"Yes, of course." The inspector's deeply creased Scotland Yard detective's face was the picture of sympathy. "I think that's all for now, Miss Dors. I can have one of my men drive you home if you like."

Diana smiled wanly. "No, that's fine, Inspector. I have a driver."

"Thank you, Miss Dors. We will be in touch."

Diana threw her arms around Priscilla dramatically for a final embrace before swaying away, the eyes of the policemen in the room following her out—to ensure her safe exit, of course.

As soon as Diana was gone, the inspector reluctantly turned his attention to Priscilla. "Well, Miss Tempest, here we are again."

"Your favourite suspect is back," Priscilla said.

"Yes, unfortunately. As I recall, you were also involved the last time we had to deal with a murder at the Savoy."

"I didn't kill Miss Kane if that's any consolation," Priscilla said.

Inspector Lightfoot looked at her in such a way that suggested he wasn't ruling out that possibility.

"But you were one of the last persons to see her alive, Major O'Hara tells me."

"Not necessarily. Skye performed in the Cabaret show after she left the party that we both attended."

"Was Miss Kane alone at this party?"

"No, she was escorted by the American theatrical producer David Merrick."

"I see." Inspector Lightfoot was now busily scribbling into the notebook he had produced. "And how did Miss Kane seem to you?"

How did she seem? Not good, Priscilla remembered. Not good at all...